STORM DAMAGE

STORM DAMAGE

ED KOVACS

Minotaur Books ⚏ New York

STORM DAMAGE. Copyright © 2011 by Ed Kovacs. All rights reserved. Printed in the United States of America. For information, address St. Martin's Press, 175 Fifth Avenue, New York, N.Y. 10010.

www.minotaurbooks.com

Library of Congress Cataloging-in-Publication Data

Kovacs, Ed.
  Storm damage / Ed Kovacs. — 1st ed.
      p. cm.
  ISBN 978-0-312-58181-7
  1. Ex-police officers—Fiction.   2. Murder—Investigation—Fiction.
  3. Mixed martial arts—Fiction.   4. New Orleans (La.)—Fiction.   I. Title.
  PS3611.O74943S76 2011
  813'.6—dc23

                                                            2011026757

First Edition: December 2011

10 9 8 7 6 5 4 3 2 1

For Alex and Ginny, John and Margaret, Albert and Dorothy, Robert and Irene, A.J., Judy, Aleta, and Joseph Paul.

Aho Mitakuye Oyasin.

AUTHOR'S NOTE

Many thanks to my readers for understanding that while numerous locations depicted in this book are real places and worth a visit, others are purely fictional.

ACKNOWLEDGMENTS

Thanks to Neungreuthai Chanphonsean for having all of her vowels and consonants in the right places.

Carl Scholl is a softie pretending to be a hard case; thanks for coming through time and time again.

Ed Stackler arrived via serendipity and I love serendipity; Ed's gifts are present throughout this work. Richard Curtis is the kind of mensch you just want to hang out with. Thanks to Richard and his posse for everything and more.

Michael Homler had just the right touch at just the right time; he and the SMP gang are terrific.

Captain Eric Morton could talk a cat out of a shrimp boat, and doesn't miss a trick. Tough guy Eric K., former bar impresario and NOPD Reserve Officer, never sold me the building he pretended to own, but he got me going on a novel sure as hell. *Semper Fi.*

Inventor, international MMA instructor, and Jefferson Parish Sheriff's Detective Myron Gaudet, a true warrior/monk,

ACKNOWLEDGMENTS

deserves to be singled out above all others for a whole lot of reasons, all of them good. Myron is an outstanding individual, and this book has a huge chunk of him in it. I stand humbly in his debt.

STORM DAMAGE

CHAPTER ONE

Five months and nineteen days into the New Normal of New Orleans, she walked into what was left of my dojo and casually flicked back her long, dark hair as she took in the mess of reconstruction, distracting me just enough so my right block sank too low and my student's rocketing left hook caught me square, breaking my nose yet again, spinning my head, and dropping me hard onto the fight cage mat.

I've always had a high tolerance for pain, but since my marriage broke up two years ago, I'd hardly been able to feel anything. Lack of feeling comes in handy when you've just been knocked on your ass, literally and in other ways.

As I sprawled there staring up at the disintegrating blue tarp that covered the huge gap where my roof should have been, I remembered the last time I'd seen the young Asian-American woman: at the murder scene of her father, Tiki Hut Sam, the last homicide before a Category Five hurricane wiped out my adopted city.

What was her name again? She had found the body, a body

that we'd been forced to leave in place as we retreated from a fury we'd greatly underestimated.

And now she had just strolled into my place, unannounced. Not that there was anyone to announce her. I was lucky to have a front door.

She looked even better than I recalled; late twenties, slender, with creamy-fresh skin, but her name didn't come. It should have, even though we'd never really met, at least not under normal circumstances. I'd known her dad pretty well and he had bragged her up more than once and shown me photos of her. Her father, Sam Siu, had been the chief building inspector of the City of New Orleans during the scandal-plagued administration of Mayor Marlin Duplessis. Sam also had owned the Tiki Hut, kind of a low-rent Trader Vic's, a tacky South China Sea–themed bar where the power elite of City Hall could drink and scheme in privacy or, if they chose, rub elbows with visiting pro athletes, Hollywood actors in town on a production, or the retro-arty crowd, which seemed to revel in the cheesy palm thatch, year-round Christmas lights, electric blue drinks in oversized glasses, and a jukebox that still spun Elvis singing "Blue Hawaii" on 45 vinyl.

The night the Storm hit was the last time I'd seen the Tiki Hut. I'd answered my last radio call ever that night, my final night as a cop. I'd had four hours left until 10-7—end of shift—and the end of my eight-year law enforcement career with the New Orleans Police Department. I'd resigned for good reasons, but Fate made my last day on the thin blue line a true day of reckoning for many other people than me, none more so than Tiki Hut Sam.

When the radio call crackled, "Signal 29U, unclassified death, possible 30, at 4800 Toulouse," I recognized the address right away, since I'd spent plenty of time in the Hut. So I ignored the mad-dog wind screaming through the trees, the terrified city already devolving into chaos as the stubborn hunkered down and the opportunists sought opportunity, and drove straight for the scene of the crime.

Not doing what I was supposed to do had been something of a theme during my tenure at the department. In fact, I'd just completed a last-minute unauthorized banzai run to give a friend's grandfather a .357 revolver out in Lakeview. The old guy would need the piece if looters showed up.

Having done that, and continuing my cowboy leitmotif, I responded to a homicide call far outside of my district. Citywide curfew had kicked in at 1800, two hours previous, phones and radios still worked, and we had a break in the rain bands. Brute blasts of heavy, moist air bounced the traffic lights on North Carrollton up and down like piñatas trying to avoid the stick as I made a wild left turn onto Orleans Avenue. Since the winds blew steady at over sixty miles per hour, we were in a mandatory citywide lockdown; all officers were supposed to be hunkered down at their District HQs or other designated staging areas for storm duty. So I wasn't surprised to be the only uniform to show as I rolled up to the Tiki Hut. A single detective's unit sat parked askew, and I knew instantly who it belonged to by the dent in the driver's door, a dent I had personally installed after learning that Detective Sergeant Dice McCarty was screwing my ex-wife.

As I got out of my unit, I powered up my concealed digital video recorder—something I did with almost any encounter, at least since the chief had made it his mission to get me fired. The pinhole cam was hidden in a lapel pin. A separate voice-activated digital audio recorder was connected to an ink-pen mike in my front shirt pocket.

The electricity was still on inside the bar, and the first thing I saw was Sam's daughter alone at a table, trying to get a cell signal for her smartphone and sobbing as she spoke Vietnamese to no one in particular. I knew the bar's layout well and crossed the gray concrete floor toward the open door leading to Sam's office and living quarters.

Sgt. McCarty sat at Sam's desk checking out Sam's laptop as I entered. Dice looked tall, even sitting down. He had been a decent cornerback for the LSU football team back in his day, before the gambling and drinking problems and the straight Fs got him kicked out with a one-way ticket to UNO, the University of New Orleans. He had big rough hands, the reddish enlarged nose of someone who drank and fought too much, bloodshot blue eyes under tossed sandy hair, and couldn't whisper if he wanted to. He glanced at me with a look like I had caused him a gas bubble, then barked, like he was calling out a defensive formation in a loud and unfriendly stadium, "Don't touch nothing, we'll be outta here in a second."

It was then I saw the body of a man on the floor. Naked except for a green bath towel around the waist. Blood pooled around the head, which angled awkwardly to the side.

"Jesus." I stepped closer, careful to avoid any blood spatter, bone, and gray matter, then bent down. A metallic whiff of blood invaded my nose. "Gunshot wound to the back of the head. Face blown away. Had to be a large-caliber slug, don't you think?"

"Just put Sam's kid in my unit," said Dice. "I'm taking her downtown."

"What about the coroner, the crime scene techs?" I eyed the lividity, trying to roughly calculate a time of death. Rigor mortis hadn't set in yet; I figured the corpse was four or five hours' fresh.

"Nobody's coming out in this. We're about to get hammered by a Cat Five hurricane, case you hadn't noticed."

"You know the regs. Coroner's office has to respond to a death, especially a homicide."

"State of Emergency's been declared, St. James. The rules are out the window."

I stood up and faced him. "This isn't some stiff on the levee. That might be Sam Siu down there on the floor, but I can't positively ID this body, and I knew Sam well. If it is Sam, then this is *big*."

Dice started to argue, but I cut him off.

"Sam was chief building inspector for the city under Mayor Duplessis. They were cronies. Duplessis is under investigation by the FBI."

"That FBI shit's a rumor."

"Like hell. This is a murder scene. We can't just walk away."

"Look, ace, power's out at the coroner's office, and the backup generators ain't working over there. I'm hearing two-thirds of the coroner's staff evacuated with their families and ain't reporting for duty. The coroner's assistants that are there, they can't get the damn electric gate open, so they couldn't roll a vehicle if they wanted to. EMS ain't rolling, FD ain't rolling, nobody's rolling. You and me ain't even supposed to be here."

"Have you gathered any evidence, taken photos? Is Sam's wallet here, his keys?" I scanned the room.

"Car keys are here, but I didn't see no wallet."

"Look, the safe is open." Sam had a heavy safe bolted to the concrete floor. The door hung wide open, the inside empty.

As I moved toward the safe, Dice closed whatever window he'd been viewing on Sam's laptop and stood up to his full six-foot-four height.

"Look, man, I know you want to play Mr. Detective. And hey, I knew Sam, too, all right? I liked him. But nobody else is coming and we need to book, ASAP."

"If we need to book ASAP, what the hell are you doing on Sam's laptop? Checking in with your sports bookie to see if he'll extend you some credit?"

Dice flushed red. I knew he wanted to hit me, and I knew he knew better than to try.

"CSI'll deal with this after the storm's passed. It ain't going to matter much to old Sam here."

"Yeah? Well, in case you forgot, this is a bar. Who will stop the looters from coming in here and trashing this place after they steal everything?"

Dice didn't have an answer, and when you can't destroy the message, go after the messenger. "You seem pretty stressed out for a guy who resigned from the department and is working his last shift," he said, with a somewhat mocking tone. "Or maybe you're just bugged because I'm sleeping with your ex-wife."

I gave him a look I usually reserve for subhumans. "You want to have that conversation, save it for when we're off duty, and not at a murder scene." I wouldn't give him the satisfaction of showing just how much I hated him or how much I still loved my ex-wife. The divorce ate at my soul; I'd simply been unable to let go of Sharon. I glanced down at the body. "Sam—if that's really Sam down there—deserves for us to do it the right way, not the Southeast Louisiana way. We could at least put him in a body bag and take him to the morgue ourselves."

"We ain't moving the corpse." A crashing sound from out on the street was accompanied by the building shuddering and creaking from a massive explosion of whining wind. Dice looked to the ceiling.

"Did you bother to check the security cams?" His look told me he hadn't. I crossed past him and entered a small room about the size of a walk-in closet.

A half-dozen black-and-white CCTV monitors showed views of the exterior of the front and back doors, and four different views from inside the bar. One monitor revealed Sam's daughter still sitting in the next room.

Sam had been old-school and recorded onto VHS tape. Racks of VHS cassettes, all neatly labeled and cataloged, cramped the cluttered room.

"The cameras are running, but the recorder's not recording."

Dice squeezed in behind me. "Maybe the tape's still there." He slipped on a purple latex glove and gingerly pressed the edge of the eject button, so as not to smear a possible print. No tape came out.

"Look," I said, pointing to some empty racks. "Someone took all the security videos going back about a year or so."

Dice sighed. There would be no easy ID of the killer or killers. "Yeah. And that would be a lot of tapes."

"Boxes full," I said, calculating in my mind. "The killer knew he'd been recorded and went to a lot of trouble to remove the evidence. This was premeditated."

My police radio crackled; Dispatch instructed us in no uncertain terms to 10-19, return to station, "Right damn now," as the female dispatcher put it. The rain had kicked in again, and the winds were hitting seventy-five miles per hour.

We locked the door to Sam's office. Sam's daughter, still weepy and stunned, didn't want to ride with Dice but agreed to follow him in her car to give a statement at headquarters. There, we assured her, she could take shelter until the hurricane passed. She locked up the bar—I didn't see any signs of forced entry to the front door—and we ran to our vehicles through needles of horizontal rain. Branches, roof shingles, and trash tore at us, flechettes of detritus, advance scouts of a massive army of debris that was about to rise up over thousands of square miles.

Dice peeled out, with Sam's daughter directly behind, me following. I veered to narrowly avoid a falling tree limb, and figured that the night was going to get interesting fast. It did, much sooner than I anticipated, because at the next corner, Sam's daughter hung a sharp left and screeched off into the darkness as Dice drove on imperviously.

I recall seriously considering following her, then changing my mind. A few more hours and I would no longer be a cop, and already my wipers couldn't keep up with the rain as the devil wind buffeted my patrol unit and the assault on my city began in earnest.

"Good luck," I'd said aloud to Sam Siu's daughter as she fled into some unfolding chasm of her own making.

Now, she stood in my dojo at the edge of the octagonal fight cage, the wire mesh screened-in ring that the looters had been too lazy to dismantle and steal, looking at me as I lay inert on the mat. Another, far less attractive face entered my field of vision, that of my MMA—mixed martial arts—student, Kendall "The Killer Creole" Bullard. Kendall used cheap peroxide to color his nappy hair something resembling blond. His fat nose looked worse than mine—not an easy feat—thanks to years of taking beatings, and his caramel skin tone bespoke his Creole lineage.

Sam's daughter glanced through the wire mesh to Kendall. He looked back at her, then back at me.

"Coach, ya'll right?"

"Good to go." Although it seemed like an eternity, I'd only been down for a few seconds as the memories of the Tiki Hut murder scene flashed through my mind. Maybe Sam's daughter wanted to sign up for classes. A paying student would be nice, since I no longer had any, so it occurred to me I should demonstrate who the master was here and who the student was.

I rolled clear, jumped up, and tapped my red leather Hayabusa gloves together.

I expected Sam's daughter to step back from the edge of the cage, but she didn't; she laced her fingers through the mesh and leaned in even closer to see what was going to happen.

As soon as Kendall resumed his fighting stance, I advanced, expecting him to throw a kick, which he did. I easily intercepted and quickly executed a textbook-clean foot sweep known as *o uchi gari,* taking out his supporting leg and dropping him like a sack of rocks.

Now it was I who stood over Kendall.

"You could be a UFC champion," I told him, "but you're screwing up."

Kendall squinted guiltily.

"That's right," I said. "I hear who you're running with, taking X every weekend. Vodka and Red Bull all night long. Sound familiar? If I just knocked your ass down in two seconds, what's gonna happen when you go up against a serious fighter? You want to win this fight coming up in Miami? You want to be a champ, Mr. Ten-Thousand-Friends-Who-Want-to-Be-Your-Ho-on-MySpace? If you do, get serious. No more raves with your Bourbon Street stripper girlfriends or you lose me as a coach and you can kiss K-1 and any chance for the UFC good-bye."

I held out my hand and helped him to his feet. He hung his head hangdog style, thinking about what I had said.

"Yeah, you right. I know dat. Can I take a shower, Coach?"

"Sure, go ahead."

Kendall opened the small steel mesh door and we stepped down from the raised cage. I feigned nonchalance as I crossed toward the large mirror on the wall, letting Sam's daughter follow. I thought my speech to Kendall had sounded pretty good: firm, succinct, final. Not too preachy, didn't beat a dead horse, and left the ball in his court.

"Officer St. James, do you remember me?"

I checked out my broken nose in the mirror, then turned to her. "You're Sam Siu's daughter."

"Twee Siu." She held out her hand and gave me a surprisingly firm handshake.

"Call me Cliff."

"Looks like your nose might be broken. Do you need me to take you to a doctor?"

I firmly grabbed my schnoz and forced it back into the general location it should inhabit. The crunching sound caused her to wince. "Not too many doctors in New Orleans these days, and that just saved me about a hundred bucks."

Twee Siu looked a helluva lot better than she had five months ago when she was an emotional wreck. Her cheekbones, framed by an expensive haircut, reminded me how photogenic she was. The pewter Chanel business suit helped project the confidence and intelligence that emanated from within. A single strand of pearls graced her delicate neck. Eye shadow and a pastel lipstick comprised her makeup suite, and I'm not sure she needed that. She sported a Prada bag that I doubted was fake.

Her smooth and dainty hands, though primly manicured, incongruously bore old scars; I was curious from what. For someone so petite, she projected a good deal of authority and confidence. Not too many people ran around in the ruins dressed like this, looking this beautiful, so if it was for my benefit, I felt complimented. But I figured she must be a banker, or maybe a greedy real estate agent getting fat on others' misfortune after all the devastation.

"Listen, I'm real sorry about your father. I knew Sam. He helped my ex-wife and me quite a bit. He was a decent guy."

"Thank you."

"You called me 'officer,' so maybe you haven't heard. I'm not a cop anymore."

"That's why I think you can help me. I'd like to hire you to find out what happened to Dad."

It suddenly dawned on me. Sam's killing had been completely overshadowed by an epic onslaught of chaos, misery, and upheaval as an American historic metropolis was essentially destroyed. Sam's murder was ancient history from another epoch that didn't hold much concern for those of us coping with the New Normal.

Unless you were Twee Siu.

"Well, I'm not a private investigator."

"I heard the state is waiving the steps and preconditions for most business licenses, due to the State of Emergency. I bet you could get certified in a day, being ex-police and all."

I had heard the same thing. Two Bourbon Street strip-club managers who'd been getting FEMA execs laid after the Storm had launched a security company in a matter of days and were now on their way to becoming millionaires, thanks to those grateful FEMA boys steering lucrative contracts their way. Hell, Louisiana was so desperate for expertise and workers in dozens of fields, it had been handing out temporary licenses to roofers, plumbers, electricians—anyone who needed a license to do something—like Tootsie Rolls at Halloween.

I'd developed a good poker face while working as a police officer, to the point where it ranked as one of my most effective tools. I used it now to conceal my interest in her proposition, giving her just a shrug. "I suppose that might be true."

"I'll pay you five hundred dollars a day, plus expenses. If you find out what happened to my father, you get a bonus of thirty thousand."

Now she had my attention. I was broke and going deep into debt. The first thing I had done after I stopped volunteering in the initial post-hurricane search-and-rescue effort was to sublet my undamaged condo in the French Quarter to a Shaw Group executive for $2,500 a month. I soon realized I could have gotten much more due to the acute lack of housing in a city flooded with out-of-town relief workers. That $2,500 covered my monthly nut, but it had left me homeless.

Mother Nature and the looters had destroyed my place of business; my students fled to points unknown around the country. I had no job, no income. Me and a couple hundred thousand other people.

With business insurance and FEMA money not forthcoming, I had quickly maxed out my credit cards to start repairs to the dojo, where I had moved some personal belongings and slept on an extra mattress. Six NOPD buddies who had lost everything had crashed with me for the first few months, helping me rip out the drywall and wiring and to gut the place. Now it was just me on a dirty mattress, with a badly damaged roof, and a partially collapsed wall you could drive a forklift through, which is exactly what the looters had done to gain access. Demand far outstripped supply, sending prices for Sheetrock, lumber, and other building materials—if you could find any—skyrocketing. All of this made the money Twee dangled look like manna from Heaven.

"You'll need to deposit the thirty thousand into an escrow account, with stipulations we agree upon given to the bank, so there's no question I'll get paid if I find out who killed your dad."

She clearly hadn't anticipated this condition. She thought about it for a second. "Okay, sounds reasonable. If you drive to Baton Rouge today and get your license, we can meet at my beauty salon first thing tomorrow, then go to the bank. I want you to start right away."

She handed me a business card. Now I remembered Sam had told me that his daughter owned hair salons and a beauty school out in Metairie. It was one of those facts that you just don't hold on to, but it explained why she looked so great: a walking advertisement for her business.

"No problem," I told her. "Can I ask you something? Why'd you come to me?"

"Because my father trusted you."

"What do you mean?"

"He told me about you a long time ago, said that if something ever happened to me, I should ask you for help. He said I could count on you, that you were an honest cop. The night I found the body, I didn't realize you were the officer Dad had told me about."

It took me by surprise that Sam thought that way about me, and more so that he would have said all that to his daughter. I hadn't even seen Sam all that much in the year or so before the Storm.

"I heard what you said to the detective that night," she said, looking down. "You said you couldn't be sure that the body was my father. Neither could I, although I assumed it was Dad at the time."

"What do you mean? Haven't they ID'd the body by now?"

"Oh." She looked genuinely surprised. "You didn't hear? The body in my father's office was never recovered. It disappeared. And the Tiki Hut got looted and flooded out. See, maybe you're looking for my father's killer. Or maybe you're looking for my father."

CHAPTER TWO

I made it to the offices of the Louisiana State Board of Private Security Examiners in Baton Rouge by one thirty. The fact that I already had business insurance greatly expedited the process. After filling out forms, taking a test that was easy for me after eight years as a cop, and schmoozing and flirting like hell with the all-female staff, I got my temporary PI license. The bag of pastries I brought from the Winn-Dixie didn't hurt, either. The ladies were hungry for Danish and juicy tidbits of what it had been like during those first days after the Storm in the Big Easy, and I wasn't above sharing in order to win their confidence and sympathy. I wanted that license *today.* So I told them true stories of boat rescues, body retrievals, and waxing a few dirtbags in gunfights. They were the stories I was comfortable telling to strangers, the ones I had become dispassionate about. The memories that still got to me, the ones that made me wake up in a sweat in the middle of the night, I didn't share with anyone except my buddies-in-arms who were there and who understood completely.

The biggest hurdle was my background check, which I finally

got the director to do over the phone with the local FBI office. No matter how much the ladies liked me, the reputation of NOPD being what it is, they really needed to confirm that I didn't have a rap sheet.

Setting up the escrow account with Twee at her bank in Metairie, the somewhat upscale suburb adjacent to Orleans Parish, went smoothly. Portions of Metairie got hammered hard and flooded, but, being in Jefferson Parish, Metairie seemed light-years ahead in terms of recovery. Sure, the parish was more affluent and suffered less damage, but they also had a tough sheriff—one of the most powerful politicians in the state—and the political will to get things done and make the hard decisions, devil-be-damned. On the other hand, in Orleans Parish it was always the "Nero fiddled while Rome burned" scenario.

So a good deal of Jefferson Parish was coming back, as it were, at least compared to their neighbors in New Orleans. Thousands of FEMA trailers sat on the front lawns or driveways of middle- and upper-middle-class homes that had been flooded or damaged, signaling that residents had returned. Restaurants on the main drag, Veterans Boulevard, reopened if they could find staff. The blue tarps disappeared as new roofs were installed. Debris got picked up at a pretty good clip. Oh, and there was power. Jefferson Parish had that thing called electricity. In New Orleans five months after the Storm, if you weren't in the Quarter, the CBD, or Uptown, there was no guarantee you had juice.

"So what work have you had done to the Tiki Hut since the Storm?" I asked Twee as we stepped outside of her bank into the humid, chilly morning. I glanced across the street and noticed that one of my favorite martini bars had no less than three huge Dumpsters brimming with rubble in their parking lot.

"Nothing. The front and back doors were broken open so I had them padlocked shut. That's it."

"And the police CSI team, what did they say?"

"What CSI?" she carped. "They barely looked around. The body was gone, the crime scene trashed. The detectives said it was pointless. Seemed to me like they were just lazy and didn't want to get dirty."

"They're not lazy, but they tend to think in terms of a conviction. So from their point of view, they were right. It's like triage, but for dead people. They're overwhelmed with murders in this town. They tend to focus on the cases they think they can solve. From our point of view, this is good news. Clues might be preserved. I need to get into the Tiki Hut right away to nose around. But first we'll need to make a pit stop."

Having helped gut a few homes and even my own dojo, I knew what Twee and I needed to outfit ourselves with. A two-hour shopping ordeal at a swamped Home Depot in Kenner had netted us lightweight disposable biohazard suits, knee-high mud boots, latex gloves, and high-end respirators. For tools, we got a couple of battery-powered lanterns, flashlights, a pry bar, and a shovel.

Shopping spree finished, I followed Twee in her new black Honda Accord with deeply tinted windows. Crossing the parish line into Orleans was instructive. Far fewer FEMA trailers sat anchored in the moonscape of Lakeview, one of the neighborhoods that took the brunt of the flooding from Lake Pontchartrain. Abandoned cars, trucks, and boats still littered what looked like a battlefield in oblique and illogical positions. Houses teetered off foundations. Clutter and wreckage of every stripe lay strewn everywhere. White goods outside of a couple homes—ruined stoves and refrigerators—signaled determined owners making the statement that they intended to come back. But few homes in Lakeview were being gutted or sending such signals. The whole muck-encrusted neighborhood looked like it had been wiped out by some kind of angry force, a plague that killed all living things.

In the era of the fifteen-minute news cycle, the Storm had dominated the nation's airwaves for months. The magnitude of the catastrophe staggered the imagination. The mantra I had repeated to friends around the country always rang the same: TV usually makes something seem worse than it is; this time, TV didn't do justice to representing the scope of the tragedy.

We turned off Brooks onto Canal Street, going south toward Mid-City. There was still no power for the traffic lights, but FEMA-funded debris removal crews traversed Canal. These crews were mostly out-of-town workers, motley groups who encamped in City Park or deserted shopping center parking lots, sleeping in tents pitched on concrete or in battered old RVs. They worked seven days a week, twelve hours a day, hauling debris to temporary dump sites in the parish. The men, and sometimes women, usually operated one or two small Bobcats that scooped debris into dump trailers towed by pickup trucks. The crews looked sickly, tired, and dirty, but the lucrative FEMA money spurred them on.

Mid-City looked bad, but a lot better than Lakeview. The thousands of homes with blue tarps covering roof damage provided the only splashes of color to the otherwise bleak streets. On City Park Avenue, Twee got tangled in a convoy of out-of-state power company repair trucks and tree-trimming truck crews from Ohio.

We waited patiently till we could shoot the gap, then headed south into a residential no-man's-land toward the Tiki Hut.

As we stood in front of the Tiki Hut getting into our gear, I scanned the residential neighborhood, which reminded me of one large panoramic sepia-toned photo, everything either dead or encrusted with shades of mud brown, devoid of color and life. Cars and trucks sat overturned up and down the street, deposited arbitrarily where the murky waters had left them. Huge uprooted trees, like fallen soldiers, rested everywhere in awkward moments of death, awaiting a burial detail. The streets and sidewalks were caked with a sludge now dried and disintegrating into noxious dust, lifted on every gentle breeze. Brown water lines on the homes across the street suggested the water had settled at about eight feet on this street. The initial depth of the killer surge had been much higher.

Children's toys, a single sneaker, a broken chair, a grungy pillow, a couple of CDs, a rusty can of hairspray, and a strangely intact perfume bottle created an impromptu mosaic in the mire near the Tiki Hut's front door, now padlocked shut.

A sour stench of rot and decay, garbage and waste, hung unpleasantly like it did in so many parts of the city, pervasively invading the nostrils, an insistent reminder that something wasn't right. Shit, nothing in this town *is* right. One could become inured to the endless images of destruction, as an emotionally charged visceral reaction simply couldn't be maintained if you spent much time in the ruins, but it was tough to get used to the invasive stink that could seize up your esophagus with an involuntary urge to retch.

The tableau here resembled thousands of others I had seen over the last five months and it deadened my soul. It was part of the New Normal. No doubt an odd beauty could be found in the unusual juxtaposition of material goods at my feet, whose functions were now rendered meaningless, but I remained too closely connected emotionally to my personal losses to look for such artistic imagery. I preferred to stay slightly out of focus to keep my sharper memories at bay.

"So where are you living now, Twee?"

"My condo in the Warehouse District wasn't damaged. Nothing. Sometimes I feel a little guilty."

"Don't feel guilty," I said. "Feel lucky."

"I don't like coming into these neighborhoods. All the destruction . . . it makes me depressed. It's so ugly now, and sad to think of the people who lost everything."

"If you want to keep your sanity, allow me to suggest disassociation. Works wonders."

"It's amazing that five months after the Storm, this block, this neighborhood, still looks like this," she said, frowning.

"Yeah, I think the only cleanup being done around here is from looters and scavengers."

"But everything is ruined, what can they steal?"

"Copper pipes and wire, aluminum to sell at the scrap yards. More sophisticated thieves go after the classic architectural details of these Creole cottages, the shotgun homes, the fine Southern mansions. A four-panel cypress door is worth seven hundred dollars or more. Old-growth hardwood windows, the decorative brackets under the eaves, Victorian shutters and cornices, ornate mantels. Those things are like gold to collectors or dealers around the country." I scanned the homes across the street. "Look at the double shotgun house on the corner. The wrought-iron fence is partially dismantled, and the cast-iron grates that covered the crawl spaces are gone. They strip the outside, then work their way inside."

"This isn't like stealing food and water to survive. This is greed. This is like vultures picking at a carcass. They should be shot," she said angrily.

Her fervor surprised me. Although I think the best way to stop widespread looting is by shooting a few of the miscreants and spreading the message via the media, Twee hadn't struck me as being a kindred spirit in this regard. The problem now: who is a looter, who is a contractor, who is a resident? Who is going to ask? Most of the law enforcement help that had initially poured into the city left long ago. There simply weren't enough police or National Guard MPs to protect every street, or even every neighborhood. And with the murder and crime rates soaring, those scarce law enforcement resources were desperately needed for other duty.

I turned to face the task at hand. Like most structures in the city, the Tiki Hut had an X spray-painted on the front wall, with quadrants of the X containing information such as the date the building was searched, who searched it, and coded markings as to what was found inside. The use of placards or spray-painted Xs to denote the condition of a building was designed by FEMA USAR—Urban Search and Rescue. I had spray-painted my share of Xs on houses in Gentilly, Lakeview, and elsewhere, working alongside my fellow officers as a volunteer. Chief Pointer's hatred for me was such that he held me to my resignation date and seized my badge and duty weapon even as the city collapsed into mayhem at a time when he needed every available officer in the field. Those were brutal, surreal, hellacious days and nights, and I didn't care to think about some of the things I had found inside some of those homes.

"NOFD searched the bar on September tenth," I said, reading the code. "That was after the water receded. No bodies found inside."

"The police seemed to think it was looted before it flooded, but they don't know when the body was removed," said Twee.

"No way to know how much water it took initially, but it had at least seven feet in it for a couple of weeks, since the building is a foot or so off the ground. You've only been in once?"

"Yes, when the police came."

"When was that?"

"I think it was the eleventh or twelfth."

"So what did the detectives say about not retrieving the body?" I asked.

"You've heard all the excuses. Hundreds of cops abandoned their jobs to evacuate with their families. The ones who stayed were rescuing people or dealing with looters and criminal gangs, they lost communications, the roads were blocked or underwater so they couldn't get around, the district police stations were destroyed, paperwork went missing, the cops had lost their own homes, it was chaos. I know all of that was true. I know the city was a mess. More than a mess. If they were truly focusing on helping the living, then I'm not upset. But I think more than a few police were doing some looting themselves. They were looking out for number one."

"Trust me, it wasn't easy to be NOPD back then, Twee. The Storm hadn't fully passed, we had winds over ninety miles per hour, and the city was already flooding. If the detectives and coroner could have come before the Tiki Hut flooded, they would have."

She opened the padlocks and we switched on our flashlights

and entered. The place had been locked up tight for most of the last five months. The fetid stink of mold, filth, and rot would have been overwhelming if it weren't for the expensive respirators we wore.

The destruction that mere water can cause inside a building is testament to mankind's folly in thinking that we have any kind of real control in this world. The fragility of our little individually organized material universes, when placed against the forces of Nature, would be laughable were it not for being so tragic. The Tiki Hut looked similar to hundreds of other flood-damaged structures I had carefully traversed. Time had dried and solidified the mud and silt, cementing the cacophony of jumbled tables, chairs, and bar stools to unwise locations in the room, where they had been deposited by fiat as the waters receded.

Video gaming machines, their screens broken, their money boxes long ago liberated, had been tossed about like corks; one of them now rested sideways on top of the bar. Another had smashed down the door to the men's room and sat atop the long urinal trough. A filthy doll, a child's shoe, and a Wiffle ball that had likely floated in from the neighborhood now perched poignantly on higher shelves behind the bar. Hundreds of shards from broken bar glasses speckled the dirty, crusted floor like flecks of silica on a sandy beach.

We didn't speak as I led her toward the murder scene. Black, green, and brown mold crawled the damp walls like a spreading virus in off-kilter, asymmetrical paisley patterns. This was the visible mold. What lingered unseen could only be known by ripping out the drywall, pulling up the flooring.

Sam's office and living quarters were in no better condition than the rest of the bar. A junked, tangled mess of dried muck, battered office items, and ruined, rearranged furniture. Mother Nature has a bizarre sense of interior design. Only the heavy safe, bolted to the floor, remained in its original place, and I set one of the lanterns on top of it.

"So the police didn't do any kind of search at all?" I asked. The respirator made my voice sound nasally and like I was deep in a cave.

"Not really. They checked the walls for where a bullet might have went if it exited the skull, but they didn't find anything. They said even if they found something, it wouldn't hold up in court as evidence."

"It's true. Some of this crap floated in from outside," I said, as I used the shovel to move some of the smaller items on the floor. "And NOPD didn't maintain chain of custody of the scene. Bogus evidence could have been planted. A crime scene doesn't remain a crime scene very long. Twenty-four hours maybe. The CSI folks get what they need and that's it, the location is released. It's not like on old TV shows where the detectives return days later to a murder scene, break through the yellow tape that has 'sealed' the area, and then find the master clue that had been overlooked. That wouldn't hold up in court."

"I'm not worried about court, or even an arrest."

What the hell did she mean by that? She wanted answers, for sure, and probably had a very good sense of what she intended to do once she had those answers.

I carefully climbed over Sam's upturned desk and used a flashlight to search the nooks and crannies in the room. "The good news is, I have crime scene photos. At least that's something."

"What photos? I thought you guys didn't take any pictures that night."

"The detective didn't. But I had a hidden video camera running. The quality is decent. I can crank out some stills. And I'll be able to estimate measurements, maybe determine where the killer stood when he took the shot."

As I climbed back over the desk toward her, I saw Twee perk up a little through the plastic lens of her respirator. The fact that I had photos seemed to give her some hope.

"You want me to have someone clean this place out carefully?" she asked. "You know, catalog everything, in case there was a bullet or something?"

"You mean a shell casing."

"Yes. I can hire a crew of people. If they find something, even if it can't be evidence in court, maybe it could be useful to us, to your investigation."

"You need to clean this place out anyway. So if you're willing to pay extra to have it done slowly, that would be great. I can set up the protocols for your crew. How soon can you get them going?"

She thought for a second. "Noon tomorrow."

She took a step forward and tripped, letting out a small scream. I caught her in mid-fall, and held on to her lithe body a moment longer than was necessary. Even with all the cumbersome gear, it reminded me of how nice it was to have an attractive woman in my arms.

"You okay?" I asked.

"Yes, thanks. If you've seen enough for now, I think I'm ready to go."

She turned to the door but I stopped her with my voice. "Sam always kept a laptop on his desk," I stated.

"Would have been looted, don't you think?"

"I suppose so." I flashed on how Dice had been so preoccupied with the laptop the night of the murder. At the time I'd cavalierly assumed he'd been surfing the Internet, simply because there was no other logic to it. It was a reasonable assumption to make at the time, precisely because Dice was known to be such an inept slacker. But of all the things he could have done at a fresh murder scene, his preoccupation with the laptop now bugged me, and I wondered if some other dynamic had been at play.

I took one last look around Sam's office. "You need to make some lists for me. I need to know who your dad's enemies were, who were his friends, family members, people who hung out here in the office, business associates."

"Okay. I don't think Dad had any enemies. None that I know of. I mean, he lived and worked here at the bar. I'll put a list together, but I don't think there will be many names."

"Did he have a lot of friends in the Vietnamese community, maybe belong to a social club out there?"

"Not really. He'd go out and eat in some of the restaurants, shop at the grocery stores, church sometimes, but he wasn't really involved in all that."

"Who else had keys to the bar besides you and Sam?"

"Only Kiesha."

"The black girl who worked here?"

"Yes. Kiesha Taylor. She and Dad were the whole staff. Sometimes they'd hire a bar back, but not usually. Dad said it only took two hardworking people to run the bar."

"I'm sorry to ask this question, but the body only had a towel around it, like maybe the victim had just come out of the shower. Think it's possible your dad might have brought a prostitute in here?"

"Not likely. He and Kiesha were lovers. Judging from all the Viagra he kept in his desk, and from what I gathered, they were very close. He wouldn't talk about it much, out of respect to my mom, even though they divorced when I was a little girl. I think Dad loved Kiesha. He was happy with her. He made her keep her own place, but they were together all the time."

"Have you spoken with her?"

"No. I don't know what happened to her."

"Know where her place was?"

"The Upper Ninth, I think."

Outside in the crisp sunshine, we stripped off the protective suits, gloves, and boots and left them in a pile at the front door. They were contaminated, and I was tired of getting sick. It had taken me months to get rid of a nagging bronchial cough that I was certain was "Storm residue related."

"This wasn't just water that flooded here, Twee. More like a toxic chemical soup. Think of all the toilets that backed up, all the broken sewer lines, the hundreds of thousands of gallons or pounds of household chemicals, the stuff every house has in the garage, under the kitchen and bathroom sinks; all of that got mixed into the soup. Gasoline and oil, industrial contaminants, poisons of every kind. And then think about the mold that's been growing inside the Tiki Hut over the last months. Make sure your debris crew keeps the equipment and themselves sanitized."

I reached into my pocket for a Partagas cigarillo and lit up. "You know, all the time I spent in Sam's office, I never once saw that big safe open. Did Sam keep valuables in there, and if he did, who knew about it?" I asked.

She fluffed her hair, which had been matted down by the respirator straps, as she calculated an answer. "Dad took out a half-million-dollar bank loan about a week before the Storm hit. He gave me a hundred thousand in cash and told me to hold it for him. The rest of the cash was in the office safe."

I looked at her as evenly as I could and tried to keep my sarcasm from leaping off the scale. "Well now, that's an interesting little tidbit that you were, what, not going to mention to me?"

"I'm not a very trusting person." She didn't fidget; she looked me straight in the eyes.

"That makes two of us," I said, exhaling in her general direction, drilling her with a stare that demanded an explanation.

"I guess I was hesitant to tell you I had one hundred thousand dollars of Dad's money. Some private investigators might try and bilk their client out of more fees, if they think there's an opportunity."

"What was it your dad said about me? That I was an honest cop who you could trust?"

She looked away from me. "I should have told you about the money up front. I apologize for holding back on that."

The wheels in my brain spun at full tilt as I tried to imagine what else she wasn't telling me. "A half-million-dollar bank loan, taken in cash, is pretty unusual."

"I don't know if that's unusual or not. But the money he asked me to hold on to is how I can afford to pay you. I have businesses, but I'm not rich."

Not rich, my ass. The little sensors in my gut told me this girl was loaded. "Why would he give you that kind of money? I mean, he gave you twenty percent of the loan. Why? Had he done anything like that before?"

"No. And I don't know why he gave it to me. I didn't ask, it wasn't my place to ask. Dad had lots of secrets. More than you and I will ever know."

"What was the loan for?"

"He got a business loan."

"For what?"

"Maybe you can find out."

Or maybe you could just tell me? "So he didn't give you the hundred grand as a gift, he intended to take it back?"

"Absolutely. He told me not to touch it, and he knew I wouldn't."

"But you're touching it now."

"I think I've waited long enough to find out what happened to my dad. In a couple more weeks I can have him declared legally dead. It's not something I'm looking forward to."

"Who else knew about the cash in the safe?"

"Dad was no fool. I can't think of anyone he would have told, other than me."

I seriously doubted that only Sam and Twee knew the money was in the big steel box. And with four hundred large sitting in Sam's safe, one didn't have to look far for a motive to his murder. Not that I was a cynic, but in a town like New Orleans, I figured maybe half the population would have waxed Sam for four hundred thousand bucks. So at least I was narrowing the field.

CHAPTER THREE

People take their drinking seriously in New Orleans, especially during Mardi Gras time. And with only ten days left till Fat Tuesday, even in this hurricane-hampered Carnival season, reduced to eight days of parades instead of eleven, locals ratcheted up the festivities.

Whether there should be a celebration so soon after the Storm decimated the city with great loss of life generated heated debate. The pro-parade crowd stood behind the concept that the city needed to send a message that we stood open for business and couldn't be defeated by a mere Act of God. Tradition is a powerful motivator in these parts, and the show must go on, especially when there's a party involved.

The pomp-and-circumstance types argued, legitimately, that Mardi Gras wove inexorably into the culture here and simply must be honored. In the last several hundred years it had usually been due to wartime that the season wasn't celebrated lavishly. In addition, with a tourist-related economy perhaps being the faded city's last possible saving grace, business interests never wavered from the position that there must be a Mardi Gras to pump badly needed money into the economy. Where tourists were supposed to stay when there were few available hotel rooms, none afford-able, was another matter.

The opposing camp countered that it would be disrespectful to stage the festival when the city was still obviously so broken and in need of outside help. What kind of message would it send to revel in the usual drunken debauchery, or even sobered pageantry, when few schools, hospitals, or basic services operated? So many had died, so many lost everything, and so, the city, claiming to be broke, shouldn't be throwing a big expensive bash with parades and floats and balls and TV cameras back on Bourbon Street showing that all seemed normal, when indeed it wasn't.

The money crowd won out, of course, and so a trimmed-down Mardi Gras season had officially kicked into gear, as it always does, on January 6—Twelfth Night—when the satirical group of masquers known as the Phunny Phorty Phellows boarded a spe-cially decorated streetcar at around seven o'clock. Since most of the streetcar lines were still torn up, the masked revelers, holding coupes of champagne, and tossing the first beads of the season, embarked from Canal Street and Crozet and rode to the River-front Line, accompanied as always by the Storyville Stompers Brass Band.

I don't belong to any krewes or organizations that require my attendance in a suit, much less a tuxedo, although I scrub up well in one. Truth is, I dislike Mardi Gras. Eight years on the force meant eight years of working the teeming insanity of endless pa-rades and the mayhem of the almost daily French Quarter street parties, especially on Lundi Gras and Fat Tuesday. I dislike crowds, especially chemically altered, hyped-up ones, and the potential for trouble they hold. If I never have to slam another belligerent vomiting drunk onto the pavement, it will be too soon.

Still, I am not one to shy away from a fine adult beverage, expertly prepared and served in a pleasant setting. I sat at my usual corner table at Pravda, a Russian-themed lounge on the edge of the Quarter. Pravda is a bastardized take on a turn-of-the-twentieth-century post-Bolshevik revolutionary salon, and Michelle, the Goth chick owner in a studded dog collar, serves up a mean absinthe the old-fashioned way. I liked the fact Michelle had classical music playing right across the street from Jimmy Buffett's Margaritaville. The music, the neoclassical antique furniture and Oriental rugs, the old Victrola in the corner, and the Cyrillic graffiti on the walls confused and repelled the run-of-the-mill low-rent drunks, gutter punks, and clueless tourists who might otherwise stink up the place. It was the antithesis of a French Quarter Bourbon Street hang.

I lit a cigarillo and scanned the list of names connected to Sam that Twee had given me. I only recognized a few of the names under "Friends," "Family," or "Business Associates." She had no names in the category "Enemies." I knew a couple of the people in the "Employees/Former Employees" category. The category that most intrigued me wasn't on this sheet: "People Who Knew Sam Had a Shit-Load of Cash in the Safe."

My good friend Honey worked swing, 4 P.M. until 12 P.M., in the Sixth District, so, it being Mardi Gras season, we had agreed to meet on her 10-40. Sgt. Honey Baybee walked in, sat next to me at the marble-topped table, and ordered a coffee from Michelle without saying hello to me. This was standard operating procedure. Honey never said hello, she'd simply sit down and pick up a conversation thread. She opened an aluminum posse box and pulled out a manila file folder.

"Copy of Sam Siu's case file. Notice the thinness. Some telephone and credit card records. Interview transcripts. Dice's report. Not much else. Chief bumped this over to cold case detectives. They're stumped." Honey often spoke in a clipped staccato of incomplete sentences, like she was popping off rounds from her 9mm.

"The homicide dicks couldn't find their ass in the dark with a flashlight," I groused, sipping my Argentinean malbec.

"Now, now. No sour grapes. Be fair. I think their solution rate has skyrocketed to twenty percent," she said with a wry smile.

There were plenty of sour grapes on my part and they had nothing to do with the red wine I drank. I should have made detective years ago, but the chief thwarted me at every turn. All because of one little miscue on Magazine Street. Well, not just because of that, but primarily because of that.

Honey took off her nylon patrol jacket, revealing her starched, pressed, dark blue tactical BDUs. Her strawberry blond hair was pulled back per usual in a French braid. She had a cute pug nose, a smattering of freckles on her wrinkle-free face, pale blue eyes, and perfect white teeth. At five six and 122 pounds, she looked athletic without being overly muscular and carried not an ounce of extra body fat. She came off tomboyish without being masculine, but what really endeared her to me was that she loved to fight. Whether her predilection to roughhousing originated from the unique nature of her name, I couldn't say. She could pass for an Uptown debutante, not that I recalled ever seeing Honey in a dress, but the girl shone happiest breaking up a bar brawl or running down a perp in an alley.

I'd seen Honey deck a new partner who towered well over six feet because he refused to let up on the "Hey, baby," "C'mere, honey baby," "Honey child, baby girl" tease patter. After she cleaned the guy's clock, no one called her anything but "Officer" or "Officer Baybee," and they did it without a smirk. Since she made sergeant, most people just called her "Sarge." She graduated from the Academy at twenty-one, making her a nine-year vet, and there wasn't a lummox left in the department who didn't acknowledge that she was a heads-up copper who carried her own weight.

I smiled at Michelle as she placed Honey's coffee on the table. "DJ Isis tonight at the Dervish," she said to Honey.

Honey looked up, thinking. "Probably not tonight."

Michelle smiled, then moved off to take the order of a long-haired guy in a black cape, and he wasn't in costume.

"You hang with Michelle at the Dervish?" The Dervish was an alternative club a couple doors down.

"They're open late," she said by way of explanation, which was no explanation since most New Orleans bars stayed open as long as they had customers drinking, but I let it slide. Honey kept plenty of secrets from me and I knew better than to push.

"Got any theories about Sam?" I asked.

"Rule Number One, follow the dope. Rule Number Two . . ."

"Refer to Rule Number One. Was Sam Siu into drugs?"

"Kiesha Taylor used. But maybe nothing hard. Far as I know," she said, spooning three sugars into her coffee.

"I never knew the Tiki Hut as being a place to score dope."

"I don't think dealers hung there. Bartenders peddle on the side. You know that."

"Doesn't sound like something that would get Sam killed," I said. "I'm thinking it was the four hundred big ones in the safe.

Unless he was blackmailing someone, you know, from all the surveillance he ran."

"Almost every murder in town is dope related. Leave it to you to go against the grain," she said, taking a tentative sip of the strong, dark-roast brew.

"Dope is the easy angle, but look who Sam was. The guy was big-time connected, and the Feds are crawling up his ex-boss's ass."

"Duplessis," she said, nodding.

"And Sam's body conveniently disappears? Please. Dope dealers who whack somebody don't disappear the stiff. They leave merchandise samples as calling cards to make a statement."

"The body didn't float away?" she asked facetiously.

"Would have been found by now, don't you think?"

"Yeah. We're not finding bodies these days. From the Storm. Except in a few attics that weren't searched well. So yeah, Duplessis is a suspect."

"The mayor might have had very strong motivation to call in a professional hit. That keeps Sam from testifying and sends a neon-sign message to anyone else thinking about cooperating with the Feds. A professional shooter could have gotten in without leaving a trace," I said.

"Since when do assassins empty out safes? They whack the target and jam."

"I think a local hit man would take the money if he or she had a chance," I said. "Maybe the safe was already open."

"Already open?"

"Sam had been in NOLA long enough to know what was going to happen to the Tiki Hut with a Cat Five about to hit. No way he would leave the money in the safe. Anything valuable in the whole bar, he would pack up, then go get Twee and evacuate to Houston."

"So the killer comes in and the safe just happens to be open? Yeah, maybe."

"The only reason the looters didn't physically remove the entire safe is because they could see it was empty. Otherwise they would have found a way to drag it out of the Tiki Hut. So yeah, why not assume the safe could have been open when Sam got surprised? The bar was closed and locked. He's taking a shower before he hits the road with his stash. The shooter comes in, sees all the cash, Sam comes out of the shower. Boom."

"Maybe. But like you said on the phone, what if Sam bugged out? If he knew the Feds were after him, he gets the bank loan. Gives some to his daughter. Kills a guy in his place to stall the investigation. Books out to Asia." Honey took a big gulp of her coffee.

"Well, Sam spoke Vietnamese, Chinese, and I think some Southeast Asian hill tribe dialects. But the timing would have to be so . . . I mean, Sam couldn't have known there was a Cat Five hurricane coming when he got the bank loan," I stated. "No way he knows the crime scene will be destroyed with no CSI done, no blood taken, no DNA. So why even kill a patsy? Why not just take a vacation and don't come back?"

"Could be that was his plan. The hurricane presented a new option," she speculated.

"Could the Feds have done this?"

"What?" Honey smiled, trying not to look incredulous.

"Think about it," I said. "Sam could be in witness protection, ratting out Duplessis and a hundred other of New Orleans's finest public servants. Sam was in the inner circle for eight years."

"FBI ain't gonna kill some Asian dude to take Sam's place," she said flatly.

"No, but I wouldn't put it past them to put a few rounds into the head of a corpse they could get their hands on. I've seen the Bureau do some crap over the years, Honey."

"So explain the missing surveillance tapes. Somebody had been coming in. Probably met with Sam over the last year. Maybe selling dope, maybe not. The five hundred Gs he got from the bank? Maybe it was for a drug buy."

"I can't rule it out. Sam knew drug dealers, that's for sure," I said.

"You need to find out who knew about the money. Don't rule out his daughter."

"If Twee did it, she's not going to hire a guy like me to come in and stir up the shit pot. She's got a cold case on her hands that isn't going anywhere, handled by a homicide unit that couldn't find a two-by-four in a lumberyard. Anyway, I saw her at the murder scene; you can't fake that kind of grief."

"Women can do amazing things."

"Indeed they can, and that means beginning with Kiesha Taylor, Sam's girlfriend," I said, then downed the last of my wine.

"You located her?"

"I'm about to."

Honey glanced down at Sam's case file and pursed her lips in a way that signaled unease. "You sure you want to work this case?"

"What do you mean?"

"I'm saying be careful. Watch your back. This ain't your typical murder. There were lots of big players all around Sam."

"If you want to run with the big dogs, you have to piss on the tall trees."

"You're not PD anymore, you're on your own. Careful who you piss on."

Her uncharacteristic concern surprised me. Honey brandished more bravado than most coppers and never held back or shied away from a confrontation. She had given voice to a disquiet I'd been pushing aside; namely, the niggling sense that I was about to grab a tiger by the tail.

CHAPTER FOUR

Perhaps more than any other street in the city of New Orleans five months after the Storm, Bourbon Street looked normal, with stumbling tipplers, garish neon, blaring music, and the smell of vomit and urine never too far off. Not all of Bourbon's establishments had reopened, but many had.

Unlike more recent real estate developers, the city's forefathers had a little common sense and built on the highest elevation around, hence, the French Quarter didn't flood and luckily suffered only minimal wind damage. The hurricane shutters on windows and doors in this historic district are not decorative, they're the real thing and they work well. So the Quarter was mostly spared from the Storm and logically became a staging area for the thousands of federal, state, and local law enforcement and military elements. High ground and high times, that's what the boys were looking for.

To be fair, we desperately needed their help. Local law enforcement kept our embarrassment to ourselves, but the outside elements that swarmed in to shore up NOPD restored order to what had become a city-wide battleground. And that was no euphemism; the city had been a free-fire war zone in the unfolding disaster.

One month after the Storm, with the city under strict curfew and before evacuees had been allowed to return, you might have seen a thousand pedestrians on Bourbon, mostly men, mostly off-duty cops, soldiers, security operators, firefighters, repair techs, or contractors—all from out of town—looking for some drink and some company. A few watering holes remained open right through the Storm and its aftermath, staffed by hard-partying skeleton crews of employees who would have ridden flaming chariots into Hell without an afterthought.

But there weren't many local women around back then. The few girls working in the few open bars and clubs were generally not A talent. Or B. But they were female and no doubt their mothers loved them.

Now, as we neared the first Mardi Gras since the Storm turned everything topsy-turvy, most of the strip clubs were again operating, if with limited staff. The college crowd had returned to the Quarter en masse as the universities ramped up to resume classes. More clubs, bars, and restaurants had reopened. And higher-end ladies of the evening had wiggled their way back, eager to earn their share of the money storm the recovery generated. Bourbon Street was getting back to a semblance of normalcy, even if the rest of the city wasn't.

Kendall Bullard, the aspiring UFC fighter I coached, worked as a Bourbon Street bouncer at Player's Club, a mid-level strip joint. I'd gotten him the bouncing job and had been coaching and mentoring him pro bono for three years. Kendall had long been my best street source, and seemed to have a better intel net than the NOPD Criminal Intelligence Bureau.

He was waiting for me on the corner near Player's Club, about to take a cab to Louis Armstrong Airport and a late flight to Miami for his upcoming K-1 bout.

"How'd the workout go today?"

"Solid, Coach. I'm good to go."

"I know you are, man. And I know something else: you've got what it takes. But talent is only part of the equation. When everything comes together for you, which could very well happen in Miami, you'll be unstoppable. And you know I don't bullshit about stuff like this."

"I know."

"Anything on Kiesha?" I asked.

"Easy as pie for you, boss. You gots about a block and a half walk to Utopia. She a shot girl, working a shift there right now."

"Sweet. I'll call you in Miami tomorrow."

Kendall nodded and got into the back of the taxi. As he closed the door, I called out, "Try to stay out of the South Beach clubs till after the fight, Mr. Stud."

"I'll try, Coach."

As his taxi lurched forward on the side street, I turned and set off on Bourbon toward Canal. In this abbreviated season, parades in the city rolled this weekend then paused until the Thursday before Mardi Gras, when they would roll daily through Fat Tuesday. And while the parades no longer entered the French Quarter itself, a pretty good crowd should be tearing up the Quarter tonight since all the parades this season ran the St. Charles route and ended on Canal, just up ahead. But this was the New Normal, and a fairly thin crowd populated Bourbon.

I greeted the two security guys I knew at Utopia's front entrance and entered the first bar area, which was uncharacteristically dead. I had the cute barkeep mix me an Original Tequila Sunrise, made with 100-percent blue agave tequila, crème de cassis, fresh lime juice, and club soda.

Drink in hand, I headed deeper into the darkened club, into the outdoor courtyard, past the big fire pit and more bar stations. A few couples and small groups of guys were here, so I angled back indoors all the way to the dim dance area with hip-hop at a decibel level approaching permanent hearing damage. Frenetic computer-controlled stage lights alternating the primary colors swept the dance floor in such a way as to ensure that no matter where you were on the floor, you would be featured in colorful light, you would be a star. But there were no dancers, so it was easy to spot Kiesha leaning against yet another bar and talking to a skinny blond guy who stocked beer into a standing cooler. She had a 1960s thing going, wearing hot pants, a halter top, and knee-high vinyl go-go boots.

I caught Kiesha's eye and subtly motioned for her to follow me out to the courtyard, where it would be easier for my hidden recording equipment to function more effectively. I sat on a café chair with no armrests and lit up a cigarillo as I watched her approach holding a rack of thin shot vials full of brightly colored alcohol. She'd always been into wigs, and tonight her hair was long, thick, very fake, and very purple.

"Hey, I know you!" She smiled that slow, sultry smile that came so naturally to her. She put a hand on my shoulder and bent over to kiss my cheek. "Nice to see a familiar face among all these new ones on the street."

"Good to see you, Kiesha. Have a seat." She put her rack of shots on the small table and pulled her chair up close so when she sat, our legs were touching. "You look great."

"Well, thank you for lying, but I do what I can under the circumstances," she said.

Kiesha was a short, thin-waisted, well-proportioned twenty-five-year-old with an ass you could set a beer on. Half black, half Honduran, the word "languid" barely sufficed as a way to describe her slow-paced, sensual, erotic demeanor. Lovely as her natural attributes were, there was no hiding an acute underlying sadness that informed her every movement. Her eyes were the big give-away.

"You making out all right?" I asked.

"Well, you know, everybody's in a mess now, yeah?"

"That's the truth. Where you staying?"

"Oh, I got lucky. I already got me a FEMA trailer front'a my old house. Some FEMA boys who come in here and drink helped me out. Electricity and everything."

Her eyes told me she was already half drunk and probably high. It's called self-medicating. I never knew Kiesha to be a lush or a complete stoner, but when your heart has been ripped out, it's easy to indulge in the pity party of chemical adulterants. I had crawled into a bottle for six months after Sharon and I split, barely holding onto my job, hardening myself in a crucible of booze and pain. Now my pain was gone, and I only had an emptiness, and a desire to make up to Sharon for all the ways I had failed her. It was a sucker's hope I held, but at least I was stable again. Kiesha, however, clearly wasn't. "Where you living now?"

"Upper Ninth, on St. Roch."

"I know how tight you and Sam were. I'm real sorry about what happened to him."

On cue, she lowered her eyes and went silent for a long beat. "Thanks." She looked up like she'd gotten a psychic signal. "Hey, buy a shot, will you, my manager's watching."

I pulled out a twenty. "Sure. One for both of us."

She slid a vial full of red liquor from the rack and downed it in a graceful flick of the wrist and head. She pulled a second vial and surprised me by straddling me on the chair. She tilted her head so she could hold the bottom of the vial in her mouth, then maneuvered herself so the open end touched my lips. She was grinding her hips onto mine when she suddenly thrust up and the upturned vial spilled its contents into my gullet. She undulated on top of me, her face inches from mine, our mouths connected by the glass tube. She gave me a mini lap dance for a few seconds before touching my face, taking the vial from my lips, and giving me a soft kiss.

"You have the most beautiful green eyes," she said, then gave me another quick kiss. "Was that okay?"

"No complaints," I said.

"I think I feel your little brother waking up."

Before I could respond, the skinny blond guy stopped by our table to empty an ashtray that didn't need emptying. He glared, she ignored him, then he moved off.

"Coworker?"

"Oh, that's Eli. He's a bar back. Stays at my place sometimes. Don't pay attention to him. He's got some stupid ideas about 'purity.'"

"And he's living in New Orleans, working on Bourbon Street?"

"Well, he's not bothered by something like prostitution, because that's a straight-up transaction between two consenting people. But he gets jealous if I talk to a customer for a long time."

"So a quick lap dance doesn't bother him?"

She smiled, showing slightly crooked but white teeth. "I guess not. Funny, huh? Kind of like a pimp; he doesn't feel threatened unless I'm making a meaningful connection."

"He's your boyfriend, then?"

"Oh, I don't know. After the Storm, everything is upside down. Who knows what he is?"

She slowly removed a pack of smokes from her cleavage and lit one. Her exhale was sexual. She stood up and pirouetted. "I might go back to dancing now all the clubs are coming back. The street is lousy with roofing contractors making twenty-five grand a week. Those boys like to throw it around and party."

"Kiesha . . . this isn't just a social visit."

She looked at me for a long moment, then sat back down. "Okay."

"I'm not with the department anymore, but I'm working as a PI. I'm looking into what happened to Sam."

She took another drag. "Good."

"You had a key to the place, right?"

"Yeah, but not to every room."

"What do you mean?"

"I didn't have a key to his bedroom or some other rooms."

"What was in the other rooms?"

"One had the closed-circuit TVs, the other was next to the pool table. I don't know what was in there, never saw Sam go in that room."

"But your key opened the office?"

"Oh yeah. I mean, we ran the bar together. I had to have access to the office."

"Why no key to the bedroom?"

"What did I need one for? I slept there five nights a week. We locked the bedroom door at night in case a burglar got in the bar."

"Where did you keep your key?"

She slowly lifted a gold chain around her neck, and a single key emerged from her marvelous cleavage. "It's been right here since the day he gave it to me. I never took it off, except to open the bar." She let the key slink back down between her breasts. "I don't have an alibi, you know."

I nodded.

"Sam and I had been arguing a little before the Storm. He had promised to marry me. I wasn't pressing for a date, but I wanted a ring. Sam didn't show emotion much. I knew he loved me, I just wanted him to show it sometimes. Eli had worked off and on at the Hut as a bar back for a little minute. I started seeing him to try and make Sam jealous. Buy me another shot?"

I peeled off another twenty and put it on the table. She easily downed the vial and returned the empty tube to the rack with a flourish.

"Didn't seem to work. Sam was occupied with some other business. Stuff he didn't tell me about. We closed up day before the hurricane came. He called me at home the night before it hit. I don't drive, so he sent a Vietnamese taxi driver over to evacuate me up to Baton Rouge. I wouldn't go. Wish I had. So I got no alibi."

"What do you think happened to him?"

"People liked Sam. I keep thinking it must've been a robbery. Some local thugs."

"Look, I know how close you two were. What was he going to do with all the cash?"

"All what cash? The bar receipts?"

"No, I mean the four hundred thousand."

She laughed. "Where'd you get that? Sam didn't have that kind of money."

If she was acting, she was good. "You knew the combination to the safe?"

"The big safe? No. He kept papers in there. He paid extra to have a Vietnamese armed courier service pick up the money every night after closing. He didn't think it was safe to keep cash in the bar and he didn't want to be making bank deposits late at night." She thought for a second. "Who told you he had all that money?"

I just shrugged.

"Sam wasn't so corrupt, you know. Not like the mayor and all the others. Sam could have made big money if he wanted to. But he . . . mostly, he just helped the mayor out. Sometimes he might take something small, like if the air-conditioning was busted, and he was doing a building inspection of some big corporation, he might mention he had a busted air conditioner at his bar and needed a new one. And the next day a truck would pull up and a crew would put a new air-con unit on the roof. Sam would just smile. But he wasn't like the others, with all the kickbacks and everything."

"How can you be sure?"

"Because I was with him for five years. We loved each other and he told me things." She casually scanned the room. "My manager's making eyes. I gotta work the room." She scooped up the money, stood, and picked up the rack of shot vials.

"We need to talk some more," I said.

"Not here. Come by my place. It's 1210 St. Roch."

"Tomorrow?"

"No, sweetie, day after. Not too early."

She leaned in and gave me another of her soft, wet kisses that suggested just what kind of a lover she would be, and then she was gone.

CHAPTER FIVE

The next morning I cycled up Magazine Street in the dark on my GT Avalanche mountain bike, arriving at Audubon Park at first light. I stretched, then ran three laps on the asphalt path, a little over five miles. I biked back to the dojo, and practically inhaled two small tins of honey barbeque salmon and a tin of tuna that I spooned onto rice cakes while standing over my desk. The Way of the Bachelor, St. James style.

I showered for fifteen minutes, alternating between hot and cold water and spending several minutes, as I did every day, trying to clear my nasal passages that were damaged from all the fighting and all the nose breaks I have had over the years. Broken noses, like the one Kendall had given me the other day, were simply one of the costs of doing business in my line of work. I washed my face carefully, wondering why I could tune out physical pain, but heartbreak from my failed marriage held me like a prisoner in leg irons.

I dressed in pale blue jeans, white sneakers, a heavy cotton khaki long-sleeve shirt, and a tan wool pullover sweater. While I couldn't rule anything out, I tended to think Sam Siu was deader than a doornail. And in a city that can seldom solve a murder, I had chosen a helluva case to make my bones with.

I sat at my neatly organized desk. It was easy to be neat when you had very little in the way of material possessions, courtesy of the neighbors. I popped the air card into my laptop, and logged online to check e-mail. Kendall had just sent me a video of his morning practice session in Miami. His fight was tomorrow night and he wanted any last-minute input. I called his cell phone as the short video came to an end.

"Hey man, you behaved yourself in Miami last night?"

"You know it, Coach," he said. "You found Kiesha, yeah?"

"Right where you said she'd be," I said, taking a sip of coffee. "Okay, I just watched your video. Honestly, you look solid. Only thing is, when you shoot in to initiate the takedowns, you're still dropping your hands, you're not protecting your face. One punch can change everything."

"Yeah, you right."

"Stay relaxed, rest up, and go kick that guy's ass tomorrow night, will you?"

"Yes, sir."

Just then I heard the back door open. I stood with the cell phone and crossed over to see who had come in.

"Hey, Cliff, ya decent?! Where y'at?" a male voice called out.

"Yeah, come on in, Bud," I yelled.

Into the cell phone, I spoke with a reassuring tone to Kendall. "Listen, Kendall, you're good to go. Don't be afraid of this guy, just fight your game. All right? Gotta go, my contractor is here."

STORM DAMAGE

I closed my cell and smiled as if Bud Begnaud, salt-and-pepper haired and paunchy at forty-two years old, was the best thing I had ever seen. That's because Bud was a contractor, a real, local, well-respected contractor, not some out-of-town shyster. Bud fixed buildings up better than they had ever been and had been doing so for decades. Landing a bona fide contractor like Bud in the New Normal was like hitting the exacta at the Fairgrounds on Thanksgiving Day. Come to think of it, no, it was much better than that. Of course, landing Bud, and having Bud actually do any work, were two different things right now. Contractors seemed to spend more time taking long liquid lunches at Parasol's and signing up new clients with fat cash deposits than they did fixing anything. But who could blame them in an environment where property owners stood in line dangling wads of money, begging the repairmen to take on the job? No one seriously labored under the notion that just because you'd hired a contractor the work would get done in a timely fashion. The amount of rebuilding, remodeling, renovation, and repair awaiting attention staggered the imagination.

My repairs were small in comparison to many, and I'd only paid a deposit—I hadn't been able to pay all the cash up front—so I understood I was low on Bud's totem pole. But at least I was on his totem pole; I knew the work would get done and get done right and that he wouldn't slink off in the dead of night with my deposit, never to be seen again, as so many other "contractors" were doing. Still, to try to speed up the process, I'd given Bud a set of keys.

"I'm just here for a minute, partner. Gotta take these here power tools over to another job site."

As he stooped over to get the tools, I touched his arm. "Bud, you need to get my wall fixed. If the crackheads around here knew I had nothing but a piece a plywood covering that hole, I wouldn't have so much as a pencil."

"Thought you was a tough guy, Cliff." He smiled.

"I'm not kidding. Come on now, we go way back."

"How many years you lived in New Orleans?" Bud pronounced it "Nu-whohr-lins."

"Okay, so maybe we don't go *way* back, but I'm a previous client. I'm not somebody you never met before. It's been five months since you hung the plywood, and that's been about all you've done. I deserve to be treated better than that."

There was a seriousness in my tone that Bud didn't miss. He secured the cordless tools in their red plastic carrying cases and snapped the lids shut. "Man, you know how it is. I don't use no illegals. My crews are good men who know what they doing. I'm working them to death."

"Well, work them to death over here. I mean, crap, how long do I have to wait? You finally show up, not to do more work, but to take the tools away. I'm not even pressing you about the roof, just fix my damn wall." I was frustrated, and he could tell.

He stood up, leaving one plastic case on the floor. "Tell you what, soon's my crew finishes Sharon's new bar, I'll bring them straight here and fix you up, roof and all. I'm even going to leave a cordless drill here as good faith."

"What do you mean, Sharon's new bar?"

"Her and Dice McCarty bought the old Jupiter Lounge."

"The place Uptown on Freret?"

"Yep. Bought the building and transferred her liquor license. They gonna live upstairs."

"Bought the building? She doesn't have money to buy a set of Legos, much less a building. And everybody knows Dice gambles away every dime he makes. The guy's always broke. Was the place a shambles, so she got it cheap?"

"No, not much damage at all. I'm just doing some remodeling. And building a secret room for Dice's guns."

It was an open secret in the department that Dice owned over two hundred firearms, not all of them being legal.

"When did she close escrow?"

"I heard they paid cash money. Got it for three fifty, something like that."

"Really?" *How in the hell could they have pulled off that purchase?*

"Sorry, Cliff, but I had to put them in line in front of you 'cause they paid the full bill in advance. Hope you understand."

"Yeah, yeah. I get it."

"Got to go, partner. Promise I'll get a crew here soon's possible. I mean that. Even if I have to do it myself, I'll get you fixed up."

"If the crackheads kill me, you won't get the rest of your money!" I jibed.

"No problem, I'll just keep your deposit," he said, winking.

Bud slammed the back door on his way out, but all I could think of was Sharon and Dice buying a place for $350,000 in cash, when I knew she had bad credit and Dice didn't have a pot to piss in.

I biked toward the Tiki Hut just before noon. On the way I cruised past the studio of an artist friend of mine in Mid-City. Her studio had flooded and all of her paintings, her life's work, were destroyed. Her place now stood abandoned; she'd told me she wasn't ever coming back to New Orleans.

I kept pedaling, which was about all any of us could do, as my mind flooded with thoughts of how so much had changed since the Storm, none of it for the better. But then, all of us residents currently wrestled with those kinds of thoughts, which was why the suicide rate skyrocketed, why people keeled over from heart attacks while trying to gut their homes, and why fights broke out over five P.M. supermarket closing times and two hundred people in front of you in line at the cell phone store.

I managed to make it to the Tiki Hut in another five minutes without getting a flat, something of a minor miracle considering all of the nails, screws, and broken glass still littering the streets.

Twee's debris removal crew lingered outside the Hut. They were older Asian men and women whose homes were demolished out in New Orleans East. They now lived with friends or family on the West Bank and had arrived together in a beat-up cargo van. I introduced myself to the leader, Michael, a florist whose shop had been destroyed and clientele decimated. He spoke English well, walked with a cane, and chain-smoked Marlboro Lights as I led him into the Tiki Hut. I was just going in for a minute so I didn't wear a respirator.

"Clean out Sam's office first, then his bedroom. Everything—every last toothpick—from those rooms goes out onto the back patio. Keep the stuff separated. Cordon off what you find in the office from what you find elsewhere."

"Does it matter where we find something? Do you want me to write, for instance, 'north corner of the office,' something like that?"

"Ordinarily, yes, but everything got moved around by the

water, so the exact location doesn't matter. Organize the debris into small items, and then larger items. Catalog everything you remove from the two rooms. And everyone has to use gloves at all times."

"Do you want us to clean things, remove the dirt?"

"No." We had entered Sam's office and I looked around at the mess. "Have you ever seen a bullet hole in a wall before?" I asked.

"Many times. The gangs are a little trigger happy out in the East," said Michael.

"Look for bullet holes when you pull out the drywall."

"Yes, Twee told me to do that."

I tried to visualize how Sam's office used to look. I'd spent a lot of time in here. My ex-wife, Sharon, and I had owned a bar a few blocks away. Our small place never enjoyed the kind of clientele or business Sam had, but we stocked high-end booze. Sam had visited often. He generously advised us and helped us get better deals with liquor distributors. Before long we were covering each other; if Sam needed a hundred ones or a roll of quarters I'd run them over to him; if we ran out of Patrón Silver or Grey Goose or lemons, Sam had them to spare. He was always smiling, always joking. I remembered all the times I had sat at his desk and he had me recount a big pile of cash because he couldn't get the count right. Those were good memories.

But that was then.

I coughed at the whiff of something putrid and gestured for Michael to follow me out. "I didn't see any kind of protective gear in your van."

"We have gutted many homes and businesses. We wear cloth gloves and scarves. Hats."

"Twee will pay for better gear. At the very least you need—"

"Not necessary. We have faced far worse danger than mold and bacteria."

"What do you mean?"

"We're Montagnards, hill tribe people from the Central Highlands of Vietnam. Our people have faced genocide by the Vietnamese government since the end of the Vietnam War in 1975. Rape, torture, 'reeducation.' Even today it happens, but no one cares. The media, governments, ignore it. We all risked our lives to escape for life in America. A rotting old wooden building is no problem for us."

"Okay, that's up to you. I hope Twee is paying you well."

"We would never take money from Miss Siu."

"You're volunteers? Part of a church group or something?"

"Yes, something. We take care of each other."

I inhaled deeply as we stepped out into the sunlight. The workers wore shabby clothes and old baseball caps. The whole exercise suddenly struck me as a big joke and a waste of time, yet something that demanded being done. I simply smiled and nodded as the elderly crew filed past me into the Tiki Hut like itinerant laborers heading to the fields.

"Nice to meet you, sir," Michael said to me, then turned to follow the others inside.

"Good luck." I didn't envy them the job they faced, but I had my own work cut out for me. I needed to catch a snake in the grass, off guard. And for that I would need the help of a snake-handler. A very rich one.

Galatoire's had reopened on Bourbon, and the Flaunt-It crowd reappeared in worshipful reverence like pilgrims to Mecca. Old money, new money, visiting dignitaries, power players, schemers, major and minor celebrities, wannabes, artistes with their patrons, sexy Metairie hairdressers looking for some short-time sugar, and even the occasional tourist vied for seats in the legendary boîte. The food was good, the owner treated you like family, and it was a convivial atmosphere. Friday lunch reigned as an A-list institution, making it impossible for the *hoi polloi* to get a table. Some of the waiters had been serving Café Brulots there since before I was born, and you knew you had arrived as a patron when they stopped bringing you a menu.

This being Sunday, I made it past the door and into the small, wood-paneled bar area upstairs with my freshly printed business cards. I'd ducked into my condo while my tenant wasn't there to grab a blazer, even though jackets were only required at dinner. At the well-worn darkly stained oak bar, under a Mission-style light fixture, I ordered a champagne cocktail. No haute cuisine or trendy drinks here. They don't stack your food vertically, and anyone ordering a Sex on the Beach would be laughed out onto the street. The restaurant is a New Orleans institution so rich with tradition and authentic old-school elegance that the computer screen behind the bar simply looked wrong.

The after-church, pre-parade lunch crowd packed the place. When Dorris Sylvester, one of Galatoire's longest-serving employees, walked past, I palmed my card and a twenty into his hand. I could live large; I was on an expense account.

"Mr. Sylvester, I'm an acquaintance of Robert Galvez. He's not expecting me, but if you could discreetly let him know I'm here, he may want to speak with me."

He glanced down at my card and the double sawbuck, then said with his syrupy French Cajun lilt, "I'll look into it, sir."

Galvez was old money. His great-grandfather had owned one of the more prosperous cigar manufacturers in the city, back when New Orleans and Tampa made more cigars than any place on Earth. The family bought thousands of acres throughout Louisiana, some of which so happened to contain that thing they call Black Gold. That made the Galvez family *very* Uptown. A true Southern gentleman in his sixties, Robert Galvez brokered more business deals and political arrangements behind the scenes than could be guessed. He mediated solutions to scandals in ways that saved face to all concerned miscreants, yet somehow remained untainted and above the fray. He was the most connected person I knew, he was known to lunch at Galatoire's five days a week, and I had reason to believe he would do me a favor.

I studied my heavily calloused knuckles, and just when my thoughts started to drift back to the far-off morning that connected me to Galvez . . .

"Cliff St. James, it's so good to see you."

I turned around from the bar and Galvez warmly shook my hand like we were the oldest of friends.

"Nice to see you, Mr. Galvez."

"Please, would you call me Robert?"

"As long as you call me Cliff."

"Well, Cliff, I've been looking forward to this day for a long time." He showed no trace of insincerity.

"If I'm interrupting something, I can—"

"Nonsense. Let's go somewhere private where we can chat."

He led me into a small, wood-paneled private dining room. Two drinks sat waiting on the table: scotch and soda, and a champagne cocktail. I was duly impressed. "Tell me how badly the

Storm treated you," he said as we pulled up chairs at right angles. He took a short sip of scotch, a polite gesture to show that he was having a drink with me even though I was interrupting him.

"My condo in the Quarter is fine. My dojo—my martial arts studio—got torn up, but it's slowly getting repaired. I didn't do so bad." I sipped my drink. Lunch at Galatoire's was all about drinking. The waiters could be your best friends by helping you pace your alcohol consumption during a three-hour meal.

"How about you, the family okay?"

"Yes, everyone's fine," he said. "The city is a mess, and that's not good for business, but perhaps we can fix some things better than they were before."

"I'm not so sure New Orleans likes change very much."

"This is true." He paused, as if to measure his words carefully. "You know . . . my family hasn't forgotten what you did. We don't talk about it, of course, and you can't put a price on something like that, but I assure you we haven't forgotten. It's a debt I can never repay. So I hope you're not offended, but, as a gesture of friendship, it would be my pleasure to help you with some cash, to get you through these tough times. I heard you quit the police department and I imagine that most gyms aren't doing so well these days."

"Thank you, but no, I'm fine. What I need is some information."

"The most valuable currency of all," he said, smiling.

"I'm working as a PI now, private investigator. I need to talk to Marlin Duplessis." If ever there was a snake in the grass, it was Marlin Duplessis. What was the phrase? He would sell a rat's asshole to a blind man as a wedding ring.

"Our former mayor. Okay, that's not difficult. Do you want me to arrange a meeting, is that it?"

"No, I'd rather catch him off guard, preferably at a location that might make him a little nervous, if you know what I mean."

"I see. I'm assuming you can't divulge the nature of why you need to speak with him."

"Wouldn't be very professional of me if I did."

"That's correct, forgive me for asking," he said.

"I heard he has a mistress. I need to find out when and where he sees her. And, of course, I didn't get it from you. We never had this conversation."

"Is the goal of your investigation an honorable one?"

"One hundred percent."

"Then I'll call you with the information within the hour. Please forgive me, but I have to get back to my guests, who are probably getting very drunk in my absence."

"I understand." We both stood and shook hands.

"A lot of people in this town, most people, would have accepted the reward I offered you. But you refused it, and until today, you haven't asked me for anything. And what you just asked for isn't very much."

"You don't owe me anything, sir."

"Please, it's Robert to my friend Cliff. And I mean that." He handed me a business card from his coat jacket. "My personal cell number is on this. Not many people have it. Don't hesitate to call me anytime, for anything."

"Well, I may just do that."

"I hope you do. And you are going to be getting some invitations from me soon, so don't insult me by turning them down." As he opened the door to the hallway, we were hit by a cacophony of laughter from some shrieking Uptown ladies well into their cups.

"Your friends?" I joked.

"I'm afraid so. The next time I see you at Galatoire's, you'll be sitting at the head of my table."

As I walked toward Rampart I thought about Robert Galvez and wondered if he was really as decent as he tried to come off. Then I thought about that morning three years ago when I had biked up to Audubon Park at first light, heard a muffled scream, and saw a female jogger being dragged into a van by two men. The van started to drive off, then inexplicably pulled over and parked. I was there within thirty seconds, shattered the driver's window with my elbow, and pulled the driver out. I quickly immobilized him, then climbed into the van where the second man, stoned out of his mind, had forced the jogger into oral copulation. Knowing full well the wretched state of the criminal justice system in New Orleans, I decided to exact justice myself, and let God be my judge. I beat both men within an inch of their lives before PD arrived. I broke bones in both of my hands, I beat them so hard, and I have strong bones. Since I was off duty I was taken into custody for a long and not always friendly debriefing, until it emerged that the suspects were wanted serial rapists from Jackson, Mississippi, who had killed their last three victims. Even the chief couldn't throw water on that, although he tried to.

I didn't take the reward for rescuing Galvez's granddaughter because I'm old-fashioned and don't think people need to be rewarded for aiding their fellow man. I knew I would represent a painful memory, so I had stayed clear of the Galvez family. But if

I was going to solve Sam Siu's murder, I needed all the help I could get.

By the time I got to the lamppost on Dauphine where I'd chained my bicycle, my cell phone rang. It was Robert Galvez. He gave me a time, he gave me an address, and he gave me the mayor's cell phone number.

CHAPTER SIX

I biked past Duplessis's bodyguard dozing behind the wheel of a black Suburban parked in front of a small condo complex in the Marigny Triangle. A half block away I spotted two FBI agents in a gray Crown Vic keeping an eye on the Suburban. I had stopped at the dojo for a quick change and resupply; I wore a tan knit cap, wraparound Wiley X sunglasses, Kevlar gloves, jeans, a sweater, and hiking boots. A black Pacsafe daypack snuggled tightly to my back.

I circled around to Spain Street, locked the bike to a pole, jumped a fence, and entered a rear door to the condo's small parking garage. This was not a high-end condo building with a doorman and security so I wasn't worried about the security cams; no one would be watching them. If an incident took place, the footage could be reviewed, but there was no one to stop me from picking the lock on the door leading from the garage to the rear stairwell.

After taking two stairs at a time, I checked my watch at the third-floor landing. Duplessis had a reputation for extreme punctuality, and I was a little behind schedule. From my pack I retrieved a gray steel box about the size of a thick paperback book. I peeled waxy paper off the back of the unit and attached the box to the wall with the self-adhesive tape. I pushed a recessed button that powered up the motion-activated video-recording device. The box had a Bell South sticker on it, which masked the tiny camera lens, and looked like some kind of official unit that belonged on the wall.

My pack also held a telescoping pole with a trigger assembly on one end. I shook a can of black spray paint, then snapped it into a bracket on the other end of the pole. Pulling the trigger on one end of the pole would cause a lever to press on the spray can nozzle at the other end.

In the hallway I found unit number 313 and located the nearest security cam. I extended the pole, pulled the trigger, and spray-painted over the camera lens. As I collapsed the pole, a door opened. Unit 313.

I had just enough time to get the pole back into my pack and spin around, as if I were coming from the elevator. Duplessis stepped into the hallway and the door quickly closed behind him.

He wasn't pleased to find another person in the hallway, and riveted his piercing eyes on me as he strode toward the elevators. Duplessis is a big man, six foot two, 280 pounds, short gray hair. He was known to be a bully, and seeing as how bullies in positions of power are usually cowards, I stepped in front of him, blocking his way.

"How was it, Marlin, she do you right today?"

Not exactly a polite opening line, but I wanted him off balance. He flashed a look of utter shock, followed by a second of fear, then he flooded with anger and reached for his cell phone without saying a word, now staring daggers at me.

"Your cell phone won't work, I'm jamming the signal." The jammer was in my backpack. All the rage in Tokyo, frustrated passengers used them to silence rude chatters on subways.

Duplessis took a couple seconds to realize he had no signal. I moved in closer, more challenging to him. "I've got you on tape coming out of a whore's apartment on Sunday, when you should be home with your family. I can see it on YouTube already."

"Why you . . ." He lashed out with his right, as I assumed he would. I stepped aside, caught his forearm, and easily spun him into an armbar compliance hold that I knew to be very painful. "Son of a . . . !"

"That was assault. And I've got it on tape."

"Screw you!"

I applied greater pressure to the arm lock and he grunted. "Step into my office, Mr. Ex-Mayor."

I led him into the stairwell, keeping him in the compliance hold. I positioned him close to the metal box I'd attached to the wall. Insurance in case my lapel pin cam malfunctioned. He squirmed; probably afraid I would throw him over the rail. A man who has stepped on a thousand toes has plenty to fear.

"Sam Siu," I said, and he stopped fidgeting. "Sam Siu, Mr. Mayor."

"What about him?"

"Why'd you have him killed?"

"What?"

He started to struggle again, but he was no fighter. His thick wrists made it more difficult, but I altered my hold and applied pressure. He yelped.

"Stop resisting and start talking or I'll break your wrist."

He relaxed. "I didn't have anything to do with that."

"You are a corrupt, thieving, cheating SOB, Duplessis. The Feds have been investigating you and your dirty business during your eight-year reign of stealing from the people. Indictments are coming down from the FBI."

"If I am tried, then the courts will decide if I am a thieving SOB. But I'm not a killer."

"Really? I hear Sam was about to roll over for the Feds, so you took him out. Sends a strong message to anyone else thinking of doing the same."

"Hey, dumb shit, Sam was the one guy I didn't have to worry about. Sam Siu was the most loyal man I've ever known. He would have stacked time in Angola before he would have given me up."

"So what happened to him?" I asked evenly.

"Sam always liked to be in the middle of something, he liked to keep his blood pumping. After I left office, maybe he got involved in some things that weren't in his best interests. Something that might have got him killed."

"Like what?"

"Don't ask me, ask T-Boy," he said.

"T-Boy?"

"Don't you know anything, man? T-Boy! Tommy Boudreaux. Sam's CIA handler from the old covert-ops days. T-Boy is the CIA station chief in New Orleans and has been forever, even though he says he's retired."

CIA station chief? Crap.

"Now just who are you?" he demanded, sensing the advantage returning to him.

The dozens of things I'd wanted to ask Duplessis suddenly seemed less important, and I couldn't focus on a line of questioning. It was like I stood frozen in a bell tower that kept clanging the warning "CIA." "I won't be posting those videos, Mr. Mayor. This isn't blackmail and I'm not out to destroy your marriage, but I will be talking to you again." I gave him a little shove as I released him, so he wouldn't get any fancy ideas.

He glared at me, wanting to lash out, wanting to say something to put me in my place, but I stared him down. I wasn't afraid of him and he knew it. He turned away and walked back into the hallway. I removed the gray box from the wall and flew down the stairs like a wanted man. Pissing on the tall trees, indeed.

I spent the rest of the afternoon and early evening working with video files. I uploaded the Duplessis video onto an external hard drive. I also examined the footage I'd taken the day I responded to Sam's murder scene and I generated stills of the crime scene. I again got a funny feeling about Dice's preoccupation with Sam's laptop. Knowing Dice, he'd probably been trying to crack into Sam's online bank account.

I set thoughts of Dice aside. I hadn't done diagrams, but speculated that the killer stood near the open safe when he fired. Unless the shooter had just been intimate with Sam, I figured he or she had somehow gotten in while Sam took a shower.

The police case file wasn't helpful. No suspicious phone calls. No credit card or bank activity that raised red flags. And no expenditures for plane, train, bus, or cruise ship tickets. The transcript of Twee's interview with homicide detectives reiterated what she'd already told me: she went to the Tiki Hut that evening to look for her father after waiting for him to pick her up at her condo and evacuate to Houston; the front door was unlocked and she called 9-1-1 as soon as she saw the body in Sam's office; Dice McCarty arrived within seven minutes of her call.

I rechecked the lists Twee had given me; friends, family, associates of her father. Tommy Boudreaux's name appeared as a business associate, but there was certainly no mention of him being the NOLA CIA station chief.

I knew that since 9/11 CIA officers had been assigned to work with the Terrorism Task Force of the New Orleans FBI office. And of course, New Orleans has a long, cloudy history of being an unofficial CIA stomping ground. America's own banana republic, as it were.

Apart from that, the CIA's National Resources Division has HQs in many major U.S. cities, including New Orleans. As a police officer, I'd never had any dealings with the New Orleans CIA station, but it was common knowledge that they were staffed by officers from the Clandestine Services and their primary mission was supposedly to recruit foreigners living temporarily in the United States—students, scientists, diplomats, business executives—to spy for the CIA when they return to their mother countries. The local CIA spooks also performed voluntary debriefings of Americans, usually business executives and academics, who have returned from overseas. And rumor had it that they carried out some counterintelligence ops as well.

Was Sam Siu a full-blown CIA case officer, a "NOC" operating with nonofficial cover, or just an asset? Did Twee know of her father's involvement? The idea of investigating the murder of a CIA officer or asset, without the force of authority behind me, was not terribly appealing, even for thirty thousand bucks.

After her shift Honey joined me at Peedy's Place, a grubby cop hang in a dismal little mini-mall on Cleary in Jefferson Parish. Peedy's doesn't serve food, which is probably a good thing, so I'd stopped at the Swamp Room on Veterans, which had just reopened for business, to get us "dressed" Swamp Burgers and cheese fries.

About a dozen off-duty coppers were getting hammered in Peedy's, where a Jack and Seven cost three bucks, not the nine bucks you'd pay in the Quarter, and you could blow off steam among peers. I recognized officers from NOPD, and deputies from St. John the Baptist, St. Charles, and Plaquemines parishes. Two female JP deputies used warped cues to shoot eight-ball on a seven-foot table with dead bumpers. Four Hispanic laborers sat at a corner table nursing beers and smiling like their face muscles were frozen. They were probably very nervous illegals who realized too late they had stumbled into a cop bar.

After allowing several coppers to snake some of my fries, Honey and I focused on watching Kendall take a beating in Miami live on Spike TV. The K-1 fight wasn't even close and ended quickly. So we hunched over the high table, returning our attention to the junk food and cheap cocktails.

"Your guy didn't look too good. Bet I could kick his ass," said Honey as she took a bite of her huge burger.

"You want to go pro, I'll coach you."

"Haven't been in a fight since the Storm. I'm ready for one."

"Careful what you wish for." I had already filled her in regarding the day's developments. She hid her disapproval of how I handled Duplessis and had no idea who Tommy Boudreaux was.

"Ever hear of Jimmy Nguyen?" she asked, licking cheese dip from her finger.

"That's a pretty common Vietnamese name. It's like John Smith,"

I said as I cherry-picked the crispiest steak fry from Honey's paper basket, then dipped it in the gooey cheese. Fries and burgers aren't on my dietary regimen, but it's hard to eat healthy in New Orleans; people down here never met anything they didn't want to deep-fry.

"He's head of the RVB," Honey casually stated.

The RVB, or Rolling Viet Boyz, is the most violent local Vietnamese gang. "Thought Larry Dinh ran that outfit."

"Larry got retired early, out in the swamp."

"By Jimmy?" I asked.

"Probably. You know how it is. When the Asian gangbangers start killing each other, NOPD stays the hell out of it. Just tell us where the bodies are."

"I assume you bring up Jimmy because . . ."

"He did some kind of business with Sam Siu. That's according to Ron Charbonnet, who works Seventh District," she said, then washed a bite of hamburger down with a slug of Jack and Coke. Honey had a good metabolism and a perfectly functioning liver.

"I'm hearing that drug wars between the Asian and black dealers are heating up. Turf, supply chains, everything's up for grabs since the Storm."

"Big time. What bugs me is Wal-Mart, Winn-Dixie, Walgreens all close at five. Yet the bars, massage parlors, and dope dens the RVB runs on the West Bank and over on Chef Highway all operate twenty-four/seven," groused Honey. "In fact, they're about the only things open on Chef."

"Hey, a thug has to earn a living, too," I cracked wise. "And all of these out-of-town workers are cash flush and need some place to blow their dough . . . like the four homeboys over there in the corner. Think I could hire them to fix the hole in my wall?"

"Probably."

I snagged another steak fry from Honey. "I'll pencil Jimmy Nguyen onto my growing list of suspects."

"Trust me. Use ink."

CHAPTER SEVEN

The crisp dawn became my friend once I heated up from the bike ride on Magazine to Audubon Park. I never cared for cold or chilly weather, but it made strenuous outdoor exercise a lot more tolerable, if you don't mind searing lung pain from sucking in frozen air. As I finished chaining my bike to the rack on the edge of the parking lot, a white GMC Yukon stopped right next to me and the passenger window came down.

"I hear you want to talk to me, so climb on in."

I eyed the driver, but couldn't tell if anyone else occupied the SUV. I couldn't imagine it to be anyone except Tommy Boudreaux, even though I hadn't put out any word that I wanted to talk to him. The driver had done to me what I did to Duplessis; he caught me off guard. My Glock 36 backup weapon I carried at all times was nestled in the small of my back in a special stretch waistband. It would take two seconds to pull it, an eternity if your life was on the line.

"I'm T-Boy. C'mon, it's cold. Get in."

He reminded me of a well-preserved TV game show host. The

man had to be close to seventy, but had a full head of perfectly coiffed salt-and-pepper hair, perfect white teeth, a tan, and not nearly enough lines or skin sag where there should be some. The guy looked handsome. And tall. Even sitting in the vehicle, I pegged him for basketball-player height.

I saw no logical option, really, but to get into the vehicle. If he wanted to harm me, well, I made an easy target biking all over New Orleans. What I regretted most was not having my recording equipment, but I stepped forward and got into the vehicle.

"Would you do me the courtesy of turning off any recording devices and placing them in this compartment?" He lifted a lid from a section of the console. His Southeast Louisiana accent had been virtually erased by what must have been decades operating overseas.

"I'm not usually wired when I go running at six A.M."

"Lift up your sweatshirt."

"No." He caught me off balance, but I wasn't going to stay there.

"Word is you were always wired when you were NOPD."

"That's true, but at the moment I'm not. I do have a forty-five auto in my pants."

"Anything less than a forty-five isn't worth carrying."

"What's CIA standard issue these days?"

T-Boy laughed heartily and whipped the Yukon out of the parking lot back onto Magazine, toward the lake.

He wasn't going to confirm or deny he was CIA. He wasn't even going to acknowledge the query. "How did you find me so fast?" I asked.

"Let's just say I maintain a robust network of information sources."

We chatted amicably for a good twenty minutes as he took backstreets into a part of town called Seabrook. He asked lots of questions about my background, travels, likes and dislikes, and travails of laboring in the police department under a chief who wanted my head. I peppered him with similar inquiries, wondering whether any of his responses bore even a semblance of truth. Nonetheless, it was a friendly kind of patter, like one might have with an amiable seatmate on an airline flight.

When we passed the heavily damaged, closed FBI headquarters building on Leon C. Simon Boulevard, I casually asked where we were going.

"Lakefront Airport. Or at least what's left of it."

I knew Lakefront Airport well. Built in the mid-1930s on a man-made peninsula sticking out into Lake Pontchartrain, the terminal reigned as a fabulous example of Art Deco architecture. Before we opened our bar, Sharon and I sometimes dressed up and drove out for a Tom Collins or Brandy Alexander and to soak up the elegance of another era.

As T-Boy turned into the main driveway, elegance wasn't the word that came to mind. The airport looked as though it had been carpet bombed.

The front doors stood wide open and we made our way into the main lobby of the terminal building. The graceful curves of the art deco design remained intact, but jumbled rubble pimpled the badly damaged building. Grime and sludge covered the large compass design in the terrazzo flooring. Pieces of the polished marble support columns had been chipped off. The antique Coca-Cola signs in the Fly Away Lounge dangled askew, the classic chrome-and-leather bar stools crushed into heaps of scrap.

T-Boy led me silently down a battered hallway, drinking fountains hanging awry, the walls stained by rancid water, toward the Walnut Room. We gingerly climbed over heavy fire doors that had been smashed off their hinges and crumpled like they'd been hit by a train. As I watched him scan the room with sad eyes, I pegged him for six-foot-six minimum. He cut quite a striking figure, even in the ruins.

The Walnut Room retained no hint of beauty or sophistication. I held sweet memories from this place, but I couldn't connect them to the shambles in front of me. The antique art deco furniture had probably been either looted or washed away. There was only dirt and mold and broken glass and a sense of horrible loss.

"Did you know Sam was a pilot?" asked T-Boy, breaking the stillness.

"I don't know much about Sam, actually."

"Rotary, fixed-wing. Sam could fly anything. He used to keep an old Beech AT-10 Wichita in a hangar right over there," he said, pointing through a broken window toward large debris piles on the tarmac. "I remember his little girl, Twee, when she was about ten years old, running around at a party we had for Sam in this very room."

"I spent some time here myself."

"Is that so? And look at it now." As he took a step, broken glass crunched under his alligator-skin cowboy boots. "You want to know about Sam and me, but that's a much bigger subject than you realize. I first met Sam Siu in sixty-nine. Some of what I'm going to tell you is still classified, but screw it. I led eleven indigenous troops—Montagnards—on a wet mission into Communist China. We'd been inserted in Laos and had to hump it a long way to the target. We were gonna kill General Giap, the top general of the NVA and their master strategist. We found out about a meeting he had with some PLA generals up in southern China and decided to take him out. Can you imagine the audacity of that? The CIA suits, even the field guys don't think that way today, it's all about CYA."

"Cover your ass."

"Exactly."

"You were the only American on the hit team?"

"Correct. We required maximum deniability. Anyway, I didn't need any Caucasians, those Montagnards were outstanding troops. We carried Russian-made weapons and radios and nothing that could identify who we were."

"You conceived the plan?"

"Correct again. We infiltrated successfully and were good to go. But the brass chicken-shitted out at the last minute and scrubbed the mission. We had Giap in our sights, literally. I should have just killed the sucker."

"But you obeyed orders," I said.

"To my great regret." He stared at a wall and didn't say anything for a few moments, lost in far-off indelible memories as he searched for new words to tell an old tale. "Anyway, the exfiltration didn't go so well. We got chased into North Vietnam and the team was shot up pretty bad. They wouldn't send an American pilot or an American plane for us. A Raven out of Thailand borrowed a Cessna and came for us, but crashed and was killed."

"Raven?"

"Volunteer forward air controller. Secret air force shit going on in Laos. Anyway, we had the entire NVA Four Hundred and Fifth Brigade crawling up our ass. Long story short, Sam Siu volunteered to fly a suicide mission in an old French Broussard to try and get us out. When they denied him permission, he took off anyway. Under heavy fire, he made a three-point landing on an eight-hundred-foot stretch of dirt track, turned the bird around, and got us out while he was shooting an M-3 submachine gun out the open cockpit window as he sang a Montagnard folk song.

"Three of us made it out alive. That was the *first* time Sam saved my life." T-Boy turned and moved toward a side exit. "Come on, let's get out into the sunshine, this place is too depressing."

We circled around toward his Yukon, dodging large pieces of siding, chunks of concrete, downed light poles.

"Anyway, I ended up bringing Sam with me to Thailand."

"Let me guess: CIA paramilitary operative and young Asian bad boy pilot equals secret air force shit run out of Udon Thani or Nakhon Phanom in Issan."

T-Boy stopped and turned to me. "It was petty of Chief Pointer not to promote you to detective."

"So Sam flew his share of dope out of the Golden Triangle."

He started to flash angry, then smiled instead. "You know, it's a shame how a Hollywood movie and a couple of half-assed books can convince the world that the CIA was doing nothing but running drugs in Southeast Asia. What we were doing was fighting a complex war where a lot of good people were being killed. We didn't fly to Point A to pick up dope, and then fly to Point B to deliver the dope. It's probably fair to say that every one of our planes at some time or another carried drugs. But our pilots and the Agency weren't in on it. It's probably also fair to say that at some time every Greyhound bus in America has ferried drugs, and so has most every sampan plying the South China Sea, every shuttle van between Phnom Penh and Bangkok, every train in Europe, and probably every taxi in Cali, Colombia. That doesn't make the drivers complicit."

"Are you categorically saying that Sam hasn't been involved in drugs in the recent past?"

"Sam tolerated the fact that his girlfriend was a recreational drug user. Beyond that, to my knowledge he wasn't involved in consuming, selling, or distributing dope."

"Do you have any knowledge of federal or FBI interest in indicting Sam?"

"I think the Feds have been looking into Mayor Duplessis and most folks from his administration, so that would have to include Sam."

"Somehow I think you never would have let the Feds indict Sam. As a professional courtesy, right?"

"This is New Orleans. There's a lot of courtesy given down here, as you may know. But I don't run this city and I don't decide who the federal prosecutor is going to indict."

"Sam's bank loan . . . what was that about?"

"You should ask the bank why they loaned him the money. Sam was a legitimate businessman or he wouldn't have gotten the loan."

"But keeping it in cash? That stinks to high heaven."

"The money had nothing to do with drugs, I can tell you that."

"But you won't tell me what it was for, and I think you know."

"It wasn't my money. Like I said, feel free to talk to the bank."

"What happened to Sam Siu? There's no body. Am I looking for a killer, or am I looking for Sam?"

"I'm rooting for you to find out. Why do you think I'm taking the time to talk to you? I don't owe you anything. Sam has been a close friend of mine for over forty years. I'd like to think he was on a beach somewhere with a Mai Tai, a backpack full of Benjamins, and a shit-eating grin. But as you learn more about the man maybe you'll come to the conclusion that he wouldn't do that to his family and friends."

"When was Sam's last op for the Agency, or his last op for you? Officially or unofficially."

"Sam and I are a couple of old dogs whose glory days are behind us. I'll speak in the present tense until you prove otherwise." He started to walk off, but I didn't follow.

"You know, thanks for your time, but for a guy who says he's rooting for me to find out what happened to his dear old friend, you haven't told me anything, really. Except a couple of old war stories. Makes one wonder."

T-Boy's eyes hardened into a look that wasn't very pleasant. If he was trying to be intimidating, I wasn't biting. I crossed my arms and looked directly at him, dispassionately, as if he were insignificant. It was a technique I had often used on local gang members and it drove them crazy. There was nothing disrespectful in my posture, and yet the message was unmistakably "screw you."

As I stared at him blankly, I had the sudden flash of intuition that it wasn't his idea to speak to me, that someone else had made that call, someone was jerking his chain. But I had no idea who.

He kept my gaze, saying, "A taxi will be here in a few minutes to take you back to the park." He got into his Yukon and slowly drove off, perfect teeth and all.

CHAPTER EIGHT

I found an open phone store in Harahan, and in a mere one hour and forty-seven minutes I had three prepaid cell phones: one for me, one for Honey, one for Twee. If I was going up against the CIA, I at least wanted semi-secure comms.

Back at the dojo, the cordless drill case hadn't been moved. Thanks, Bud, you butthead. The four-by-eight sheet of three-quarter-inch plywood Bud screwed to my rear wall five months ago was still all that separated me from the legion of unsavory elements in the Lower Garden District. I understood Bud had many high-dollar massive restoration projects on his plate. Still, the long delay ticked me off. The fact that so many NOPD vehicles and heavily armed cops were constantly at the dojo in the months after the Storm had provided a good measure of insurance. But now it was just me, and I wondered if that insurance policy was still in effect.

I went to work on the Internet. Sam Siu had a number of LLCs registered by the State of Louisiana. One caught my attention: Bayou Aviation, with an address in Lafourche Parish. His partner? Tommy Boudreaux. The Bayou Web site indicated it performed helicopter repair and maintenance as well as air services catering to the myriad of oil companies on the Gulf Coast. Apparently Bayou did a lot of work shuttling workers and supplies to offshore rigs. Curious how T-Boy had neglected to mention to me he was Sam's business partner in an aviation concern.

T-Boy had more LLCs than the Acme Grill has oysters: aviation companies in southern parishes, trading companies, import/export, wholesale, retail, and service business located in Lafayette, Baton Rouge, New Orleans, Shreveport, and elsewhere. Each of his companies had simple Web sites that didn't give many specifics.

Quite a few Google links led me to, of all places, the society pages of the *New Orleans Times-Picayune.* T-Boy socialized with the city's heavy hitters. I wondered how well he knew Robert Galvez.

Try as I might, I couldn't crack a home address for T-Boy. But that could wait; I had a more pressing engagement with a lady at her FEMA trailer.

St. Roch Avenue looked like a garbage dump. I found a parking space between piles of discarded soggy mattresses, broken TVs, and mildewed clothing, hoping I wouldn't pick up a nail and get yet another flat. I'd driven my 1986 midnight blue and white Ford Bronco instead of biking because I knew the neighborhood to be in such poor shape. In this lawless area where the dope dealers had been some of the first to return, I'd make too easy a target on my bicycle. The pot-holed street itself had been cleared, but just barely. The neutral ground, the wide grassy median strip between the north and southbound lanes, ran overgrown with weeds and uncut grass and buried under teetering piles of tree limbs, rotten wood, shards of drywall, household debris of every imaginable type, and bags of fresh garbage. As I got out of the Bronco, packs of rats scurried at will up and down the street. The whole city was overrun with the rodents, but no money or manpower existed to do anything about it.

One block away, Independence Square Park bustled, but not with children at play. FEMA subcontractors busily fenced in the park, laid out PVC sewer pipe, and installed electrical and water hookups for hundreds of FEMA trailers slated to arrive at the site. Neighborhood folks with unlivable residences would be assigned a trailer at the park until they could move back home. From the looks of things, that might take years.

But Kiesha, a sexy young woman with FEMA friends, didn't have to wait for an official trailer park to open in her neighborhood. Her trailer took up her front yard and most of the sidewalk, which had to be a code violation. As if there was anyone left in the city to enforce code violations. The trailer was leveled using cinder blocks, and the PVC pipe connection to her sewer line gave off the faint but potent stink of raw sewage. I walked up the custom-built wooden steps to her door, and she opened it before I could knock.

"Hey, Cliff, c'mon in." She wore a low-cut diaphanous ivory-colored top and black tuxedo pants. The wig today was medium-length golden curls.

If you've seen one FEMA trailer you've seen them all. Two things always came to mind: they're cheaply built and they're small. But it was a roof and it was free and quite frankly a godsend, even if the government, i.e., us taxpayers, grossly overpaid for them. I handed Kiesha a cold bottle of French champagne and sat on the built-in couch that could fold out to a bed. "Pop this now if you're thirsty." I selfishly wanted her drinking, the better to answer my questions.

"Later, baby. I been working on a gallon of piña colada daiquiris since noon. Have one with me?" In New Orleans, a "daiquiri" referred to any kind of slushy alcohol drink. I generally didn't drink them, but didn't refuse when she handed me a brimming plastic cup.

A toilet flushed and the narrow bathroom door opened, revealing Eli, looking more emaciated than ever.

"Eli, say hello to my old friend Cliff."

He nodded sullenly as he neared, while struggling to zip up his pants. Unshaven, greasy haired, and scraggly, he looked wasted. Three adults congregating in the tight space for only a moment made me wonder how entire families could live in such confines for months, even years, without going stark-raving mad and killing each other.

She sensed it, too, and took bills from her purse and pressed them so they disappeared into his large palm. "Sweetie, why don't you go over to Office Depot and see if they got your flyers ready." She turned to me. "Eli's lead singer in the Junkyard Dogs. They're playing at One-Eyed Jack's day after tomorrow."

I nodded.

He turned to me. "You a cop?"

"Used to be."

He thought about that, then, "Our set's early. Starts at eight."

"I'll try and stop by."

He turned and left without saying good-bye.

Kiesha topped off her drink, leaving the pitcher of blended booze on the table, then sat next to me on the small couch. She scrunched so close to me it felt more like a first date than an interrogation.

"It's not my business, but is your buddy on smack, crack, or meth?" I asked.

"Well, probably one of those three. He's got a habit, but he's better than he was. His music is not bad, you know. And he actually holds down a job now, so he's not so bad. 'Course, he's not so good, neither." We both laughed. "You know, I got to know your wife, your ex-wife Sharon, after you two split."

"Yeah, how's that?"

"Well, you used to always come into the Hut to borrow something or lend something, but after you two broke up, Sharon came, and then later it was Dice."

"So Sharon said bad things about me?"

"Not really. I could tell she was angry with you, but she didn't badmouth you none. She wanted it over and got what she wanted. But somehow I could never see how you two got together. Sam said you'd be better off once you got over her. He didn't trust Sharon and he sure didn't trust Dice."

No surprise that Sam hadn't trusted Dice. No one did. But it intrigued me that he felt that way about my ex, Sharon. I couldn't fathom why. "Why didn't he trust Sharon?"

"Other than the fact she drank too much, I can't say. But he was strong about it."

I nodded. Sharon had become a heavy drinker, and by the time we broke up was flirting with being an alcoholic, but that didn't make her a bad person. "Not to change the subject, but tell me about Jimmy Nguyen."

She let out a big exhale. "Jimmy, huh? Well, Sam didn't like him much. He certainly didn't approve of Jimmy dating his daughter."

"What? Twee dated a gang leader?"

"You didn't know Twee has a rap sheet?"

"No," I said, putting on my poker face to hide my surprise, "but I'll look into that." I could have kicked myself. I should have performed due diligence on my employer right off the bat. "Did Jimmy hang out at the Hut? Was he dealing there?"

"No and no." She took another hefty gulp of the slushy booze, rolling it around on her tongue as the ice melted. "Like I said, Sam didn't like him. They were doing some kind of business, but not because Sam wanted to. He needed him. But no, Jimmy didn't hang there."

"You don't know what kind of business?"

"No."

"Who was your dealer, then? I know Sam looked the other way, but I need a name."

"Deon Franklin."

"He delivered to you at the Tiki Hut?"

"He never carried, his boys did, but yeah, he'd stay for a drink sometimes."

"You were buying for yourself and selling a little on the side, right?"

"True," she admitted readily.

"Crack?"

"Never. I may be dumb but I'm not stupid. Pot, X . . . occasionally a little toot. Nothing hard, nothing injectable, and never crack.

Small amounts, low-key. Deon and I went to high school together at Thirty-five."

"McDonogh?"

She nodded.

"So Sam didn't do business with Deon?" I asked.

"They knew each other because Sam knew he was my old class-mate. And because Sam loved me he indulged me in my little rec-reational use, you know. But Sam didn't like dope, so no, he didn't have nothing to do with Deon."

"Could Deon have known about . . . humor me for a second. Let's say Sam had four hundred Gs in his office safe. Is there some way Deon could have found out about that?"

"Did Sam really have that kind of money in the safe?"

"I'm not sure, but that's what I hear."

"From who?"

I just looked at her. Her hazel eyes told me, with a bit of sad-ness in them, that her lover had kept it from her, that she had no idea about the four hundred large.

"You must be working for Twee, so it had to be her who said that. I don't know, I don't know about that kind of money. Sam trusted me, but I guess he didn't trust me four hundred grand-worth."

Her cup was empty. As I leaned forward to get the pitcher of daiquiris from the kitchen table, she placed her arm on my shoul-der. After I topped off our cups and sat back, she eased her arm around me, as casually as if we were two lovers sitting on a bench in Jackson Square on a spring afternoon.

Her perfume smelled of night-blooming jasmine, and as I in-haled the sweetness I noticed a framed picture on top of the re-frigerator of Kiesha and Sam in a Caddy convertible on some country road. I nodded toward the photo. "I remember that Caddy Sam used to have. You really did love him, didn't you?"

She glanced at the picture. "He loved me, too." She took a huge gulp of her fresh drink, finishing half of it. "Didn't have no engagement ring, but he gave me this." She flashed a large ruby ring, square cut, set in diamonds. If it was real, it had to be worth $10,000.

"Sam gave that to you?"

"Had it appraised for thirteen-five."

"Really? Maybe Sam wasn't as tight as I thought he was."

"Sam wasn't tight. Well, maybe he was. He never lent money to people who asked." Like many in New Orleans, Kiesha pronounced it "axed." "But I saw him give it away so many times to people who needed help. Don't you know how many people he helped? Ask around in the Vietnamese community, they'll tell you."

"I'll do that." I took a healthy slurp of the drink and cold shot up through my nasal cavity into the front of my brain. I closed my eyes, trying to focus. The concoction tasted extra-strong and I could feel the effects of the alcohol relaxing my normally tight shoulder muscles.

"You didn't sweeten these up with a little extra something, did you, darling?"

"Oh, I always doctor my daiquiris, baby, the way Momma taught me."

Who was trying to get who drunk, here?

"All of the electronic bugging Sam was doing of the customers. You know, the video and audio recording. Tell me about that."

"Yeah, he did that. He got a big kick out of that. But he kinda stopped after the new mayor got elected."

"He stopped recording?"

"No, he kinda stopped paying attention. I mean, sometimes, the next day we would go listen to the conversation, if it was a movie star or if it was some big players, but he didn't pay so much attention like before, when he was in with Duplessis."

"Be honest with me on this . . . think Sam ever blackmailed anyone with what he got on tape?"

She thought for a second. "Sam liked excitement, he liked to be in the middle of things. But he was a decent man. He wasn't some rat bastard. I don't think he would have blackmailed anyone, even if he didn't like them. He just wasn't that greedy."

I refilled her glass from the gallon pitcher. We were plying each other with her alcohol. Part of me felt guilty. I obviously wanted her tongue loosened, her answers to be delivered spontaneously, without parsing her words to withhold information. Another part of me knew that Kiesha didn't need any prompting to cop a buzz. She would be getting toasted this afternoon whether or not I had showed up. And her physical openness suggested an avenue that I had never considered and probably shouldn't. Certainly, I couldn't deny how comfortable it felt sitting so close to this exotic, sexual female, whose seemingly offhand, unconscious caresses were sending shock waves into my system. For essentially two years, I hadn't been touched by a woman. There had been no dating, no sex, no cuddling. I hadn't even had a massage. Handshakes were probably the full extent of my physical contact with women over the last twenty-four months. That and having to handcuff a few felonious females in the line of duty. But something was changing in me, something had changed, and I felt no desire to pull away from Kiesha's embrace.

She took a sip and smiled the kind of smile that suggested her cooperation was total. I fought that notion, and focused.

"What about T-Boy, would he use blackmail?"

"T-Boy? That crazy man is capable of doing anything. He's the only person I know who truly scares me. Well, maybe not the only one. There's a few, in fact."

"Like who?"

"Deon, for sure. He's power tripping and don't think nobody can do something about it."

"But you're old friends."

"We're old *classmates*. I maintain a healthy respect for what the man's capable of doing. Namely, anything he wants."

"Deon I get; he's a thug."

"Then there's some bad cops like Dice McCarty. More than a few black folks gonna be limping around the rest of their life because they owed some money. And when Dice came to get it, they didn't have it."

"Who was he collecting for?"

"Loan sharks. And don't forget, he became the new you. He helped run your old bar with Sharon after you two split, so it was him coming into the Hut to borrow something or lend something. But he's an ass, and just as big a thug as Deon. He always scared me."

"Why does T-Boy scare you?"

"His eyes. He can freeze you with 'em. They're just stone ice-cold dead killer eyes. And Sam told me—he was drunk—he kind of warned me to always be nice and respectful to T-Boy. They were good friends, and Sam knew a lot about T-Boy's past, all the people T-Boy killed for the CIA. It was some serious shit and it scared me. Even Sam was . . . he wasn't scared of T-Boy, but he was careful, you know what I mean? He'd never do nothing to antagonize him, no way."

She very gently started to rub the back of my neck, making circular motions with her long, soft fingers, then lightly scratching her painted fingernails down my skin, under my collar. I locked my eyes on her. "So they never had a falling-out, arguments, business disagreements?"

"Not that Sam ever said. They got along good."

"You know anything about their company, Bayou Aviation?"

"Probably less than you know. I've been down there to Lafourche with him, but Sam didn't get into details and it wasn't my business to ask."

I took another sip, easing myself toward a place I wasn't sure I should go. I had an engorged penis, a pole tenting up my thin cotton slacks. Her eyes darted to my crotch, and then met mine again.

"Was there anybody else that you and Sam knew who scared you? Maybe someone who scared Sam, too?"

"Sam wasn't really scared of anybody. I don't think you are, neither." She tugged on my shirt, pulling me a little closer to her. "Eli understands I wanted to seduce you, so he won't be back. 'Course, maybe you *are* scared of something. Maybe you're a little scared of me." She took a gulp of her drink, holding the frozen mush in her mouth. She reached over and ran her hand over my crotch, then found the zipper and eased it down. Without breaking eye contact, she leaned over, the drink still icing her mouth. She'd somehow had a condom hidden in her palm, and expertly encased my swollen member. Then she swallowed the mouthful of daiquiri and enveloped me.

I blinked from the jolt of cold pleasure. She moved to kneel in front of me now, and as I looked down, she stared at me, never stopping her ministrations.

STORM DAMAGE

I was having sex with a suspect in the murder case I'd taken on. I was way, way out of line here. And I absolutely didn't care.

Was there anyone in this battered shell of a city who wasn't either physically injured, emotionally scarred, or psychically damaged? A collective pathology of quasi-post-traumatic stress hung like a cloud over the delta. Scores of thousands harbored an unfocused rage at feeling abandoned or forgotten. At having suffered horrific indignities at the hands of man or nature or both. There was the grief of losing loved ones, the utter shock of losing every single possession of a lifetime save the clothes on one's back. Careers disappeared along with life savings, certain lifestyles simply ceased to exist along with entire neighborhoods. When you've been poor all of your life, one of the working poor, and "they" even take that from you, along with your self-respect, then what is left? More indignity and humiliation waiting for the handouts of survival—cast-off clothes, bottles of water, a roll of toilet paper—with little hope for anything amounting to anything good. The $2,000 in FEMA money was great, when it finally came, after navigating a maddeningly inefficient bureaucracy, but the small money didn't make anyone whole.

Now, as the first Mardi Gras after the Storm approached, there was only survival for the survivors, the basest of instincts: to keep going, no matter what, no matter how broken or battered everyone felt, how cheated and abandoned, discouraged and depressed, forsaken and alone.

The people of New Orleans five months and change after the Storm were hurt bad. The few public mental health clinics that existed before were gone, shuttered, destroyed. Private mental health professionals had not returned, just as most MDs in private practice had not. They chose to adopt a wait-and-see attitude from the comfort and safety of Dallas or Memphis or Atlanta to see if the city would come back. Some of the most sorely, desperately needed professionals who had made their fortunes here now stayed away. With only one hospital operating, the city still struggled mightily to fix broken bones, much less broken hearts, shattered nerves, and wounded souls.

Hence, comforts were taken where comforts could be found. So the drug and alcohol rate, never a low figure in New Orleans, skyrocketed. Self-medication.

Other comforts were taken as well, in a city that needed all the love it could get. Or if not love, affection. Or, in my case, if not affection, physical intimacy. The basest salve to temporarily assuage what only time, if even that, could possibly heal.

But I needed no such rationale or justification as I made love to Kiesha for the rest of the afternoon, our lovemaking alternately as gentle as holding a newborn, then as ragged as repulsing the throes of death. Most of the damage I nursed was pre-Storm. A fast healer physically, I felt embarrassed that my inner hurt had lingered and had defeated my attempts to move on. The guilt of my failed marriage had been crippling, and I needed to release it. Which meant letting go of Sharon, an act that went against the grain of what I felt had been my destiny. And bucking your perceived destiny is not always so easy. It made me afraid. Kiesha was wrong about me. There was something I *was* afraid of.

As we undulated to an unheard rhythm and merged our energies, I knew I was taking a step forward. What a gift, what a gift, what a gift she gave me.

As for Kiesha, she hadn't evacuated, most likely meaning she spent a hellacious four or five days either in the brutal nightmare of the Convention Center or the Superdome. I couldn't imagine and didn't want to know, didn't want her to have to dredge that up. I only wanted to give her something back, right now, as she was giving to me. In this short time we would be together today I wanted her to feel protected and loved and whole in a consecrated space of two people giving everything. And maybe I wanted to feel the same.

Later, as we lay in each other's arms and fluids and scents, my jaded, cynical, ex-cop self emerged. I'd have to keep her as a suspect until proven otherwise. Having sex to gain the sympathy of an investigator is not exactly a new ploy. I had to consider it, even though I knew it didn't apply in this case. The odds of her killing Sam and taking the money, then remaining to work as a shot girl while living in a tiny, cheap trailer in a filthy, rodent-infested war zone, seemed remote at best.

She hadn't even known about the money. I had seen that in her eyes. It was one more stab in her heart when I had told her about the cash, and she compartmentalized the hurt almost instantly. I wondered if she could teach me how to do that.

CHAPTER NINE

After freshening up at the dojo, I set out walking the seven dark blocks of uneven pavement to the Bridge Lounge, over by the Crescent City Connection overpass, to meet Twee. Our arrangement was that every few days I would update her on the progress of the investigation. She would pay me in cash for the previous days' work plus expenses, and decide whether she wanted to continue with the investigation. Considering what I intended to show her, I figured it was fifty-fifty as to whether I would still be employed tomorrow.

Earlier I'd stopped in at the Sixth District station and caught Honey at the beginning of her shift. She griped about the prepaid cell phone I forced on her, but stuffed it in a cargo pocket. She also handed me a printout of Twee Siu's rap sheet. Twee's last arrest was twelve years ago, for felony assault. Sam's little girl had put a rival gang girl in the hospital after slicing her face with a razor blade that Twee had been wearing in her hair. Her other arrests were typical for a female gangbanger: burglary, shoplifting, auto theft, possession of stolen property. She had been a busy teenager. An FIC, Field Interrogation Card, filled out by a patrol officer when she was just fifteen indicated she was already a jumped-in member of the RVB street gang.

The dark intersection where the Bridge Lounge sat still had random debris scattered about, making it a bit of an obstacle course for driving. Walking was no less challenging, but I loved walking in New Orleans, regardless of the neighborhood; the whole city was one large historical district that deserved every preservation effort possible.

I entered, spotted Twee at a table, and signaled to Alex the bartender to send over my usual.

Over an Original Tequila Sunrise I filled her in on what I'd learned from T-Boy and Kiesha. We watched a short "highlight" reel on my laptop of the interrogation of Duplessis and of the video I'd shot at the murder scene the night the Storm hit. I gave her one of the prepaid cell phones and made it clear I would only talk to her using these phones.

"Good," she said. "You've been doing good work."

"So your dad was CIA?"

Twee let out a short laugh. "Hardly. He could have used the pension, though. He flew for the CIA during the Vietnam War. He was just a pilot, and that was a long time ago."

"But Tommy Boudreaux, the New Orleans CIA station chief, is your dad's business partner? Come on."

"Tommy helped Dad relocate to New Orleans after the war. They were friends. Dad ran his bar full-time. Before that, he worked for the city and ran the bar. He certainly didn't have much time for me. And he had his aviation company, although he really didn't run it, he was more of an absentee owner. It was a tax deduction for all the flying he liked to do. Trust me, he was no spy."

"He spied on his Tiki Hut customers," I stated.

"I'm sure the CIA wants to know who the head of the Sewer Department is screwing. I mean, yes, he illegally eavesdropped on some of his customers. That was when he was in city politics, which is pretty cutthroat around here. I told you, Dad had secrets, but CIA spy was not one of them."

"You're sure about that?"

"Yes. He would have told me."

"Okay, then that brings us back to T-Boy."

"Tommy . . . we knew he was CIA, of course. He was a career guy who retired a couple years ago. I mean, he's ancient, he's so old."

"Could they have been up to something together?"

"You mean like some kind of geriatric *Mission Impossible*? That doesn't make sense to me, but you're the detective."

"You're right about that, which brings us to this . . ." I handed over the copy of her rap sheet and the FIC stating she was a made member of the RVB. I put my laptop away as she scanned the documents. This was the revelation that I thought might possibly end my work for Twee.

"I didn't expect you to turn this up so soon, but if you hadn't found out by the next time we met, I would have fired you. You wouldn't be a very good private investigator if you didn't find this." She slid the documents back to me.

"Jimmy Nguyen runs the RVB and you were his girlfriend."

"Yeah, Jimmy and I were tight once. I was a bad girl in those days. Drove Dad and Mom crazy."

"You took it a little bit farther than just driving your parents crazy. You're a convicted felon with multiple arrests."

"Yes, I am. Guess I can't run for president."

I looked at her evenly. I wanted some answers and she knew it.

"I was an immature, stupid, rebellious teenager. I fell in with a rough crowd and did things I'm now very ashamed of. Dad finally had enough and when I was seventeen he kidnapped me. I was literally smuggled out of the country against my will and taken to Vietnam. T-Boy made the transportation arrangements. They took me to a small village in the Central Highlands. A Montagnard village where some of Dad's relatives still lived. My introduction to tough love. I ran away several times, but they always found me. I had to work hard and learned a lot of things, including discipline and respect for elders and authority figures. I was whipped into shape; I became a different person over two years. Two years."

"Go on."

"Dad brought me back and I got jumped out of the gang."

"How were you jumped out?"

"Well, I wasn't gang-raped, if that's what you're asking. Dad had money, so he bought me out. Girls who don't have money and want out, they get gang-raped."

"You dated Jimmy after you were jumped out?"

"No. I got an associate's degree from Delgado and then went to beautician's school. Jimmy and I have stayed friends, but his lifestyle is not something I choose to be a part of. End of story."

"What was your dad's business with Jimmy?"

"I think it was some kind of off-the-books arrangement. Jimmy transported fresh fish to Dad's aviation company and Dad flew the fish to high-end customers around the state. I told you before, Dad didn't tell me a lot about his business activities."

I looked up and saw three Asian men in their twenties heading right toward us. Too late, I realized that others were coming up from behind. I jumped to my feet just as six men surrounded our table. Twee looked completely surprised and stayed seated.

"You get out. Stay away from Asian girls. Stay with your own kind," said the taller one in a thin black leather jacket.

"You guys Asian Pride?" I asked, doing a quick 360-degree scan of my adversaries, checking for weapons and to judge which men looked the most formidable—I'd have to go after them first. I was also checking to see if Alex had caught what was happening. He had, and I saw him reach under the bar to press the panic button, a direct alarm to NOPD.

Patrons sitting near us scooted away. Smart customers started exiting the bar, while the thrill seekers grabbed their drinks to see if there would be a show or not.

"Shut up and get out," said the stocky one closest to me on my left. He looked like one of the toughest ones.

"Twee, do you know these guys?"

She didn't answer me but spoke in Vietnamese to the stocky guy, who listened for a good thirty seconds, enough so that I thought this was going to be diffused. Then he cut her off abruptly. It felt like he was dressing her down, but I had no way to know what he had said.

"Last chance," said the stocky one, taking a step closer to me.

I maintained a healthy wariness regarding organized crime in Louisiana, whether it was the Italian mob, the black gangs, or the Vietnamese. Pissing them off was usually not in one's best interests. Asian Pride, if that's who these guys were, was a ruthless local gang who enforced a "no-fraternization" policy. They seriously didn't like Asians mixing with non-Asians. Politically correct types called them insular immigrants experiencing difficulty assimilating into a foreign culture; I called them racists. Either way, I don't like being pushed around for no reason.

"Look, I haven't done anything to you. My friend and I are minding our own business. This isn't your turf. This is one of my neighborhood bars. You don't live around here. *I* live around here. So no, I'm not leaving. If you insist on making trouble, then okay, there will be trouble. And maybe I can't take all six of you, but at least two, maybe three of you are going to the hospital to-night, seriously injured."

Just when I thought the fight was on, the front door burst open . . .

. . . and two NOPD officers rushed into the bar. Sgt. Honey Baybee had the lead. Alex pointed to our table and Honey bar-reled over with her partner on her heels.

Before anyone could say anything, Mr. Black Leather Jacket, all smiles, stepped in front of Honey.

"Officers, there's no problem here." He very smoothly took her hand and pressed cash into her palm. I saw him mouth the words "three hundred" to her. To anyone watching, it was just a hand-shake. He looked at the name tag on her chest. "I'm sure, Officer Baybee, we can all agree there's no problem here." He smirked when he said "Officer Baybee."

Honey looked to me, looked at the other five Asian men, and smiled coyly.

"You just tried to bribe me. And you touched me, you assaulted an officer. And it's *Sgt. Baybee* to you, *noodle dick*." As she flung the bills into his face with her left hand, she reached down to her duty belt with her right hand, drew her collapsible baton, and used it as a striking tool to smash him in the ribs.

Now it was on.

I cracked my elbow into the stocky guy's face, with a crunch that I knew cost him some broken bone, and he went down. As Honey and her partner each grabbed a thug, I spun to grab the guy on my right. I got lucky, got him by the hair, and slammed his face hard onto the heavy table, breaking a wineglass and making enough of a mess that Twee finally got out of her seat and moved to the side.

That's when I got tackled from behind and hit the deck with somebody kidney-punching me. Grappling is a big part of kick-boxing and MMA, so it took me about five seconds to put the thug in a scissor lock. As I tightened my leg vise on his neck, I looked up to see Honey knock a gangbanger through the front plate-glass window with a right that came all the way from Alabama. Her partner was cuffing the only other thug still moving.

Honey beamed until she looked around and spotted Twee. Jealous, her fair skin flushed red, then she looked down where I still sprawled on the floor, nonchalantly choking the gangbanger with my femurs.

"Bailed your ass out once again, St. James," she said as she crossed over, then cuffed my playmate.

"Yes, Sgt. Baybee, you surely did." I got up and caught the bartender's attention. "Alex, a round for the house." I'd busted up some of his furniture. The least I could do was spend some money on drinks to keep his customers from leaving.

Twee approached and touched my arm. "It's better if I don't get involved in this."

Honey heard the remark as she used plastic flex cuffs to secure the prisoners who weren't getting iron bracelets. "Go on, get out of here."

"Honey, you haven't met my client, Twee—"

"I said get out, now! Before I change my mind. I'll take care of this."

"Okay, let's go," I said to Twee, grabbing my laptop as I threw money on the table for Alex. As we hit the door I looked back and winked at Honey, but she gave me a dirty look.

Twee drove me to the dojo. We sat in her car with the engine running and the heater on as a couple of drunken Hispanic laborers staggered along the dim, crumbling sidewalk, impervious to the chill damp of the night.

"Okay, who were those guys back there in the bar? Straight up."

"They're gangbangers, but mostly low-level, junior members. I've seen them before, but I don't know all their names."

"So they're RVB?"

"Yes."

"And what did they want?"

"This isn't about Dad, and it's not about you personally. It's about me, a private matter, and believe me, I will take care of it."

"What kind of private matter? Are you out of the gang or not? You need to be honest with me. That was no joke back there. I hurt a couple of those guys, and I know they're not that forgiving."

"You will have no fallout from this, I can guarantee that." She reached into her oversize purse and handed me a thick manila envelope. "Three days' pay plus extra for expenses. Call me tomorrow; you're still on the case."

Honey called me using the prepaid cell to set up a "meet and eat" as soon as she was 10-7. So I found myself sitting at a window table with her inside St. Charles Tavern. I figured she was ticked off about Twee and that whole mess, but we were well into our second chess game and she'd yet to mention the pugilistic activities of earlier in the evening. She had half a BLT in her right hand, her gun hand, and a bottle of Pabst in the upturned palm of her left hand. While keeping the beer balanced, she used her index and middle fingers to move her white queen diagonally, killing my knight. It was 1:43 A.M. and she was uncharacteristically being very aggressive with her queen and kicking my ass.

And there was an afterglow about her.

"You got what you wished for."

"What, your knight?"

"No, the fight."

"Oh yeah." She had changed out of uniform and wore a green T-shirt and no bra. Her tight low-rise jeans provided a panoramic view of her tramp stamp—the tattoo just above her butt—of two crossed lightning bolts. A couple tables of guys who looked like out-of-town construction workers kept looking over at her rear view, and I couldn't blame them.

St. Charles Tavern stayed open twenty-four/seven, one of the few places able to do that these days, and the bar food wasn't bad. I recognized one of the waitresses as a former stripper from Rendezvous that I used to bang, before I got married. Her nose stud was now ruby instead of cubic zirconium and she had a few more tats, so tips must be good. A table of Orleans Levee District Police officers were here on a meal break, but then, the levee cops are on a perpetual meal break. I pegged a few gangbangers and their girlfriends, at another table some drug dealers I recognized, several couples out on dates, and a few drunks trying to sober up by getting a burger in their stomach.

"You're killing me tonight," I grumbled, as she took my other knight.

"That's because I'm happy. We booked all six gangbangers into the jail ward at Touro Hospital. See, after you left, they kept resisting. I took them outside for further interrogation. You know, dark, no civilians with a cell phone camera. It was fun. My knuckles hurt so good. Threw all six of them into my unit after that."

"They all fit in the backseat of your unit?"

"I stuffed two in the trunk. I blew off so much stress. That's the only reason I'm not mad at you."

"Mad at me. For what?"

"For being stupid. I suckered your knight just now. Just like your girlfriend is suckering you."

I knew she was a little jealous, but I wasn't expecting this. "My girlfriend? C'mon, she's my client."

"You're being played by that little Vietnamese bitch."

"Look, I'm peeling an onion."

"Really? Ron Charbonnet told me that Twee Siu spends time at a RVB hangout on Chef. Club Bamboo."

"Twee told me she was still friends with Jimmy."

"Maybe you can be too, now that you met him."

"What?"

"The stocky guy whose face you broke? That was Jimmy Nguyen. Your client's ex-boyfriend, although the 'ex' is questionable. One of the most powerful crime bosses in New Orleans."

"I tagged Jimmy Nguyen? Why, that little Vietnamese bitch."

CHAPTER TEN

Fueled by anger, I biked up to Audubon Park at dawn. I ran three laps as I worked out various scenarios in my mind. I needed more simplicity in my life, not convolutions and chimeras. I liked Twee's money and I truly wanted to find Sam's killer, as much to prove my detection ability as to avenge his death. But I refuse to be abused, and during the last couple of years, I had suffered nothing but abuse, from nature, from government, from neighbors, from the chief, from my ex-wife, and now from a client who seemed unmoved by the fact that her duplicity was endangering me. Life was upside down; the ruminations I'd had yesterday regarding the mental stability of the city, well, maybe the psychosis applied to me more than I cared to admit.

Maybe if I left, went overseas to make some good money as a security contractor in a real war zone, I could come back in a year or two with a couple hundred large and things would be like they were before. Maybe.

Under a dull, battleship-gray sky I saw the glass all around the Bronco as I coasted my bike into the small dojo parking lot. The driver's window was broken out. I looked around and saw nothing out of the ordinary. Well, that's not true. There were lots of unordinary things to see, mind you, in this ravaged city, but that was part of the New Normal. My section of Magazine Street, Antique Row, now looked more like Skid Row. Garbage and debris stacked high waiting to be picked up. Every other vehicle on the street was a pickup truck towing a trailer full of tools or building materials. Maybe three out of four businesses remained closed. Grime seemed to coat everything. The tiny green space at Magazine and Sophie Wright was full of downed trees. No moms walked by pushing kids in baby strollers. No groups of schoolkids surged past tossing candy wrappers into the gutter. No suburban shoppers looking for antiques stubbed a toe on a jutting slab of broken sidewalk. Boarded-up windows revealed no views. A Humvee full of camouflage-clad National Guardsmen slowly rolled by, M-4s at the ready, looking for trouble. One didn't have to look far.

We were a city on life support. And my Bronco had just been violated. Insult to injury.

As I looked more closely, I realized the Bronco had been tossed, not cleaned out. I didn't keep valuables in it, but a crackhead would have taken the jumper cables and the plastic tub with extra oil, a few tools, a flashlight, tire gauge, and stuff like that. But nothing was missing, not even my handheld emergency CB radio. Everything was a jumbled mess as if someone had been looking for something. Whoever it was missed the hidden compartment in the door—the cold Browning PB .380 was still there. This was a message, and I got it.

Feeling pissed off, I started to head into the dojo, when a splash

of color on the blighted block caught my eye. From a gallery railing of the antique shop across the street, the owner had hung a
purple, green, and gold flag. Purple, green, and gold meant as much
to the people of NOLA as the fleur-de-lis or an LSU jersey. Purple,
green, and gold were the New Orleans colors for Mardi Gras. I
smiled as I looked up and down the block, more closely this time.
I noticed some Mardi Gras beads hanging from a mailbox, a tattered and faded fleur-de-lis T-shirt draped from a window ledge, a
purple, green, and gold pennant dangling from a shop's doorknob.
The hollow shell of a burned-out redbrick building on the corner
was now draped with gold lamé bunting like a Vera Wang gown
on a toothless meth head.

I remembered that after 9/11, my first instinct that horrible
morning was to fly Old Glory. I lived in St. Louis then, and I hung
the Stars and Stripes outside my apartment window in the Soulard.
The whole city did the same, as cities did all over America, spontaneously attaching American flags to car antennas, planting them in
front yards, hoisting them up on poles. It was a sign of solidarity
saying we're all in this together. And now, in our own way, New
Orleans was saying we're still here, we're not beaten, we're down
but not out, and we'll get through this continuing to be ourselves, to
carry on our way of life.

For people born here, Mardi Gras isn't just a party, it's *tradition,* it's part of their heritage. They ski and gather around the
fireplace in Colorado; they surf and luau in Hawaii; they take hay
rides and hold barn dances on the plains; and in the Mississippi
River Delta they parade and attend balls at Mardi Gras, devil be
damned.

I ducked inside and found a few strands of beads from last

year's Carnival in a desk drawer. I draped them around the exterior light fixture next to the dojo's front door.

The gesture was as much a show of solidarity with my city as it was a message to the shitbag who trashed my Bronco. *I'm here, and I won't back down.*

The sign over the parking lot on Severn near West Esplanade announced three businesses: Celadon Salon, Beauty City Supply, and Metairie Beauty College.

The beauty school and beauty supply store occupied the ground floor. I eyed a half-dozen very attractive young Asian women in white frocks taking a cigarette break outside the beauty school, and wondered if Twee owned the whole building. I took the concrete slab stairs on the outside of the structure two at a time. Celadon took the entire second floor and looked like the kind of fashionably trendy salon that lets you know a visit here costs an arm and a leg. That's why the salon was in Metairie, not Central City.

The perfectly made-up Asian receptionist looked at me with a smile. "Can I help you?"

"Probably not."

I walked past her into the salon and made a beeline for Twee at a workstation, where she was applying some kind of pasty substance to a foiled-up matron twenty years past her prime. Twee wasn't happy to see me, but she waved off the receptionist who had followed me in.

"We have to talk."

"I need about fifteen minutes. The receptionist will . . ."

."Now," I insisted. "Right now." My look told her that it was right now, and there was no other option. Whether I got fired or not, it was right now.

"Jeannie, take over for me."

An assistant stepped forward and took the pasty concoction and a small brush.

"Let's go outside," said Twee, wiping her hands.

She led me down the rear stairs to the back of the building. We stood about thirty feet from one of the many ugly canals that spiderweb New Orleans like varicose veins on a worn-out old streetwalker.

"If you are not up front with me from now on, you can take your money and shove it up your lying ass." My eyes drilled into her. She lit a cigarette and stared hard at me as she exhaled, waiting for me to continue. "No, you start, Twee."

"Start where?"

"Why didn't you tell me that was Jimmy Nguyen whose profile I rearranged last night? You lied to me, you said you didn't know those guys."

"I didn't lie to you. I chose my words carefully. I told you they were *mostly* small fish that I didn't know. That is the truth. You were recording our conversation, weren't you? Play it back and check."

"So it was a sin of omission. You neglected to tell me Jimmy was there."

"Yes."

"That doesn't work for me. You're making my job harder by withholding information that I need for the investigation and maybe for my own personal safety."

"Jimmy's out on bail. He's settled down. Mostly, he's mad at himself. He knows he acted out of emotion, and that's never a smart thing."

"Really, so who just broke into my truck, but didn't steal anything?"

She stared at me. "I don't know. Jimmy gave me his word there would be no repercussions against you or the officers. Jimmy is good for his word. If he wanted to mess with you, he wouldn't bother with your truck." She looked out over the canal, toward a subdivision of luxury homes that were all in varying states of repair. At least the Storm had been fair; the rich got hit just as hard as the poor.

"It's complicated. Jimmy still loves me. He's very jealous. He hasn't been able to let go, even after all these years, but it's starting to sink in that he'll never have me again. Never."

"You're spending time at one of his gang hangouts. Why?"

"Business. I own three salons, two beauty supply houses, the beauty college. I export beauty products to Asia. I have other legitimate local investments in the Vietnamese community here. Jimmy is a crook, but he also does lots of regular business. We help each other, but mostly, he helps me. He has a decent side, believe it or not. I've been squeezing a lot of money out of him since the Storm for local Vietnamese charities, nonprofits . . . even no-interest loans to help people get back on their feet."

"All right, fine. But don't lie to me. Are you in the RVB in any way, as a consigliere or something?"

"Do gangbangers spend ten hours a day on their feet cutting hair?"

"I don't know, maybe you're the exception. You give me lots of generalities, but not many specifics. And quite frankly, my reputation isn't for sale, or rent. You're a felon, hanging out with felons, and I'm not feeling very trusting toward you. Maybe you better find somebody else."

I turned and started to go.

"What if I said I have Dad's laptop?"

I stopped in my tracks and turned to face her. "Then I would say you lied to me when I first asked you about it."

"I didn't lie to you, I misled you. I suggested that it would have been looted. And it would have been if I hadn't gone back to retrieve it that night." She vigorously crushed out her cigarette. "You have to decide if you want to hear this," she said, "because you could become an accessory after the fact. I don't know what statutes I broke, but something like tampering with evidence or impeding an investigation."

I was too intrigued not to bite. "Keep talking."

"The night the hurricane hit, I didn't follow you guys to the police station. I circled around the block and went back to the Tiki Hut. I was scared, but figured the place was going to get looted, like you had told that detective. When I got inside, I grabbed the laptop off Dad's desk. I couldn't think of what else to take, and I didn't want to be in there by myself with the body, so I drove to my condo to ride out the hurricane."

"The money in the safe?"

"It was gone, I swear. I don't know who—"

"What was the loan for?"

"I told you, I—"

"Bull-fucking-shit! Damn it, stop lying to me or misleading me, stop leaving out important facts. I know this is hard, but tell me the truth!"

"You're going to have to live with my not answering that question. I'm positive the loan had nothing to do with Dad's death.

Having the cash might have gotten him killed, but not the reason he had it. Okay?"

"No, not okay. You're holding out on me."

"I have very good reasons. I didn't hire you to inventory every aspect of Dad's private life, or of mine. If you can't accept that, then maybe you're the wrong man for the job."

I'd come to the Rubicon. *Am I going ahead, or not?* I scrunched up my mouth, shook my head, and looked away from her. Another flat gray sky hung over the city. A chilly breeze bit into me and I involuntarily hunched my shoulders. The mirrored windows of the glass-and-steel high rises over on Causeway Boulevard reflected more of the grayness back my way. Like the city today, this case was one big gray area. Kind of like my finances, my future; one big gray area. I felt righteously peeved, but I needed the job.

"Swear to me you didn't move or touch the body, and you don't know who did."

I saw tears form in her eyes and begin to trickle down her face. "I swear," she whispered. She spoke so softly I could barely hear. "Maybe you can imagine my position. There are things I'm not comfortable telling you because I want to protect people close to me . . . but maybe someone close to me is involved in what happened to Dad."

At that, Twee Siu wept; rivulets of mascara snaked down her perfectly made-up face, now perfectly sad.

CHAPTER ELEVEN

Many of the city's coffeehouses had yet to reopen, but CC's in the Quarter was operating, so I stopped for a caramel mochasippi. I needed to work the phones and hit the pavement and run down the people connected to Sam on Twee's list. Not an easy task considering few people were living where they used to live and two-thirds of the population hadn't returned from exile yet. And I needed to figure out who Twee may have been referring to when she suggested someone close to her may have whacked Sam. *Who was close to her? Jimmy Nguyen? Family friend Tommy Boudreaux? Her dad's ex-boss Duplessis?*

My brain swam with possibilities, but I couldn't stop thinking about Kiesha Taylor. She had mentioned something I needed to follow up on, but the point escaped me. Unless I was fooling myself and merely feeling a sexual urge. I couldn't deny that the woman got me going.

Except for Kiesha, I hadn't had sex since the breakup with Sharon. I simply hadn't wanted to be with other women. I'd clung to the asinine concept that reconciliation was inevitable. A large crack had now appeared in that belief of mine.

After another ten minutes of trying to concentrate, it came to me why I was thinking of Kiesha. She had told me Sam was doing some kind of business with Jimmy Nguyen not because he wanted to, but because he "needed" him. She'd said Sam didn't like Jimmy one bit. Yet Twee had told me Sam was transporting fresh fish around the state that he got from Jimmy.

There are dozens of companies selling fresh fish in the bayou. Why would Sam buy from a guy he didn't like, a gangster who introduced his daughter to a life of crime way back when? Why did Sam "need" to buy fish from Jimmy? Or had he been buying and flying something else?

I knew there was more I could learn from Kiesha if I could jog her memory a bit and if she wasn't too inebriated. I grabbed my sweet coffee concoction and drove over to St. Roch.

The bad feeling hit the pit of my stomach as soon as I saw her door ajar. You don't leave your door open in the Upper Ninth Ward on a good day, and these weren't good days.

"Kiesha, you there?" I called out. I rapped loudly on the flimsy siding, which must have sounded like detonations inside the acoustically bouncy trailer. "Kiesha!"

I pulled the Glock from my rear waistband and stuck it in my jacket pocket, keeping my grip. I checked my watch, activated my hidden digital recorder, then entered.

Kiesha's body sprawled contorted on the narrow floor in the kitchen area. She'd been shot in the head and maybe elsewhere.

Blood, bone fragments, and gray matter had sprayed all over the stove and refrigerator. Overriding my emotions with training, I checked the bedroom behind me to make sure it was empty. The bed was freshly made, the room neat and tidy.

There was no way to clear the other end of the trailer for suspects without compromising the crime scene. It was simply too tight a squeeze.

DVDs, dollar bills, and plates lay strewn on the floor; perhaps she put up a struggle. I knew she was dead, but bent down to check her pulse anyway. Rigor mortis hadn't set in yet. I sighed deeply and said a silent prayer for her spirit. I needed to disassociate, to compartmentalize this as I had seen her do yesterday. So I swallowed my impulse to cry, swallowed my desire to vomit. I steeled myself with the vow that I would track down and kill whoever did this, so I needed to stay composed and lucid and professional.

The killer had thrown what looked like a bag of crack rocks onto her torso. As I scanned her body, I noticed her knuckles were scuffed, a fingernail was broken. With luck, the killer's DNA would be underneath her fingernails. Then I saw that the ruby ring was gone.

I moved to the couch and sat on the same spot where I'd sat yesterday. My instinct to come had been correct; if only I'd come sooner. She couldn't be more than a few hours' dead.

Twenty-five years old yesterday, a few hours' dead today.

Her boyfriend was a junkie and I knew the name of her dealer, so my plans were already taking shape.

Then I saw a photo album on the kitchen table I hadn't seen yesterday. As I leafed through it, the closeness of the relationship she'd had with Sam Siu became more evident. One photo leaped out at me, though. Kiesha, Sam, and Marlin Duplessis stood smiling, arms locked, in front of a building under a sign stating BAYOU AVIATION. I removed the photo and put it in my inside jacket pocket.

Then I found a section of the photo album labeled KAITLINN. There were many photos of a little girl, a café au lait racial mix. I didn't know Kiesha had a kid. Other photos showed the girl with an older woman who could only have been Kiesha's mom. There were report cards and birthday and Valentine's Day cards, and a couple of photos of Kiesha and Kaitlinn together. On a whim, I took one of those photos, too.

In for a penny, in for a pound, I bent over her body again, this time removing the Tiki Hut key from around her lifeless neck. The homicide dicks would write this off as just another drug murder—the bag of rocks guaranteed it. Twenty-percent homicide solution rate my ass. Whether her murder and Sam's connected somehow was subject to speculation, but of one thing I was sure; she'd now been removed from my suspect list.

I glanced around the room again. No open cupboard doors, no drawers pulled out with their contents dumped on the floor. The bedroom was neat as a pin. The place hadn't been searched. I took some small solace in that, clinging to the notion that she hadn't been killed due to my investigation, that there had been no damning evidence she possessed that would ID Sam's killer. At least that was my hope.

As I sat there, the anger welled up. I had to get out of the trailer or I was going to lose it. I stopped at the door and looked back at her for the last time.

I promise, Kiesha, I will find your killer, either on Twee's dime or my own, and I will even the score.

Outside in the cool air I used deep breathing techniques to regain my composure. I gave Honey a quick heads-up on the sterile cell phone, then called in the Signal 30 to the Fifth District. In a million years I wouldn't consider walking away without calling this in. Aside from the fact my prints and fresh DNA were all over a murder scene, I couldn't tolerate the idea of abandoning her corpse to bloat and decompose in a lonely FEMA trailer for who knows how long. I respected her too much for that. I would maintain the integrity of the crime scene until PD arrived.

As bad luck would have it, Dice McCarty showed up. The homicide detectives were centralized out of downtown and didn't operate from the individual police districts; Dice drew the straw. He ignored me, being as happy to see me as I was to see him. I cooled my heels in the Bronco, examining my video and inputting notes on the case. The purloined evidence from Kiesha's trailer I'd stashed in my hidden compartment with the Browning automatic.

After about forty minutes inside with the CSI team, Dice came over to me and lit a Marlboro. I didn't have to bother rolling down the window since I didn't have one anymore.

"Before I take you downtown and have you talk into a tape recorder, let's go over a few things."

"Nice to see you, too, Dice."

"I hear you're a PI now. Working the Tiki Hut Sam case."

"That's why I was here to talk to Kiesha."

"Couldn't be a real detective so you became a pretend one, huh?"

"Couldn't cut it at LSU, so you went to UNO, huh?"

Dice flushed red. It was a hot button of his that I knew about, a reference that usually resulted in a fight. He turned and waved two uniforms over. "Step out of the vehicle," he said to me, curtly.

I put my laptop away unhurriedly, and got out. He towered over me, and I'm not short. Two black patrol officers flanked him. "Assume the position, I gotta pat you down."

"Come on, Dice, you know I'm no drug dealer. You saw the bag of crack rocks. You mean you're not going to phone this one in like you do all the others? You know, blacks killing each other, just another drug murder so who cares?" It was a brutal challenge; I basically accused him of being racist in front of black officers. Dice literally gritted his teeth, seething. He was seriously ticked off at me, but I carried a smoldering rage that I barely kept a lid on. I wanted to hurt somebody, and maybe Dice sensed that.

"Isn't that right, Frazier?" I said to the skinny patrolman, continuing my tirade. Frazier was an okay copper I had worked with in Third District. "You've heard the word on Dice. We all have. But hey, McCarty, if you're telling me you're actually going to do your job and try to solve something, then you might be interested to know someone took a large square ruby ring from Kiesha's right hand. I saw it on her when I was here yesterday, and now it's gone. And Kiesha told me some very interesting things about you, Dice. That's one of the reasons I came back today."

The piss and vinegar drained from Dice's face and he paled as his eyes glazed for a second. Then he pretended to examine his fingers. "Do me a favor and ride with Frazier downtown to make your statement." He avoided eye contact and his usually gravelly bellow sounded more like soft sand shifting on a dry breeze. I had struck a nerve. "He'll bring you back to your vehicle." Dice turned and walked slowly back toward the FEMA trailer.

As he disappeared into the trailer, I realized that if Kiesha Taylor possessed any physical evidence linking Dice to Sam's murder, he would have it under wraps before the night was out.

———

Detective Mackie took my statement. NOPD would have to do their own work; I told them nothing about Deon being Kiesha's drug source, or of Eli. I bounced in an hour. Thirty minutes after that I stood with Kendall Bullard in front of the Player's Club on Bourbon Street. His swollen-shut right eye gave him kind of a hip Cyclops look. He should probably be taking it easy at home after his K-1 fight in Miami, but he needed to earn money and never shied away from hard work.

"The guy took you apart, Kendall, not because he was stronger, not because he was faster, not because he was lucky. He kicked your ass because he was focused. Mentally, he was better prepped. I'm not talking about being smarter than you, I'm talking about . . ."

"Yeah, you right. He was in the zone and I was zoned out."

I couldn't have said it better. "There's a time for partying, man. You don't have to give it up forever. But when you're training for a fight, forget about it. You're wasting everybody's time. And to be honest, you won't get many more chances before you're yesterday's news."

Kendall nodded in agreement. "Don't give up on me yet, Coach."

"Let's talk more about this next week. Right now, I need your help. Kiesha Taylor got waxed today. In her FEMA trailer in the Ninth. I found the body. I need to know if she did crack."

"Yeah, heard about Kiesha. Anybody can get a jones, but I don't think she was a crackhead."

"What was really going on at the Tiki Hut before the Storm? Was there some problem over dope? Maybe between Jimmy Nguyen and Deon Franklin?"

"'Course Jimmy claim it as his turf 'cause Sam be Vietnamese and they doing some business. But Kiesha's drug man be Deon for long time. So, maybe some, um, friction, but the Hut wasn't no dope hang. And everybody know Sam had juice."

"So no trouble you know of between them."

"You said *before* the Storm."

"Meaning?"

"Deon and Jimmy going at it now, man. The lead be flying. Deon Franklin?" Kendall repeated the name back to me as if I had spoken of some evil thing. He looked furtively about. "Careful messing with him. You and me ain't even having this here talk."

"That's right, we're not, but tell me about him."

"He roll large. Been backed up out of Houston by Jamaicans. Since the Storm, he move way up the chain. He act like it, too. Like he the king dope man of New Orleans."

"I heard he moved soft drugs."

"Not no more. He graduated. Jimmy and him and other dealers, too, all fighting over the H market and crack. You ain't Five-Oh no more, Coach. Don't mess with him, no shit. It ain't healthy."

"I won't mess with him, Kendall, but I have to talk to him. One hundred percent, I have to. Kiesha was my friend."

"It be your ass. Password this week be 'Arizona Cardinals.' Gonna change on Friday. Corner of Whitney and Ryan on the West Bank. Go into the rib joint. Tell the cashier the password, then they buzz you in. Starts about midnight. Name of the joint be Chi-Chi's."

"Chi-Chi's. He there every night?"

Kendall shrugged. "He the owner. Just don't think about calling for backup. Deon got Fourth District in his pocket. NOPD won't come for your ass. Not there. No way, I hear."

"Know what kind of car he drives?"

"Black Mercedes S550 with gold trim and custom gold-plated eighteen-inch wheels. The wheel spokes look like pythons. Python snakes. But he don't drive, he ride in back like he the Donald. But I think he be the Devil, instead."

The more I asked around about Deon Franklin, the less I liked the guy. He graduated with honors from Delgado Community College, where he took business classes. He essentially put himself through school by peddling pot and pills. Most college drug pushers don't have violent reputations, but Deon didn't like getting stiffed for his money or cheated on a deal. Word is he beat the crap out of a gay professor who was having trouble paying his drug debt, but the prof wouldn't press charges and the whole thing got hushed up. Vice cops told me Deon's rise in the last two years had been meteoric, leaving plenty of bodies in his wake. I wanted to know if Kiesha Taylor had been one of those bodies.

CHAPTER TWELVE

The West Bank is New Orleans without the charm. And New Orleans doesn't have a whole lot going for it except charm. The squiggly Mississippi River splits the city. The French Quarter, Up-town, CBD, Warehouse Arts District, Mid-City, City Park, Audubon Park, the Marigny—none of it sits on the West Bank.

I stood in the chill West Bank blackness next to a magnolia tree on Whitney near Ryan at 2:14 in the morning. Half a block away, a dimly lit mini-mall parking lot overflowed, making it appear that the take-out rib joint must have some pretty good food. And good soundproofing. Deon Franklin's speakeasy had to be rocking, but stillness hung over the block like someone had pressed the mute button. Then I heard an approaching deep bass thudding and felt the peripheral sound waves from a five-thousand-dollar car-stereo system. Headlights and treble riffs materialized from the south, then the blue flashers of a police cruiser lit the block with a frenetic sense of trouble. A short shriek from a siren and a black Mercedes S550 whose wheel spokes looked like python snakes pulled over practically next to me with the cruiser right behind.

Two officers got out of the unit. One held a shotgun while the other, Officer Tyrone Banks, slowly approached the Benz with his hand on his weapon. Tyrone, a divorced ex-Marine, was pretty good at Brazilian jiujitsu and had stayed at my dojo for three months after the Storm until he could find a new place to live. As Tyrone approached, another squad car appeared from the opposite direction and screeched to a stop inches from the front bumper of the Mercedes. Two officers got out of the second squad car; both held shotguns, but didn't point them at the Benz.

I have very good friends on the force, some of whom owe me big-time. And they are the kind of friends who would go to the wall for me, whether they owed me or not. Four of them—all non-Fourth District cops—were here on the street with me now. It only took a couple of quick phone calls earlier this evening to make the arrangements for this intercept of Deon's easily identifiable ride.

I hadn't asked Honey to come because I'd been leaning on her for help fairly heavily and didn't want to put her at risk in case things went south.

The four officers and I all knew the thugs in the Mercedes were most likely heavily armed and might panic, so this little favor my buddies were doing for me was not so little.

How nice of the Mercedes's occupants to want to share their ugly music with everyone within 250 yards. I was curious if there was any meltdown going on inside the car, but the window's tint made it too dark to see and the music too loud to hear voices. Was Deon calmly calling his attorney or an NOPD Fourth District bagman? Or were the thugs locking and loading, perhaps thinking this was a hit?

The driver lowered his window, but not the volume, disrespecting the officers.

"Turn that damn shit off!" My old friend Tyrone Banks didn't like being disrespected.

Someone shouted inside the car, then the music stopped.

"Which one of you is Deon Franklin?" asked Tyrone.

"What district you work?" asked the driver.

"None a your business, little man, I ain't talkin' to you, 'cause you ain't Deon. I got a gentleman ova' here wants to have a private conversation with Deon Franklin."

I stepped out of the shadows and approached the driver's side door.

"What does he want?" The deep voice came from the backseat of the Mercedes.

"I'm a private detective and I want to talk to you about Sam Siu."

After a pause the deep voice asked, "What's your name?"

"Cliff St. James."

The rear window on the driver's side came down. The male passenger looked to be about twenty-five, but it was hard to tell in the bad light and with his oversized sunglasses on. He had the "chee wee" hairstyle—short dreads that, except for the color, resembled a Southern snack food—but I couldn't get a clear picture of him. I saw the glint of a diamond ring as he looked me over, but I wanted to see his eyes. And I wanted to see if there were any scratches on his face.

"My man Trey will walk you into the club, on the corner."

I shot Tyrone a quick look, then said to Deon, "That's fine. My friends here will be coming with me."

"Oh no, they won't," said Deon. "Not without a search warrant. Uniformed cops come into my joint, my customers will run for the doors."

Now I had a problem.

I had carefully considered how to approach Deon. I had the password, so I could have just gone into his club and requested a meet, with backup waiting a few blocks away if necessary. I'm dumb, but I'm not stupid, so I rejected that avenue. Deon ran drugs and his organization was basically a Murder, Inc. Soloing it into his "house," his very own den of iniquity and HQ, without having previously established I had juice behind me, was more than risky. And having backup waiting a few blocks away didn't guarantee I'd ever have the chance to summon it if Deon decided to take me out.

So this police intercept on the street established that I had some muscle behind me and friends in powerful places. It gave me a layer of armor. Now all I needed was an audience with the Thug King. And there was something else that I very much wanted from Deon, and I wasn't going to get it by talking to him through a car window on a dark street.

I crossed over to Tyrone and spoke softly so the thugs couldn't hear. "Wait for me down on General DeGaulle. If I don't show up in thirty minutes . . ."

"Then the cavalry will come to the rescue," said Tyrone. "You sure about this, man?"

"Hell no. But let's do it." I turned to the Mercedes and raised my voice. "Whenever you're ready, Mr. Franklin."

Deon tapped his driver on the shoulder. Looking greatly pained,

Trey got out. He couldn't have been more than five foot five, with a slight build. Trey looked too soft to be a fighter so I figured him for a shooter. A bone-colored raw silk blazer matched well with beige pants and an open-collar striped shirt, making him one of the better-dressed thugs I'd seen. He flashed me a sneer without actually looking at me and sauntered off toward the club without speaking.

I nodded to Tyrone and followed Trey on foot. The officers got into their units and backed off. A thug in the front passenger seat slid behind the wheel and the Mercedes drove away, turned at the corner, but didn't pull into the mini-mall. I figured they were circling around to a back door.

The two police units then left the immediate area. I felt reasonably confident there would be no problem with Deon, at least not yet. I needed to get my foot in the door and check his face and the faces of his posse for telltale scratch marks Kiesha might have inflicted. And hopefully I would get something else, too. This would be a delicate visit and I had no intentions of pushing my luck. Still, I found myself seething just under the surface from the knowledge I'd have to show respect and restraint to pieces of human garbage like Deon Franklin and his posse.

I followed Trey right past my Bronco, which I had surreptitiously parked at the mini-mall, maybe one of the safest places to park on the West Bank, considering Deon's reputation.

I walked behind and slightly to the right of Trey, who took his sweet time. He pulled out his cell phone, speed-dialed, and started talking to a female. He stopped, making me wait as he jabbered about mindless nothings using speech that barely resembled English. He shot me a quick glance, then spit. It was one of those not-too-subtle ways certain groups in New Orleans disrespected other groups; and yet, one couldn't be absolutely certain it was a disrespect meant for you. Except I was certain.

He started slowly walking again, and I had had enough of this crap.

"Hey, you!" Trey didn't react, I figured he wouldn't, so I overtook him, put my arm out in front of him so he had to stop or bump me. He stopped. I looked around as if I were listening for something, then I spit to my left, in front of him, as he had done to me. "Never mind, slick."

I walked briskly toward the rib joint and entered. People actually were eating ribs at a few of the tables. I told the cashier, "Arizona Cardinals."

She pressed a buzzer and I walked past her through a heavy door that swung open into another world. My initial impression of the interior design was Burmese opium den meets Philippe Starck. Featuring dark hardwoods, the club had a modernly minimalist Asian vibe that seemed completely out of place given its location. A highly polished black lacquer sign inlaid with faux ivory read CHI-CHI'S.

Two guys as big as Mack trucks stood in front of a sleek lacquered table in the entryway, eying me carefully. Before anyone said anything, Trey came through the door and looked at me like I'd just screwed his little sister in the front pew at church.

"Put your hands up and turn around."

It was probably the most grammatically correct sentence Trey had spoken in some time. "No. *You* are not going to touch me. If you touch me, I'll rip your eyeballs out." I looked to the two beefy doormen in tight suits. "You guys can pat me down."

I stepped away from Trey, raised my hands, and slightly spread my legs. This was actually a fighting stance I had practiced using. I quickly gauged distances, nearby objects I could grab, and calculated how I would take out all three men if the situation went bad right now. I stood completely unarmed; there was nothing in my pockets except a driver's license, PI card, and money. I expected a search, so didn't bother packing my usual kit. The two huge doormen I didn't take for great fighters. Without question, I knew I could take all three men.

Trey reluctantly nodded his head and the two men gave me the kind of thorough pat down that suggested they had a future or past in corrections. This being New Orleans, they might be *presently* employed, perhaps by the Orleans Parish Criminal Sheriff as jailers, and were moonlighting as bouncers for Deon.

By the time the search ended Trey had disappeared. Two other thugs walked up to me. Big, hard men who had to be ex-cons, they wore trendy silk suits, white shirts, and silk ties. But you can't make a silk purse out of a sow's ear, and they looked uncomfortable in the sleek duds, reminding me of bulked-up pro athletes who tried to scrub up in Hugo Boss suits, but couldn't quite pull off an elegant look. Clothes don't always make the man. Nothing soft about these guys; they were stone killers who had probably spent a lot of time in the weight room at Angola. They looked at me with all the warmth usually reserved for bill collectors or the repo man. One of them nodded with his head for me to follow him.

I felt like the icing in a sandwich cookie, one thug in front of and one behind me, as we made our way through a series of rooms where customers danced, drank, and generally had a splendid, chemically enhanced time. One dark room contained satiny couches and huge pillows for people to lounge on the carpeted floor. Another room featured café tables and chairs made from tropical hardwood, reminding me of furniture I'd seen in Cambodia. I glimpsed a shapely waitress in a hip-hugging blue silk cheongsam, slit dangerously up the sides, carrying a black lacquer saucer holding a small mound of white powder and two straws. Cocaine delivered right to your table! No wonder the place was crowded, even late on a Tuesday night.

At the end of a hallway a heavy door opened and we entered a plush office with a very different design concept. Nothing sleek in this room—the furniture was traditional Chinese. Deon sat behind a heavy, ornately carved wooden desk. He lit a cigarette as he watched me enter. Three gorgeous young groupies sat on red velour-covered ottomans around a low-slung, boxy wooden table. A half dozen thugs posed stiffly, some sitting on massive straight-back wooden chairs whose thick armrests were carved to look like pythons. Trey leaned against a teak wet bar, giving me the evil eye. The posse was impeccably dressed, completely against type from the usual New Orleans gangsta drug dealers clad in sports jerseys, oversize baseball caps askew, sweats, or the five-times-too-large baggy pants thing. I always got a chuckle out of seeing a thug walk along a sidewalk having to use one hand to hold up his pants. It made knocking them on their ass so much easier.

Deon's men wore custom-cut blazers or suits and Italian loafers. There were no garish colors or OTT bling, no gold teeth studded with diamonds. The ladies were equally well turned out, looking like they were ready for the VIP section at the BET Awards show. Forget about Nike and Reebok, this was all Dolce and Gabbana.

The door closed and locked behind me; my two escorts stood on either side as we stepped into the room; they stopped me in the center. No one spoke. It was almost still, the soft light diffused through faux Chinese lanterns, the raucous club music muffled by excellent soundproofing. A gunshot in here would not be noticed outside. A fax machine printing out a page pierced the quiet. A thug took the document to Deon. I caught a glimpse of what looked like a photo.

Deon studied the fax, then looked at me. He was a stone-cold clotheshorse. Maybe he emulated P Diddy or Jay-Z or some other pop culture mogul. His charcoal-colored silk suit probably cost at least $8,000. Pale green silk tie, custom-fitted linen shirt. He still wore the large sunglasses. I strained to look for scratches on his face that Kiesha might have left, but he leaned back away from his desk and the dim light revealed little.

"I don't like being pulled over by the police." The deep voice didn't match the slightly babyish face.

"Can't blame you, and I apologize for that. If I could have safely arranged a meeting some other way I would have."

"I don't like Five-Oh; nobody in this room do. When I think about all the times I got pulled over, it brings back a lot of bad memories."

"I'm not a policeman."

"You an ex-policeman."

"That's correct. And I don't like drug dealers, thugs, and murderers. When I think about all the ones I sent to Angola, it brings back good memories."

The room went unbelievably still. I was either proving that I had big *cojones* or was an absolute lunatic, I wasn't sure which. But I knew I needed to establish with certainty that I was not afraid of Deon Franklin.

"Can we speak privately?" I asked.

"This as private as it gonna get for you, cuz."

"All right. Two people you knew were murdered and I'm trying to find out who killed them."

"I knows a lots more than two people who been murdered." This remark brought a nervous laugh from his entourage. "I mean, how many this week, Trey?"

"Thirty-seven, Deon," smirked Trey.

Another laugh from the peanut gallery, as Deon pulled a large-caliber handgun from the shoulder holster under his silk jacket and placed it on his desk. A .50 cal Desert Eagle.

"Yeah, dead people are real funny, but the FBI wasn't laughing when I talked to them about you. Sam was cooperating with them, you know. Some big shots are gonna get indicted. So they're not very happy that somebody killed their snitch. And people say that somebody is you."

"Who say that?"

"I put Jimmy Nguyen in the hospital last night. And five of his best friends. And before I rearranged his face, he told me you killed Sam and stole the four hundred grand from his safe at the Tiki Hut."

"You lying," said Trey with contempt. "He didn't put nobody in no hospital," he said to Deon.

"I heard Jimmy had a little trouble last night," said Deon, contradicting Trey. "If Sam had four hundred K cash money in his safe, wish I'd known."

"Any idea what happened to Sam?"

"I had no issues with Sam. People get killed in this city all the time." He said it in a way that sounded like a warning. "Who gave you the password to come in tonight?"

"Kiesha Taylor. Same person who gave you the four-one-one about Sam's money."

"Shit, only thing that woman ever gave me was her coochie. And that gets old, man, know what I mean? I did that bitch nothing but favors."

"You were her supplier for a long time. You dealt at the Tiki Hut. You telling me you didn't make any money?"

"Kiesha was small change."

"Whoever whacked her left a bag of crack rocks on her body. And you were her dealer."

"Lots of crack dealers in this city, man. Like maybe even that skanky-assed white boyfriend of hers. Who knows, maybe she disrespected the wrong person. You know, like you disrespected me by having me jacked up in front of my own house, and like you disrespected my cousin Trey, here."

"Mr. Franklin, you got pulled over, you didn't get jacked up. Nobody was going through your pants pockets while you were spread-eagle with your hands on a hot engine hood. And I already apologized to you for the traffic stop. And with all due respect, your cousin Trey over here needs to learn some manners. Respect has to be earned, not just given. I only did to him what he did to me, and he didn't like that very much."

Trey pulled a chrome-plated .45 auto and pointed it at me.

"Come on, you saw some of my backup. If I don't walk out of here in one piece," I checked my watch, hoping they would fall for the bluff, "in four minutes and fifteen seconds, then my NOPD and National Guard military police buddies will come crashing through your doors and trash this place. You might own Fourth District, but you don't own everybody, Deon."

"He bluffing," said one of the girls sitting on the floor.

I was losing control. In fact, I never had it. Coming here in this way had been a calculated risk, and getting out was going to be dicey. A heavy security door on the opposite wall probably led outside to where Deon parked his Mercedes. A private entrance. That door might be my quickest escape if things went south.

"Really?" I said. "Call the jail ward at Touro Hospital and ask Jimmy who put him there."

"Screw Jimmy," said one of the thugs. "He gonna be dead soon, anyway."

"I don't get this visit," said Deon. "You got nothing but a smart mouth. If the FBI wants to talk to me, give them my address. But I'm through talking to you." Deon looked at his boys. "Trey, put away the gun. Gentlemen, try not to break up my furniture, but you have two minutes to whup his ass and then throw the mother outside. I mean it, two minutes."

They came at me all at once. I launched myself across the room toward Deon, and took pleasure at the shocked look of fear that suddenly crossed his face. But Trey cut me off, so I kicked his knee, snapping it, and putting him out of action. He'd have to be in a cast for at least six weeks. A lesson in manners.

Trey, however, was the least of my worries. The two big ex-cons started to grab me, but I spun free and took a running leap for Deon.

Deon sprang back just as I slid across the top of his desk. I had taken him for a coward and was right; he ran from behind his desk just as the two bulls dragged me to the floor. This probably saved me. That and the fact that the guys didn't want to mess up their fancy clothes. They clearly weren't accustomed to fighting in suits.

They heaved me to the center of the room. Grappling around on the Oriental rug made it harder for anyone to land a serious blow. I took some kicks, but the guys all wore soft leather loafers—another reason I wear steel-toed shoes. The kicks, especially the ones to my head, prompted lots of cheering from Deon's posse. Mostly I tried to protect my groin and my face. One of the bulls who knew how to fight clocked me a few times and opened up some cuts that gushed blood everywhere. That helped, because it made me look much worse than I was.

"Don't get blood on my carpet, dammit! That rug cost thirty-five grand! Take his ass outside!" yelled Deon, waving the huge handgun that he'd gone back to his desk to retrieve. "Bitch tried to lay a hand on me!"

One of the bulls tried to get a finger in my eye, but luckily I got one in his first. He screamed and rolled off me. Then I got pulled to my feet and a gut punch knocked the wind out of me. Some more body blows, a couple more shots to the face, and I was a bruised, bloody mess gasping for breath. Deon, apparently satisfied, yelled, "I said get him out, now!"

In that brief flash as hands tore at me, I caught a glimpse of Deon, now standing in a shaft of light, and saw what looked like pinkish slash marks—scratches—on his left cheek. Then they hustled me out the way I came. The bloody sight of me was a nice message to send to the patrons, a little reminder they needed to behave themselves in Deon Franklin's place.

Out through the rib joint and into the parking lot, where they threw me to the ground. I rolled and completely surprised them by springing to my feet and breaking into a dead run.

The Bronco sat unlocked, the key in the ignition. As I roared off they lunged for the door handles. One of the bulls reached in and grabbed me just as I got my hands on the Browning in the door compartment, but he fell away as I picked up speed. Rounds impacted in my tailgate as I sped down Whitney. I fought the urge to return fire. Time to regroup, not to fight.

CHAPTER THIRTEEN

My body didn't normally register pain anymore so I could have felt worse. I'd broken every rule by acting based on emotion, my anger over Kiesha's murder, but so what? Were those really marks on Deon, or was that wishful thinking in the haze of a beating? DNA could solve that easily enough, except Deon had never done time, so he had no DNA or fingerprints on file. Which is why I had made the leap across his desk; I scooped up some cigarette butts from his ashtray and snatched his three-hundred-dollar gold-plated Bugatti lighter; they rested safely in my pocket. I smiled as blood ran into my mouth. I had gotten exactly what I wanted from Deon Franklin. Whether the evidence I'd gathered was worth taking a beating for remained to be seen.

I drove onto the Crescent City Connection Bridge, wiping blood out of my eyes so I could see to steer. Kendall Bullard had been right: be careful messing with Mr. Deon Franklin.

"I can't believe this doesn't hurt."

At 4:51 A.M. my third Crown Royal rocks sat on the bathroom sink at the dojo. Honey washed off the dried blood and swabbed the cuts with alcohol. The black eye wouldn't be too bad, and the other swelling would be gone in a day or so. The spreading bruises on my torso looked much worse. Altogether, I had the look of a loser.

"What hurts is my ego. I mean, I got what I wanted, but I got my ass kicked doing it." I'd filled her in on the events of the day, one of the worst in recent memory.

"You should have stayed in bed today."

"That wouldn't have kept Kiesha alive."

Honey said nothing as she applied butterfly bandages to the cuts.

"Deon said something interesting," I recalled. "He suggested that Eli sells crack."

"You think Eli killed Kiesha and left that bag on her body?"

"I think he's a junkie, and junkies do stupid things when they need a fix."

"Here's something else to think about," said Honey. "The thing you said about Dice, the way he acted at Kiesha's trailer? I talked to one of Dice's ex-partners who hates his guts. Found out Kiesha had been a stoolie for Dice."

"While she was with Sam?"

"Before Sam, when she was a young teenager. They go way back. He worked her hard, is what I heard."

"Really?" I took another gulp of Crown and started to get that warm and fuzzy feeling. "I got Deon's DNA and his cigarette lighter. I thought I saw a scratch on his face. Kiesha had a broken fingernail."

"Lab results of any DNA under her nails? Won't be in for a couple of weeks."

"NOPD still using the State Police lab up in Baton Rouge?"

Honey nodded. "Who knows when ours will be up and running again?"

I handed her Deon's cigarette butts and lighter that I'd secured into plastic evidence bags.

"I might let you beat me at chess if you can put a rush on the DNA results from Kiesha's murder scene," I offered. "If it matches Deon's saliva from these cigarettes, and if his prints on this lighter turn up in her trailer, we can get a court order to obtain a legal sample. Then we got him for Murder One."

First aid complete, Honey crossed her arms and leaned back against the door frame. "You might *let* me win at chess? Well, speaking of strategy. No, speaking of the lack of it. Think about what happened the last couple days. You fought with the top echelon of two of the largest crime gangs in the city. Meaning they want you in a body bag. You insulted the local CIA spook. You pissed off our ex-mayor, who is still very powerful. Your fingerprints are all over a murder scene. Your employer is a convicted felon who has lied to you. She withheld important evidence. She is probably still connected to a criminal organization. And your car was broken into. Which ain't no coincidence."

"It's a *truck*, okay? Don't insult my ride." I took another sip. "Anyway, pretty good for just a few days, don't you agree?" I grinned.

Not amused, she turned away, walked out into the gym, and picked up her denim jacket.

"You would think," I continued, feeling the effects of the

Canadian whiskey, "that having accomplished all that, I could at least get my contractor to fix the hole in my wall."

"It's the hole in your head I'm worried about." She waved the evidence bags at me. "I'll get these up to Baton Rouge this morning."

Just as there were never any hellos from Sgt. Honey Baybee, there were never any good-byes. She got into her Jeep Wrangler and drove away.

Dojos are, by design, big empty places, and I suddenly felt empty in a big way. I sat heavily at my desk in the corner and poured my fourth Crown Royal. Kiesha's murder gnawed at me. I kept going back to the notion that my nosing around had made her a target. I didn't know who killed Sam Siu and wasn't sure I was up to the task of finding out who did. Maybe I'd overreached. Maybe this New Normal wasn't worth adjusting to. Hometowns you're stuck with, but New Orleans was my adopted home. Why not simply walk away and put down stakes elsewhere, as tens of thousands of others had? Or just live on the road for a while. My credentials easily qualified me for overseas work, maybe a CivPol gig through the U.S. State Department, training foreign police officers in places like Kosovo or Lebanon or Africa. Or I could get convoy escort or PSD duty in Central or South Asia. A couple years of those kinds of contracts and I'd make some real money, tax free. Life would be simple. I could live some place where things worked, some place not so broken.

I booted up my laptop and within fifteen minutes had submitted my résumé to the three largest global security companies. Perhaps Chief Pointer had been right all along. Perhaps I wasn't detective material.

I climbed the narrow ladder to the small loft area that served as my bedroom. My buddies and I built it after the Storm. I rolled onto the old mattress, careful not to spill my drink. I looked down at the octagonal fight ring, remembering that I'd always wanted to have my own dojo and live in it. The Storm had granted me a bastardized version of my wish, minus students and a roof.

My living situation wasn't the only goal I had manifested in a warped fashion.

I'd always wanted to be a detective. Another wish achieved, but not exactly as planned. As a police officer, I simply assumed I'd become a police detective, not a private detective. Who was I kidding here? Private detectives in New Orleans don't hold quite as much respect as the strip club touts on Iberville Street.

Then I thought of Sharon. I'd achieved my wish of marrying a woman I felt so in tune with, a woman who, initially at least, had been my best friend and partner. But we went bust, and ever since our split my life has been off-kilter.

I forced myself to stop this line of thinking with another sip of whiskey. I'd vowed to have no more pity parties regarding my ex-wife, even though I thought about her every day, knew she didn't want me back, would never take me back. There was nothing I could do; no absolution would be forthcoming. I had blown it, there were no more chances with her, period; so I guzzled my drink, lay back, and within seconds passed out as I had done so many times since she left me.

There was no Audubon Park the next morning. Stiff as a board, I barely made it out of bed and down the ladder of my makeshift loft. And that wasn't until four in the afternoon. The hot/cold shower lasted thirty minutes. My broken nose bled as I tried to clear my nasal passages, but that wasn't so unusual. I had trouble getting into my khakis, so I wolfed down four naproxen with a gulp of yesterday's cold coffee. I called Mayor Duplessis's cell phone and was surprised that he agreed to meet.

One good thing since the Storm was that the parking situation in the CBD and Arts District had improved exponentially. Fewer people vied for spaces and no meter maids gave out tickets. Any space not occupied by debris, construction vehicles or materials, portable diesel generators, mold remediation equipment, oversized Dumpsters, mobile industrial-sized air-conditioning units, stump grinders, work trailers, portable johns, lunch trucks, or partially collapsed buildings was fair game.

I parked my Bronco in a tow-away zone—no tow trucks operated in the city—and walked into Cuvee, an elegant French restaurant in the CBD, promptly at six. Mr. Former Mayor sat ensconced in a cocktail-hour meeting with three people who had to be lawyers. Hard to say how I knew for sure, they just had the look of intelligent grifters. I caught Duplessis's eye and he immediately came over to me at the bar.

"I hope you're not going to cause another scene, Mr. St. James."

"Likewise." I casually glanced around the room. "How'd you get my name?"

"It's on the street you're looking for Sam's murderer. I've nothing to hide in that regard. I owe Sam, even in death. Out of my debt to Sam, I'll help you to the extent I can. But I want you to leave my girlfriend out of it. Completely. If you don't, there will be trouble for you." He made no attempt to mask the threat.

I nodded my assent. "Unless she was involved in Sam's murder, she's out of it."

"In that case, I'll talk to you."

"You know the FBI is tailing you, right?" I said softly, so no one could hear. "They're in the Crown Vic Interceptor right across the street."

"Yes, my shadows are always with me. Do you know the pedestrian walkway out back?"

"I know it."

"Could you meet me there in five minutes?"

"Sure."

Exactly five minutes later, Duplessis ducked out the back door and crossed to where I rigidly sat on a bench smoking a cigarillo. "I hope the other person looks worse than you do," he said, checking out my face.

"Occupational hazard."

"Have another one of those smokes?"

I gave him a stick and lit him up. "There's been another murder," I said.

"You're talking about Kiesha Taylor. I saw it in the paper this morning. Will you be looking into her death as well?"

"Already started."

"In that case, I definitely want to help you. I liked Kiesha very much."

I showed him the photo I lifted from Kiesha's trailer, of her, Sam, and Duplessis. "Can you tell me about this picture?"

"Those were happy times. On the surface, she and Sam made an unusual couple. But they were truly close. Two peas in a pod. It's odd to look at this photo knowing that Sam and Kiesha are both dead. Two friends murdered."

"Where was this taken?" I asked.

"Sam's business out in Lafourche Parish, down on the Gulf. He flew us down there from Lakefront Airport. He had a beautiful old World War Two military aircraft. A Beech . . . I can't remember the model number. Twin-engine small transport. Gorgeous polished aluminum fuselage. On a Saturday, as I recall."

"Okay."

"Sam wanted to show me his operation. He had contracts—small ones—with some of the oil and gas companies to fly employees or cargo to and from the offshore rigs."

"You know which companies?"

"Billings, National, and I think UniOil."

"So he wanted you to see his business because . . ."

"It was a weekend outing," he said, exhaling a long plume of bluish smoke. "Sam and Kiesha and I were friends. We sometimes socialized. He did a lot of things for me, and I scratched his back, too. Isn't that how the world works? I used my influence to help Sam get contracts and I opened the door at some major banks for a line of credit."

"So he got bank loans to help grow his aviation company?"

"Yes, that's correct," he said.

"Did you help him get city contracts?"

"He didn't want the scrutiny that would entail. He liked having the aviation business out in Lafourche. 'Under the radar,' he used to say. And he was close to Port Fourchon, so it made business sense."

"But he flew out of Lakefront."

"He rented hangar space for a couple of planes at Lakefront, but nothing commercial."

I looked down at the photo. "The Sam I knew was kind of a

thrifty guy. Why rent hangar space in New Orleans when you've got your own private airstrip in Lafourche?"

"Sam spent money on things he enjoyed. He loved to fly. He could have driven down to Lafourche, but he commuted using a Cessna he kept at Lakefront. Probably wrote it off as a business expense. The Beech, he only flew on special occasions."

"So this picture, this was a social visit. Who took the photo?"

"The lady whom you are going to leave out of your investigations."

I nodded. "Mr. Mayor, you told me before that maybe Sam got involved in something with T-Boy that wasn't in his best interests. Can you be more specific?"

Duplessis took a breath and looked up and down the walkway. "I don't trust spies. Like journalists, their job is to betray confidences, at the very least. T-Boy is someone who will trample anything to get what he wants. And he's above the law. A multimillionaire business-man who's also a card-carrying CIA officer. A legendary one. It's a powerful combination. Sam was bright, but he wasn't clever or calculating. I always suspected T-Boy took advantage of him, but I couldn't tell you how. I don't have any specifics. But the CIA and aviation companies have a long history of doing dirty business, don't they?"

"Indeed they do."

"And you said Sam was thrifty? He looked like a freewheeling philanthropist compared to T-Boy."

"But he's a millionaire."

"Probably still has his first dollar."

"Does it make sense to you that Sam would have four hundred thousand dollars in cash in his office safe? From a bank loan?"

"Well, sometimes legitimate business transactions have to be completed with cash. But it's not the norm."

"I'm told Sam got a half-million-dollar loan a week before he . . . a week before the Storm. Any idea which bank gave him that loan?"

"No. I introduced Sam to half a dozen bankers more than five years ago. He's gotten a number of business loans over the years since then. As far as I know his aviation company was doing well. He could have gone anywhere for that loan."

"Which banks did you open the doors for him at?"

"Let's see, Federal Fidelity, Crescent City Savings, Louisiana Mutual . . . there were a couple of others, but I'd have to check my files, which isn't so easy. I had twenty-two feet of water in my house in Lakeview. My files were upstairs, luckily, but they're still a mess. Looters trashed the place."

"Did any of those banks actually give him a loan?"

"I know he got a loan from Federal, but that was a few years ago. I mean, we're talking four or five years ago."

"If you were Sam, would you go back to where you'd gotten a loan before?"

"I'd go to where I could get the best deal."

"Sounds reasonable. By the way, do you own any handguns?"

"I do. I have a .50 caliber Desert Eagle."

"Mind if I borrow it to run some ballistic tests?"

"Do you have a spent bullet for the comparison tests?"

"Not at this time."

"Ask me again when you do."

"Mr. Mayor, I have to ask you this question. What were you doing, late afternoon, the day the Storm hit?"

"Flying my plane to my farm outside Natchez. I have a dirt strip on my property up there in Mississippi."

"You file a flight plan?"

"Matter of fact, I did. I have a Cessna 180. Kept it at Lakefront in Sam's hangar."

"Were you alone?"

"No, my lady friend accompanied me. I assume the records of my flight plan were destroyed, along with everything else at Lakefront, but I'm not sure. Feel free to check. I fueled up before takeoff, so I could probably generate a credit card statement to prove that."

"Okay. Thanks for your time. Oh . . . I can help you out if you ever want to lose your FBI tail."

"Agents Bershad and Cormier? What would I do without them? In fact, if you want to know if I have an alibi in terms of Kiesha Taylor, check with my two centurions in that Crown Vic."

I hadn't expected Duplessis to be so forthcoming. Offering to provide me a credit card statement? Was he really helping me out of loyalty to Sam and his friendship with Kiesha? I had no way to know. Duplessis was a shrewd, cool character. Perhaps he simply had nothing to worry about because he hadn't been involved in Sam's demise. Still, the level of his cooperation suggested that he didn't want any trouble from me. Was he worried about me blackmailing him regarding his mistress? He'd been married for almost thirty years, so a divorce would cost him his ass.

The FBI tail didn't concern him, which made no sense. He knew them by name and referred to the Feds as his "centurions." His protectors? A very visible FBI team would certainly discourage your garden-variety hit man. As a politician, Duplessis had a reputation for turning liabilities into positives. Was he now appropriating his FBI tail to be used as a bodyguard detail? To protect him from whom? Duplessis and Sam had been thick as thieves. Maybe they had been up to something that got Sam killed and had Duplessis running scared.

CHAPTER FOURTEEN

A couple of regulars at the bar tossed back shots of Corso gold tequila just as Twee entered Pravda promptly at 7:30 P.M. I happened to be one of them, and considered the Corso to be of great medicinal value, considering my present condition.

Twee and I settled in at my usual corner table on two antique Russian Jacob-style mahogany chairs next to the fireplace. I filled her in on recent developments and, considering the condition of my face, was fairly forthcoming about what had happened at Deon's place.

I mentioned to her the comment I'd heard that Jimmy Nguyen's days were severely numbered.

"I'll pass that on to Jimmy, but what about Kiesha's murder? Don't you think it's tied in? I mean, she gets killed the day after you talk to her in her trailer." Twee seemed genuinely upset about Kiesha. She had called me on the sterile cell phone as soon as it hit the news.

"NOPD thinks it's a drug-related murder," I stated flatly.

"I'm asking what you think."

"I think it's too soon to tell."

As promised, she brought Sam's laptop. We booted it up on the marble-topped table and spent an hour poring over the files on the hard drive. Most of it was Tiki Hut business: spreadsheets, a fax file, inventory software. The rest ranged from insignificant Internet downloads and photos to some letters relating to charity activity in the Vietnamese community.

Then I saw a video folder labeled MONEY TEST. I double-clicked and the folder revealed dozens and dozens of individual videos, each titled with a person's name and a date. I was surprised to see almost ten videos titled CLIFF ST. JAMES.

"What are these?" I asked Twee.

"Click on one."

I did. Video taken from a hidden camera in Sam's office showed me sitting in front of Sam's desk, counting a pile of cash. A few moments after I finished the count, Sam entered the shot.

"Four thousand one hundred thirty-seven dollars, Sam."

"You sure?"

"One hundred percent."

"Okay, thanks."

The video ended.

"This video was shot from a camera hidden in Sam's office."

"Concealed in a briefcase. He didn't run it continuously, only when he tested someone."

"So you're telling me that all those times I counted money for Sam, he was testing me? To see if I would skim some, put a few bucks in my pocket while he was out of the room?"

"Yes. He kept testing you with larger and larger amounts of money, but you never took a single dollar."

"I have this rule; I never steal less than ten million dollars at a time."

"Kiesha stole, but only a little. Dad didn't care; he knew she needed the money. Most people he taped, and there were a lot of them, stole something eventually. That's why he tested people repeatedly. They seldom stole the first time he had them count cash. The only people who stole the very first time and every time were Mayor Duplessis and your ex-wife, Sharon."

"Sharon stole money from Sam? Are you sure?"

"Every time. Dad showed me the videos."

I scanned the folder for a video with her name. "So where are they?"

Twee leaned in closer to the screen and began scrolling. "That's funny, they're not here. I've seen them before. Dad talked about how your wife had larceny in her heart and that you were better off without her." She looked at me, realizing that maybe her comments were inappropriate. "I'm sorry, I didn't mean to . . ."

"Sam was wrong, my wife doesn't have larceny in her heart. Her drinking has gotten worse, I'll grant you that. To be honest, from what I hear, she's become an alcoholic, but that doesn't make her a thief. I'm just wondering what happened to the videos."

"Maybe Dad erased them."

"Were there any videos of Dice McCarty, Sharon's boyfriend after she and I broke up?"

"Yes. Don't forget, he was helping Sharon run her bar. He came into the Tiki Hut to borrow or lend things, just as you had done."

"So Sam tested him. And he tested the mayor, too? That I don't get."

"Dad was suspicious of people's motives. Anyone he ever invited into his private office, he tested. Anyone he was thinking of hiring, anyone he was thinking of doing business with, he tested. He did it casually, acting like he was frustrated that he kept getting a different figure and could they please help him. Then once they started counting the pile of money, he would excuse himself to go to the toilet. Cold cash is very tempting to the dishonest."

I scanned the folder, but no Dice. "I guess your dad erased Dice's videos, too." What I actually thought was that Dice had been busy deleting files on Sam's laptop when I showed up the night the Storm hit.

I lit a cigarillo. Something wasn't right. It wasn't just a few missing videos, it was as if the laptop had been sanitized. Dice hadn't had the time to have done that.

"Where are all the files relating to Bayou Aviation?"

"He kept them on an external hard drive. He plugged it into this laptop or his desktop computer at Bayou."

Her answer was too pat, too quick. "I need to see the files."

"I don't have them. When I went back to his office that night, I was scared. I wasn't thinking about all the dozens of important things I should have taken. Maybe the cleanup crew will find it in the debris."

In a million years, I knew that wasn't going to happen. Twee was again being Twee. "Any reason I can't examine his office computer at Bayou Aviation?"

"I'll have it delivered to you."

"He have a secretary out there?"

"Of course. But his partner, Tommy Boudreaux, runs Bayou now. And I don't think Tommy will let you nose around in the company files."

"No problem," I said, downplaying my interest. "It's probably a dead end anyway. But T-Boy is a pretty interesting guy. What can you tell me about him?"

"I thought you already talked to him."

"I'm asking you."

"Well, I've known Tommy as far back as I can remember, since I was a little kid. He and Dad were like blood brothers, but still, they led separate lives, if that makes sense. I mean, they were always close, but they ran in different circles. Bayou Aviation is what connected them the last few years, but neither of them ran it day-to-day. They have a manager for that. Tommy has a lot of companies. I'm not sure that Bayou is that important to him, because he has lucrative companies all over the state. But he was CIA so he likes to keep his business to himself."

"Think he's retired?"

"He says he is."

I turned my attention back to the laptop. "Friend of mine works at the Jefferson Parish crime lab. I'd like him to take a look at Sam's laptop."

"Why?"

"I want a copy of Sharon's videos. My friend might be able to pull them up from the hard drive."

"I'm sorry, but no, I'd rather not put it into a stranger's hands. How about if I have one of my geek friends try to pull up her videos?"

"That'll work," I said, masking my disappointment. "In the meantime, I need to study some of these files. It'll only take a minute to copy Sam's hard drive onto this."

I removed a high-capacity flash drive from my backpack and plugged it into a USB port. She looked panicked.

"Ahh, wait . . . I . . . I'm not sure about this."

"Twee, you just showed me the files. I need to check them more carefully. Do you trust me or not?"

Her mind raced, then, "Umm, okay . . . sure. Cliff, it's not that I don't trust you. Dad was very private. He would never have showed this to anyone. So it's almost like I'm betraying his trust."

Her words sounded logical and reasonable. They always did. But I had already begun to understand just how craftily Twee Siu's brain operated.

"You're not betraying his trust," I said, starting to copy files. "You're doing what he told you to do—bringing me in to help because something went wrong."

My cell phone signaled that I'd gotten a text message. The message from Honey read: 10-23.

This meant that Honey had finished installing a GPS tracking device on Twee's car, parked out on Decatur Street. I wanted to start keeping closer tabs on my boss. She wasn't the only one who knew how to be crafty.

After her shift, Honey and I cruised in her unit out to the Tiki Hut. At night, this section of Mid-City was the dark side of the moon. National Guard MPs patrolled the area infrequently; they were simply spread too thin. But if they did roll up, being in a police cruiser with Honey still in uniform meant the troops would keep their M-4s at port arms and not point them in our face while we tried to explain ourselves.

A high cement wall surrounded the Hut's long back patio, extending all the way to the next block. So instead of parking on Toulouse and going in the front door, we parked on St. Peter. I used Kiesha's key to let us in through a heavy wooden gate that opened onto the very back of the property.

"Twee said her crew already finished the cleanup and were starting to gut the place. They're working fast."

"We breaking and entering?" Honey enquired with a fake smile.

"Darling, we are investigating." I raked the patio with the powerful beam from my Surefire E2D Defender flashlight.

"Don't want the boss to know you were here?"

"Why trouble her with small details? Hey, check this out. Very neat work."

The workers had used yellow crime scene tape to segregate the debris now stacked in a rather orderly fashion on the patio. I found the section marked SAM'S OFFICE. Honey and I snapped on latex gloves and silently went to work. After a few minutes, my flashlight caught a glint of brass from a shallow cardboard box full of small office items. "Honey . . ."

The shell casing was startling in its size. I picked it up using the end of a pencil, then looked at the case stamp.

Honey whistled softly as she moved in close for a better look. "Fifty caliber?"

"Fifty AE," I said, reading the stamp. "If this came from the murder weapon, no wonder the victim didn't have much of a face left."

"From a Desert Eagle?"

"Or an AMT AutoMag, LAR Grizzly Win Mag, maybe a couple of others. Big, heavy semiautos that sound like cannons and are usually used to hunt large game. Only somebody strong with big hands uses a gun like that. Duplessis has a fifty-cal Desert Eagle. Deon has one, too."

"So do a lot of idiots," groused Honey. "Trying to make like a big man. Seen guys like that on the range. Makes them feel potent."

"My contractor told me he was building a secret room in the Jupiter Lounge for all of Dice's guns. And I distinctly recall that Dice owns a fifty-cal AMT AutoMag."

The muffled crash of something heavy dropping from inside the Tiki Hut startled us. We extinguished our lights simultaneously and wordlessly drew our weapons. I pocketed the cartridge and whispered to Honey, "Looters?"

"Let's find out."

Honey was always game.

We split up and made our way onto the wooden deck leading into the Hut. We heard two men carping at each other. Flashes of their lights streaked through the windows as we crept closer. I caught a glimpse of them stacking something on top of the pool table, then the lights and voices disappeared into a small room. Instinctively, I turned on my hidden recording devices.

I held up Kiesha's key and gestured to the locked back door that led inside. Honey nodded in the affirmative. I unlocked the door and we stealthily entered the stuffy bar heavy with stale air.

"I'm telling you, this driving-across-the-Causeway-four-times-a-day bullshit is killing me. We ought to at least get reimbursed for gas, if not get travel time pay."

The male voice came from the small room near the pool table. Sounded Caucasian; thirties, maybe. Then the footsteps, lights, and voices came closer as Honey and I took up shooting positions.

"You're complaining about a little driving, playboy? I lost my whole damn house," rasped a much older voice.

Two men in dark coveralls emerged from the small room, the

room next to the pool table that Kiesha had told me she didn't have a key for. The men were removing electronics cases the size of PCs, and stacked them on top of others on top of the pool table. The older man wiped his forehead with a handkerchief.

"Okay, lock up the room and I'll start putting these into the van."

Honey lit them up with her flashlight and I followed suit. "Freeze, police! Hands in the air!"

"What the hell?" The older man squinted, turning his head away from our blinding lights.

"Shit," said the young one, holding up his hands to block the flashlight beams.

"Get your hands up or I will cap your ass!" I screamed as I moved in toward them.

Their hands shot in the air. "FBI, don't shoot!" coughed the older one.

"We're FBI, we're FBI!" The young one looked like a deer in the headlights.

Honey and I exchanged a look. "Call it in," I said.

She spoke into her radio mike, "Dispatch, this is Sgt. Baybee, Sixth District, reporting two male looters at 4800 Toulouse. Request backup, over."

"Looters? Goddammit, cancel that call. I got my credentials right here." The old one started to reach for a pocket.

"Hands up, Pops, or I will shoot you silly," I said. He reluctantly complied. Honey covered them as I moved in closer. I found his FBI ID and it looked legit. Special Agent Matthews. "So you want to show me your warrant or your letter of permission from the property owner to be here, removing these"—I shined my light on the sophisticated digital electronics that were crusty with mold and mildew—"removing this digital surveillance equipment from the premises?"

"Hey, this equipment belongs to the Bureau."

"Shut up, Ledoc," said Matthews, the older one.

I walked around and glanced into the small room that had always been locked. The room looked nearly identical to the room where Sam had kept *his* snooping gear. This room apparently had been used exclusively by the FBI. The shelves that held the equipment were now empty. Since they used digital electronics, there was no need for racks holding cumbersome tapes or even CD/DVDs.

"So you boys had the Tiki Hut wired, huh? And it's taken you this long to come and retrieve your gear?"

The two men looked at each other, then to me. "One phone call straightens this all out," said Matthews.

"Agent Matthews, you have no idea," I said, "but I guarantee you that one phone call isn't going to straighten much out. I'll give you fifteen seconds to get out that front door. Otherwise, unless you got a warrant or that letter I mentioned, you're both going to jail tonight."

"Hey, you can't do that. And we're not leaving here without our equipment."

"In that case, this little incursion on your part is going to get a lot of attention."

"Ledoc. Let's go, now," said Agent Matthews.

"But . . ."

"This will get worked out on the down-low." Matthews gave me a look like he wanted to scratch out my eyeballs. "Don't worry."

Matthews grabbed his partner and practically pulled him out

the front door. Honey and I watched them climb into an unmarked van.

"Cancel the call," I said softly.

"Never made the call. You didn't hear Dispatch respond, did you?"

"Perfect. I've got chips and beer at the dojo. Let's get this gear over to my place and see what's on every channel."

CHAPTER FIFTEEN

The bunkerlike FBI building on Leon G. Simon Road sat less than a half mile from Lake Pontchartrain. The Storm and the massive surge of water from the lake rendered the building uninhabitable, so FBI operations moved to a temporary facility in Mandeville on the north shore of the lake, a mere twenty-four-mile drive across the Lake Pontchartrain Causeway, considered by many to be the longest bridge in the world, depending upon your definition of the word "bridge."

To me, a bridge is a bridge—Lake Pontchartrain had definitely been troubled water as it broke through the levees—but semantics notwithstanding, the drive is a straight-as-an-arrow exercise in excruciating monotony, evidenced by the fair number of drivers who manage to flip their vehicles over the guardrail and meet a watery death in about thirty feet of saline solution. Just the thing weary FBI agents needed to have added to their daily workload. Nonetheless, the decision to move to Mandeville hadn't been arbitrary. No functioning structures existed in Orleans, Jefferson, St. Bernard, or Plaquemines parishes that could adequately house the FBI.

STORM DAMAGE

Honey and I had finished plumbing the depths of the Bureau's digital secrets by about 5:30 A.M. She crashed in my bed while I biked up to Audubon Park, forced my stiff body to run a lap, biked back for a quick shower, then began the long drive to the North Shore in my Bronco.

A lot of strippers, hookers, and sexy bartenders from New Orleans gravitate to Mandeville once they marry well, opting for a bit more respectability. Having a large body of water between you and your former clients provides a certain psychic buffer, and also generally eliminates the nuisance of being propositioned in the produce aisle by ex-customers, with your kid watching.

The North Shore also attracts those who want to remain within striking distance of NOLA without dealing with the less seemly aspects of the city, like the crime rate. A good rule to keep in mind in New Orleans is that regardless of how expensive your home might be or how highfalutin or trendy the neighborhood, you're never more than three blocks from a crackhead.

Irrespective of the provenance of its residents, Mandeville is a sleepy little place that has foisted its urban sprawl into the belly of a lush pine forest. Densely packed stands of conifers stood side by side with impressive lakeside mansions, apartment buildings, strip malls, and the post office. Trees were Mandeville's thing. Want directions in New Orleans?: "Go to Dos Jefes Cigar Bar, turn right and cut over to Monkey Hill, right again past St. Joe's all the way down to Bachelors III, then left to Superior Grill and the Columns is right there." Directions in Mandeville: "Go to the first tall stand of junipers and turn right, then one block to the cluster of chubby evergreens and turn left, go past the woods on your right, then take a left where you see the hundred-foot lone pine." You want bars, stay in NOLA; you need trees, go to the North Shore.

But as I drove into Mandeville for the first time since the Storm, it looked like a thousand Paul Bunyans on go-pills had had one hell of a time clear-cutting the surroundings and thinning the woods. How ironic that finished lumber was in such short supply across the lake, while megatons of perfectly good pine blown down by the winds still choked parking lots, backyards, and driveways. The *vatos* and their chainsaws beavered away endlessly on downed evergreens for miles around. Fireplace logs would be readily available for the next hundred years or so.

I chugged a latte from the Coffee Bean on Emerald Road, then found myself stacking the Bureau's electronics next to the X-ray machine in the FBI building lobby when I showed up unannounced at 9 A.M. asking to meet with the SAIC. That went over real big, and now it was 10:30 and I was sitting in the world's smallest conference room with a cold cup of weak FBI coffee, fighting fatigue, when the factotum entered the room. Special Agent Harding was cute, thirties, dyed blond, and here to blow me off.

"Sorry to keep you waiting, Mr. St. James, but Special Agent in Charge Gunderson is simply unable to break away to meet with you today. He asked me to thank you for returning the electronics and asked if you would like to schedule a meeting for next week."

I stood and stretched like a cat waking from a nap. "No, just tell him to watch the six o'clock news. It'll be on all the stations. You know, FBI agents Ledoc and Matthews caught on videotape removing surveillance equipment in the middle of the night from the unsolved murder scene of Sam Siu. Looking like a couple of Keystone Kops caught in some nefarious act. That'll knock the hurricane out of the headlines for a day or two, won't it? And Duplessis's old gang will scatter like rats, trying to remember all of the incriminating conversations they had over the years at the Tiki Hut."

I tossed a DVD onto the table. "Tell Gunderson to keep this copy of his inept agents in action. I have plenty more."

Ashen-faced, Harding scooped up the DVD as I crossed to the door. "Please, can you wait just a few more minutes? I might be able to squeeze you in after all."

"What can I do for you?"

Eight minutes had elapsed from when I played my trump card to when Agent Harding and I walked into Gunderson's very cluttered office. He was paunchy, in his fifties, and didn't look happy to see me. There was no handshake. Harding stood off to the side as I sat down uninvited across from Gunderson.

"You can scratch my back." Since he cut to the chase, so did I.

He looked at me over his bifocals and checked out my facial wounds. "Look, I don't need another pain in the ass, I have plenty already. I'm busy. And I'm not too keen about you blackmailing your way into this meeting. So what exactly do you want?"

"First of all, no blackmail, just barter. I want to know about Sam Siu. I've been hired—"

"Yeah, yeah, you're ex-NOPD, now a private dick, and you've been going around like a bull in a china shop trying to figure out who whacked Sam. I'm not impressed so far."

"Are you categorically saying Sam's dead? Because some people think he's helping the Bureau bring down the old Duplessis inner circle."

"Absurd."

"Make a good teaser to go with the video I took. Fox News will love it."

"Yeah, I hear you're a regular walking reality show." He took off his glasses and tossed them onto his messy desk.

"Special Agent in Charge Gunderson, I let your boys go last night, I returned your equipment, and I'm willing to deep-six the video. Maybe in return you can tell me how it is that the FBI was running surveillance out of the Tiki Hut. You think maybe NOPD homicide and the DA might consider that an important little tidbit you neglected to share with them?"

"Has he been searched? Do we have all of his cameras and tape recorders?"

"Yes, sir, he's clean," said Harding.

"As a rule, we don't trust NOPD. But then, as you know, they don't trust each other. It's a very broken department. Sure, there are good officers on the force, and you were one of them. Although why you hit Chief Pointer in the face with a string of beads during that St. Patrick's Day parade over in Irish Channel . . ."

"That was an accident."

"You broke his glasses while he was riding on the department's float."

"True, but . . ."

"The mayor on one side of him, the chief's wife on the other."

"I was off duty, on a gallery with other off-duty officers . . ."

"Gallery?"

"They call a balcony a gallery down here."

"Whatever. You were drunk as a skunk, right?" asked Gunderson.

The scene replayed in my mind as it had a thousand times. The moment that I self-destructed and derailed my career at NOPD.

Plenty of people have been hit by a hard, errant throw of beads from a passing float or a gallery of revelers. Usually it's an accident, though sometimes a mean drunk makes a malicious throw at a target. I can't honestly say that in that flash from idea to action that I didn't intend to hit Pointer with the beads. Stupidly, I did, but there was no malice, per se, although the police rank and file, including me, hated and resented the man. How did I even make the shot? It was a one-in-a-million throw that I made by entering "the zone" and sealing my destiny in the department.

"I was *drunker* than a skunk. Much drunker."

"Well, I think Chief Pointer is a stupid, petty, Grade-A asshole. We all got a big kick out of your little escapade."

"Didn't work out too well for me."

"Time will answer that. This all won't matter much in a few days, but you and I aren't having this conversation. Agreed?"

"Agreed."

"Sam Siu's murder didn't fall under FBI jurisdiction. But Sam was helping us, so naturally we nosed around a little. Unfortunately, in the aftermath of the Storm, there was no manpower for a serious investigation. I have no idea who killed Sam. I have to assume it was his body that was found, even though we have no evidence either way."

"How was he helping?"

"The equipment you returned? He agreed to let us install it in his bar. He wasn't privy to our recordings, although I understand he ran his own surveillance. Sam wasn't providing any other evidence or testimony, he wasn't ratting anyone out. Compared to the rest of the Duplessis administration, Sam was pretty clean. We weren't going after him. He didn't have to cooperate, we didn't have anything on him. He simply agreed to accommodate us."

"That's it?"

"What can I tell you? The surveillance computers remotely downloaded newly recorded conversations every day to our secure server right up until the power went out."

"Daily? What time were they set to download?"

Gunderson turned to Harding. "Six A.M. daily. Without fail," she said.

"Anyway," Gunderson continued, "our gear in the Tiki Hut got ruined in the flooding but the audio files were safe in cyberspace. So we weren't in any hurry to pull the equipment out. Hell, our HQ was destroyed, most of us lost our homes, we've had other things to worry about. But when I heard the Tiki Hut was being gutted, I sent Ledoc and Matthews to go get our equipment."

"Did you have Sam's office bugged?"

"No, I wish we had. Then we might know who killed him. We had a few of the 'power booths' wired, places where certain movers and shakers always sat. I think you have a good idea of who our targets are here."

"Audio only?"

Gunderson looked to Agent Harding. "Audio only," she said.

"So you listened to the recordings from the day Sam was murdered?"

"I haven't personally, but sure, that's been checked, right, Harding?"

"Sir, all the Tiki Hut audio files we possess have been examined for evidence."

"And there was nothing? No sound of a gunshot?" I asked somewhat skeptically.

Gunderson again turned to Agent Harding for an answer.

"The bar was closed," she said. "We used unidirectional mikes with a short range, the point being to pick up the conversation at the table only and not have bleed-through from the rest of the bar."

"But a gunshot from a fifty-caliber handgun might be on there, right?" I asked. "In the background. That would help pinpoint a time of death."

"The Tiki Hut is not small. The murder took place in another room, far from our microphones. The killer may have used a sound suppressor. They are legal in Louisiana, unfortunately." Harding was good, but she was squirming just a little.

"I am not aware of any gunshot having been recorded."

"What makes you say fifty caliber?" asked Gunderson.

I held up the cartridge in a Ziplock bag. "Not admissible, but found in Sam's office. And the victim's face was blown away, suggesting a large caliber. Here's a still from video I shot at the crime scene."

The eight-by-ten clearly showed a .50 caliber shell casing on the floor near the large safe behind Sam's desk. I hadn't seen it the night I responded to the homicide call, but spotted the shell when I closely examined my hidden camera video footage from that night.

"Good work. Want me to have the FBI lab take a look at that shell casing?"

"No thanks, I got it covered. Marlin Duplessis owns a Desert Eagle. Fifty caliber. Makes sense: big man, big hands, big ego."

It was subtle, but the energy changed in the room. A new tension settled in.

"Duplessis, I don't take for a killer. And a lot of guys have Desert Eagles. Either way, without the body or more evidence, you don't have much."

I smiled and nodded. I had a lot more than he realized. "You guys weren't tailing him twenty-four/seven when the Storm hit like you are now. His alibi is flimsy. Just a thought." I pocketed the plastic bag containing the brass shell. "Last question; what about Tommy Boudreaux?"

"What about him?"

"What were he and Sam really up to with the aviation business?"

"You're talking way above my pay grade. There are places we just don't stick our nose into. I mean, look around my office. We're swamped in the swamp. Corruption runs thick in people's blood down here. It's a way of life. Where I'm from in California, the politicians skim off some of the whipped cream on top of the pie. Down here, there are so many hands reaching in to steal a piece, you can't even see the pie. I put as many of these people away as I can, but it's like pissing into the wind, because the next guy, the next gal, is always just as bad. But as far as Tommy Boudreaux is concerned, all I can say is you're in the wrong federal agency."

I got Agent Harding's business card and cell phone number as she escorted me out. All very cordial for someone who parsed her words more carefully than a slick Houston attorney and who had grossly misrepresented the facts in the meeting with Gunderson. Truth was, she hadn't listened to the audio surveillance for the day of the murder. No one at the FBI had.

Power went out at the Tiki Hut at 5:19 A.M. on the 29th. Therefore there was no audio file download at 6:00 A.M. of the previous twenty-four hours of recording time. The FBI didn't have the audio file, I did.

STORM DAMAGE

And I had every reason to believe that Sam Siu was shot dead in his office at 4:47 P.M. by an unknown assailant using a .50-caliber handgun. I knew of three potential suspects who owned such a weapon: Marlin Duplessis, Deon Franklin, and Dice McCarty.

It took over two and a half hours and a triple espresso to drive from the FBI's temporary headquarters in Mandeville down to the southern edge of Lafourche Parish on the Gulf of Mexico.

Port Fourchon, right at the end of Highway 3090, provides support for about three quarters of the deep-water drilling prospects in the Gulf. Almost all of the major and independent oil and gas outfits have some kind of operations at the port. Thousands of trucks come and go every day. Barge terminals, pipe yards, shipyards, platform construction facilities, and many other kinds of service business operate at capacity in the thriving port area.

Most of the air services connected with port operations fly out of South Lafourche Airport in Galliano, about twenty miles north of Port Fourchon. The Galliano field has a 3,800-foot asphalt runway, lighting, signage, security, and refueling capabilities. It's a growing regional airport and it would have made sense for Sam Siu and Tommy Boudreaux to have located operations there.

But they didn't. Instead, Bayou Aviation sat back off of Highway 1, between Port Fourchon and South Lafourche Airport. I almost missed the small Bayou Aviation sign, and turned onto a narrow asphalt road. I hadn't been able to glean much off the Internet except to learn that Bayou's strip was a private 1,700-foot turf-surfaced runway, meaning it could only accommodate smaller fixed-wing or rotary aircraft.

I drove a quarter mile past the operations building and hangars and parked off the road amid the dark greens of semitropical bottomland plants, cypress trees, and butterweed. I hiked back, keeping to cover, and set up observation next to a moss-dappled live oak. Saw palmetto, wax myrtle, and trumpet vines closed all around me. White ibis and wood ducks worked the land behind me and the waters that were never far off in the delta.

I snapped a quick photo of the Bayou layout. A six-foot-high chain-link fence topped with razor wire surrounded the property. Massive steel-construction hangars that had to be 10,000 square feet each bookended the single-story cinderblock operations center/office.

I'd come for nothing more than preliminary recon, but was rewarded with a dividend when I recognized T-Boy's white Yukon in the parking lot next to the front door of the Bayou Aviation office. My payoff increased when none other than Jimmy Nguyen walked out of the office and climbed into the passenger seat of a silver Range Rover with mirrored windows. Two Asian men already lingered in the Range Rover, and they drove off together toward the main road.

Putting Jimmy and T-Boy in the same office—Sam's old office—at the same time kind of rang my chimes and made me stop thinking that I should be catching some Zs. Three minutes of surveillance and I had already made a major connection.

I then spent three more tedious hours fighting sleep in the mosquito-infested foliage that had a prehistoric, deeply wild feel. A few delivery trucks came and went. Huge accordion-style folding hangar doors stood open, affording me good visuals of the busy workers performing aircraft maintenance.

Finally, T-Boy emerged from the office and drove off. Now that

I had the lay of the place, I could come back fully prepared for a black-bag job, if need be.

As I made the long drive back home, the logic at play in my brain suggested that T-Boy and Jimmy must be moving dope. Could Sam have gotten in their way? Honey was right. When someone turns up dead in New Orleans, always refer to Rule Number One.

CHAPTER SIXTEEN

I'd promised Honey a night out. After returning to the dojo from my recon at Bayou Aviation, I slipped into a shirt that wasn't too badly wrinkled and popped a caffeine pill I'd bought at a Circle K. I felt jazzed about the hot leads I had generated—the .50 cal. casing, the Tommy/Jimmy connection—but I needed a night off from Sam's case. Still, I shamelessly wanted to kill two birds with one stone, and figured Honey would go along with my plan for a suspect interview over drinks.

Honey picked me up in her police cruiser. Being able to take your unit home is a big perk for police in the South, since they are so horribly underpaid. But the reason she drove it tonight was because we were going to the Quarter during Mardi Gras season, even a reduced and truncated Mardi Gras season, when parking is near impossible, unless you're in a police car.

I convinced her our first stop should be One-Eyed Jack's. Eli's band was slated to play an early set there. I considered Kiesha's murder a parallel, secondary investigation, so if Eli actually showed up and hadn't skipped town, I had lots of questions. A few drinks, a few questions, then Honey and I would move on to other venues, if I could stay awake. T-Boy and Jimmy would keep until tomorrow.

So One-Eyed Jack's it was. Most locals still refer to it as the Shim Sham because New Orleanians don't cotton to change all that much. The Shim Sham had been a popular burlesque house, and wisely, the new owners kept the physical arrangement basically intact. A bar and a few tables and chairs occupied the foyer. Management kept the raked floor in the theater proper, but removed all seating. A big circular bar sat anchored in the center of the space, smack where the best seat in the house used to be. A shallow gallery featuring brothel-style flecked wallpaper overlooked it all, and a proscenium stage crowned the space.

Honey had the next two days off and signaled she stood ready to party by looking downright delectable in tight, low-rise black jeans and a snug sleeveless black top under a short black leather jacket. I looked like crap-on-a-stick: sallow complexion, black circles under tired red eyes, bruises and scabbed cuts and scratches. I felt sapped and could have nodded off standing at the circular bar. I wearily eyed patrons trickling in as I finished updating Honey on my surveillance excursion.

"Sounds like we need to pay a visit to Bayou Aviation," said Honey.

"I figure a little B and E at oh-dark-thirty tomorrow night."

"Count me in," she said, then flashed a double sawbuck at the heavily sleeved bartender with a Betty Page kind of thing going on. "Red Bull and Grey Goose. Make it two."

"It's not even eight and you're ordering me Red Bull. Do I look that tired?" I asked.

"I don't want you to peter out on me tonight."

"I'm fine."

"I mean it. I want to go to the Dervish later," she said.

In the dim light I was able to hide my surprise. The Dervish was an alternative hangout heavy on leather, rubber, and vinyl after midnight. Michelle had said something to Honey about it the other day. The late-night dancing could be very full-contact.

Just then the lights dimmed and Eli and his band took the stage. Honey hadn't met Eli before, so her eyes lasered in like a range-finder on a moving target.

"So much for being in mourning over Kiesha."

"If you kill someone you love, do you mourn for them?" I wondered aloud.

"Which one is he?"

"Think poor man's Mick Jagger," I said.

"The tall skinny guy. So strung out he can barely stand up. Nice pants, though." Eli wore hip-hugging black leather pants laced up along the sides.

"So buy me a pair." I leaned in and impulsively kissed Honey on her temple. A platonic kiss and yet it wasn't. She didn't ac-knowledge it either way. I wondered what had gotten into me to kiss her at all, then chalked it up to exhaustion.

The music ramped up and didn't stop for the next forty-five minutes. The band generated a power pop/medium metal, high-energy sound. Eli made a slick front man, vaulting around the stage like he'd just shot up some good crank.

Toward the end of the set, the crowd swelled with new arrivals who had mostly come to see the next act. Eli and his band put on a competent, good show, but it wasn't a New Orleans sound or vibe, and I couldn't help thinking they would do a lot better some-place like Chicago or Pittsburgh.

I also couldn't help thinking about my emerging and complicated feelings for Honey. We'd been coworkers and friends for years, but I'd never lusted after her or related to her in any way but as a pal and partner. A cool hangout friend who I liked and trusted. But now I felt a distinct pull to her in another direction altogether. Had the fling with Kiesha burst the dam? My sexual urges seemed to have returned in a big way. But it was more than just sex. Perhaps I craved something I had been shut down to: the touch of another human. The simple physical contact with Kiesha nourished me more than I thought possible. And I wanted more. Not a relationship just yet, I was still too broken. But maybe to be touched by someone who cared about me, maybe that would be good.

As if on some unspoken cue from my musings, Honey wordlessly reached into my back pocket, extracted my wallet, and bought us another round. This kind of presumed familiarity was new to our friendship, and I didn't quite know what to make of it. Couples did this kind of thing. Yet we were far from being a couple, in anyone's book.

As the set ended I lit up a Partagas cigarillo—I had a source for Cuban smokes, screw the embargo—and watched Eli glad-hand friends and supporters as he climbed down from the stage and invaded the crowd.

"So what's this guy like?"

"I've met him twice. He probably spoke six words to me. Sullen personality. Intense. He's basically a gutter punk Quarter rat. Doesn't have a dime. You know the type: couldn't make it in Philly or Baltimore or wherever the hell he's from. No problem, come on down to New Orleans where you don't have to grow up, you can keep the party going, the delusional dream alive for years."

"NOLA is a forgiving place. You can fake it, endlessly," observed Honey.

"Absolutely. Guys like Eli can keep the musician's lifestyle, work in a hotel or restaurant a couple days a week, sponge off friends and strangers, keep the buzz on, pull small-time hustles. Kiesha said he had a hang-up about purity, integrity, something like that."

"A hustler worried about integrity?"

"No, you know what it really came down to? Jealousy. Kiesha said he didn't care about her giving lap dances, as long as she didn't make a meaningful connection."

"Now that's mighty pimp of him."

I caught Eli's eye. He didn't hide his feelings well. He flashed a brief look of surprise. The look when you see someone you don't want to talk to; someone you had forgotten you might run into; someone you had no choice but to speak with. He made a beeline toward us. I figured he just wanted to get it over with.

"Eli, this is my friend Honey. Honey, Eli."

He offered a traditional handshake to her. "Thanks for coming."

Honey just smiled and nodded.

"I wasn't sure, you know, if you might cancel because of Kiesha's death," I said.

"Her family's scattered all over. None of them have come back since the Storm. Her mom lives in Atlanta. They want to handle the funeral, so . . ."

"Where you living now?"

"Same as before; here and there. Just not at Kiesha's place. Can I have one of those smokes, man?"

I lit him up and ordered him a rum and Coke. We chatted about his music until the drink came.

"What happened to your face?" he asked.

"I guess Deon Franklin doesn't like me."

"Screw that son of a bitch. Deon was bad news to Kiesha."

"Because he sold to her?"

"He treated her like she was his property. He's garbage and so is his posse. Putting on expensive clothes doesn't change that. Yeah, she owed him money, but when hasn't she? She's always been good for it."

"What did he do exactly?"

"Got rough with her a couple times recently. Threatened her."

"How recently?" asked Honey.

Eli looked surprised that Honey jumped into the conversation.

"She's PD," I explained.

"Week before she died, maybe."

"How much did she owe?"

"Twenty-eight hundred."

"Well, that's not a lot to some people," said Honey, "but local crack dealers have been known to kill over twenty bucks."

Eli practically chugged his drink.

"Do you have an alibi, Eli, for the day Kiesha was killed?"

"Not really."

"Nothing?"

"I was crashed out in my van," said Eli nonchalantly.

"So who do you think killed her?"

"You read the papers. The murder rate is through the frigging roof. New Orleans was dangerous before the hurricane, now it's practically anarchy."

"Most murders are over dope," said Honey.

"You selling crack, Eli?" I asked.

"Where'd you get that?"

"A little birdie. I mean, I'm trying to figure how Kiesha ran up a twenty-eight-hundred-dollar tab with Deon. She didn't do crack or heroin or anything heavy. She was a light user. And a small-time occasional pusher. Now if she bought rocks to front to someone else to sell, you know, someone she cared about, to help them make a little money? And if that someone smoked up too much of the merchandise, or shared it with his party buds, or maybe just wasn't very good at business . . ."

"Look around, man, the city is demolished! Everybody's going into debt right now. For everything. Twenty-eight hundred is nothing. Hell, Dice owed her three times that."

I kept my poker face going in spite of this shocker. So did Honey.

"Dice and Kiesha go way back, but tell me about that," I said, nonplussed.

"Child support for the kid."

I sipped my drink and stole a look at Honey. This was news to her, too. Then I flashed on the images in Kiesha's photo album.

"Kiesha and Dice have a cute little girl, right?" I asked rhetorically. "Kaitlinn."

Honey's eyes widened a bit.

"Not so little, she's eleven now," said Eli.

"Raised by Kiesha's mom, who is up in Atlanta," I said.

Eli nodded. "Even Sam didn't know about Kaitlinn. Nobody did, really. She was afraid if Sam found out, he wouldn't want her. After Sam died, she told me stuff I don't think she told many people."

"Dice owed Kiesha how much, exactly?" asked Honey.

"Almost ten grand. She said he was good at first, you know, paying, since he raped her and she got pregnant, being underage and all. Cop doing that, even in New Orleans, that gets out and Dice is screwed."

I nodded, keeping my poker face locked in, shocked by the revelation that Dice was essentially a sex offender.

"Kiesha was twenty-five, so she was fourteen when she had the child. Must have happened after he first started using her as a snitch," said Honey.

"Kiesha and Dice, they still got it on, didn't they? Maybe a once in a while thing?" I didn't know where the questions came from, they just appeared on my lips like a jolt of intuition.

Eli flashed dark. "Yeah. Last time was three or four weeks ago, maybe. Even when she was with Sam, she'd get her drink on and be alone at her place and Dice would show up and . . . that's what's she told me, in so many words."

Cops always watch a suspect's hands. I could blame the smoky, dim light, I could blame the fact I was running on fumes, but somehow, until right this second, I had missed the fact that Eli wore a large ruby ring, square cut, set in diamonds.

Eli saw me staring at his ring finger, then bolted like a thoroughbred at post time.

Honey and I were a second slow to react. "He's wearing Kiesha's ring!"

Eli was scrawny, but agile with quick reactions. The crowd had thickened as it had gotten later, and he threaded through the patrons like a smart missile. I stumbled on the steeply inclined, uneven floor and went down. Honey raced past me and shot several yards ahead by the time I got out onto the street.

Eli cut sharp in front of an oncoming horse and buggy full of giggly, inebriated coeds and tore up toward Bourbon. The guy could run. I run for distance, I'm not a great sprinter, but Honey stayed with him until they cut left onto Royal, toward Canal.

The Quarter is fairly well-lit, so at the corner I glimpsed Honey dart into a doorway about twenty yards ahead. A gaggle of Mardi Gras bead–draped relief workers out for a night on the town and holding Hurricanes in jumbo plastic drink cups slowed me down. I flanked them and bolted into the entranceway to the Royal Blend Coffeehouse courtyard. A few patrons at wrought-iron tables looked up as I trotted onto the patio, breathing hard. I caught sight of Honey through some French doors as she checked inside. "He's a murder suspect," I said, to no one in particular. "Which way did he go?"

Before anyone could answer—not that they would have—I heard a crashing sound from the next courtyard. I kicked a chair against the wall, jumped on it, then pulled myself over the top. Eli stood jiggling an iron gate that opened to a breezeway leading back to Royal Street. The courtyard sat behind an antiques shop. Old furniture and junk loomed all around, stacked erratically. When he saw me drop over the wall and scramble toward him, he just gave up. He panted, out of breath, and kind of seemed relieved he wouldn't have to run anymore.

"Do me a favor and lace your fingers behind your head, Eli."

He complied as Honey dropped over the wall into the courtyard.

"Now slowly move your left hand behind your back."

He complied.

Honey trotted up. "You got cuffs?"

I shook my head. She cuffed him without incident, then turned him to face us.

"Whose ring is that you're wearing?" I asked.

He said nothing.

"Eli, talk to us or we got to take you in, right now. I mean, you got an explanation, let's hear it," I said. "No need to make this hard."

Eli unfocused his gaze like he was staring into some alternate reality for a few moments, then he looked me in the eye for the first time ever.

"I went to the trailer, found Kiesha's body. I panicked. I'm a junkie with a record. Didn't think it would be a good idea to call in a murder."

"You walked away from those crack rocks on her body?" I asked skeptically.

"Damn right. Those were clues to the killer. Since Kiesha was dead, I figured the ring belonged to me now, so I took it. The cops or coroner's people would have stolen it if I hadn't taken it."

Honey and I couldn't object to Eli's line of thinking on that one.

"How could the ring belong to you?" asked Honey.

"We got married about three months ago. Marriage certificate's in my van."

Eli opened the passenger door to a beat-up old red and white Ford Econoline van parked on Esplanade, not far from Port-Of-Call, an impossibly popular place known for great burgers, but I usually avoided it because of the tourist crowds. He started to reach into the glove box but I stopped him in case he had a weapon stashed. Honey held him as I fished out an official document. A valid marriage certificate from Orleans Parish for him and Kiesha. They'd been married three months and six days.

Now it was my turn to stare unfocused into some alternate reality.

Why didn't Kiesha tell me? She said he wasn't her boyfriend, that she didn't know what to call him. *Umm, husband, maybe?* They must have forged a bond in booze, drugs, loneliness, and fear. In a beleaguered city offering little but uncertainty, with the love of her life murdered and future plans dashed, maybe Eli represented a short-term salve to her heart. Maybe the guy, with all of his problems, had treated her well. I hoped so.

I pulled a blue latex glove from my cargo pocket. I reached out quickly and yanked a few long hairs from Eli's head.

"Oww! Hey, what was that?"

"Voluntary DNA sample. Eli, for your sake, I hope you didn't kill her." I dropped his hair into the glove opening for safekeeping, stuffed it in my pocket, and shuffled away.

CHAPTER SEVENTEEN

Honey and I left Eli at his crash pad on wheels and walked slowly on Royal toward the heart of the Quarter where her cruiser sat parked. The street ran lousy with the costumed revelers of a walking krewe, the Krewe of Cork. Wine aficionados in wild costumes parading on foot, they topped off their wine goblets from prepositioned supplies in shops throughout the Quarter. A brass band following them kicked into high gear, playing a hyped-up version of "Red, Red Wine," reminding me that the madness of Fat Tuesday loomed only five days away.

"Dice McCarty raped a young teen, owed her ten thousand dollars in child support, and now he's leading the investigation into her murder."

"And he was the lead investigator of Sam's murder, too. What a coincidence."

"He had a motive to kill her. Big-time." I stopped to light a cigarillo.

"And to kill Sam if he knew about the money."

"How 'New Orleans' to lead the murder investigation for someone you killed." I rubbed my eyes, beyond exhausted, but remembered my promise to Honey. "We can still make the Dervish," I offered.

"No. Buy me a drink at your place."

As if to punctuate her remark, she took my hand and tugged me forward.

This time it was the dojo.

I saw the mess as soon as I turned the light on, and quickly drew my weapon. Honey stood behind me and pulled a Sig Sauer .45 from her purse. Wordlessly, using gestures, we covered each other as we moved inside.

It took about ninety seconds to clear the place, and I tucked the baby Glock back into my pants. I crossed to the utility room and popped open the secret wall. My laptop, passport, B&E kit, cash, important papers, and other valuables were still secured into a "boogie bag," a Pacsafe backpack, exactly where I had left them. Extra magazines for my Glock and extra boxes of ammo sat stacked on a shelf along with a few knives and some electronics gear, and other tools of the trade.

"Tossed. Just like the Bronco," I said. "Doubt anything's missing."

"But they didn't find the good stuff," she said, looking at my backpack in the little hideaway, and my ammo and weapons stash.

"Yeah, maybe they're after the laptop, or rather, what's in it." I removed the computer from the backpack.

"They wanted your notes?" she asked.

I just shrugged. "The crime scene photos, Sam's files, the FBI audios, the video of Duplessis . . ."

"So how'd they get in? The back door is still bolted from the inside. The plywood is still covering the hole in your wall."

"Unless they rappelled through the huge-ass hole in the roof," I looked up at the blue tarp covering, "they picked the front door lock."

As Honey crossed to the front door and bolted it shut, I found the bottle of Grey Goose in the freezer of my battered refrigerator. "We definitely weren't burglarized," I said, holding the vodka, "by my friendly neighborhood dirtbags, or this marvelous elixir would not be here."

"Make mine strong," she said, and disappeared into the bathroom.

I mixed up a couple vodka Sevens. My dojo fridge was one of the few examples of "white goods" that didn't have to be thrown out after the Storm. I never kept anything but beverages in it, so nothing went bad, and the looters had left the door open after they cleaned it out, so it didn't get moldy.

While the place was a mess—the intruders had thrown my mattress from the loft onto the floor below—it wouldn't take long to clean up. I kept very little in the dojo. Excluding the few pieces of used, throw-away furniture, one load into the Bronco and there wouldn't be so much as a toothpick left.

I booted up the laptop, tuned in some streaming jazz on the Internet, plopped down on my secondhand couch, and had finished half of my drink when Honey emerged wearing very brief black silk panties and a revealing black silk bra.

She sat next to me as casually as if we were sitting at Pravda, took her drink, and put back most of it in one gulp.

"Smooth," she purred.

The incongruity of her sitting in sexy lingerie in my just-vandalized home seemed lost on her. We weren't even lovers. Yes, I held conflicted, confused feelings toward her. A powerful lust could definitely be summoned, but I wasn't feeling too sexy at the moment. An opponent had just violated my space, in a major way. And I wasn't in a match with a referee where everybody shakes hands when it's over.

"I'm thinking you need to back off from this, Honey. Helping me will only cause problems for you in the department, especially with the chief, and maybe even get you involved in some trouble you don't need. You warned me about this case, and—"

She cut me off with, "I never thanked you for taking that gun to Grandpa Dan."

"You don't have to mention that."

It was Honey's grandfather out in Lakeview that I'd taken a .357 revolver to just before answering the call at the Tiki Hut and finding the body. Her widowed grandpa decided, like many other elderly folks, that he was too old to bother with an evacuation. And like many others, he paid the ultimate price for the decision.

"I should have taken him an ax, too," I said, mostly to myself.

Honey and I had found his body. Five feet of water stood in his house when we paddled a pirogue I had commandeered right into his living room, through his smashed-out picture window. The uncovered attic opening at first gave us a glimmer of hope, even though I knew that his block had been submerged under twenty-five feet of lake water when the levee failed.

I climbed up through the opening and saw him right away. I

tried to stop Honey from following, but she wouldn't have it. He must have been confused, panicked. His fingers and knuckles were raw from trying to scratch and smash his way through the wood to get outside, onto the roof, as the water rose inside his house.

He drowned, trapped in his attic.

Honey broke down and cried like a baby, the only time I've ever seen her express deep emotion.

"And I never thanked you for going with me there that day."

I freshened our drinks, not sure what to say. "I don't want anything to happen to you, okay?"

"I'm spending the day with Mom tomorrow. Take her to brunch. Walk the riverfront. Afternoon tea in the Quarter. It's a little family tradition we do every Mardi Gras."

"You're changing the subject."

"Yes."

Honey was as stubborn as they come, so I just ran with it.

"You still sleeping at her house?"

"You know Mom's neighborhood. They're kind of scared. Feel safer if I'm there."

I nodded.

"I sleep on the dining room floor. A nice little corner. On an air mattress. Nine of us in a house with one bathroom." She took another drink. "We're lucky to have a place at all."

"I understand."

"But tonight, I want to sleep with you," said Honey.

My poker face failed me. Before I could stammer out some lame reply, I simply said, "Honey, I don't know if it's safe here."

"I just want to cuddle. Nothing else. Is that all right?"

I just looked at her.

"And I want you to give me a key. Okay, St. James?"

She leaned in and kissed me on the lips. It was more than platonic but less than purely sexual, and I wasn't sure what to make of anything right now.

"Go to bed. I'll be there in a second," she said, disappearing into the bathroom.

I decided to leave the mattress on the dojo floor. I stripped down to my usual sleeping attire of boxers and a T-shirt. My stiff body, thanks to the beating at the hands of Deon Franklin's boys, ached with a dull pain that I simply tuned out. I shut it off the way I had shut off all other feelings. Within twenty seconds I was asleep, but stirred when Honey crawled onto the mattress. She held a tube of something and some other stuff in her hand.

"Man, I was almost out."

"You were out. You were snoring."

She pulled the covers off and scanned my body as she lifted my T-shirt.

"Those are some ugly bruises." She crushed a couple of binary cold packs, creating an instant freeze that she placed on my torso. Then she gently rubbed mentholated cream onto my battered body. Cold and hot, ice and fire. The human touch of someone whom I suspected truly cared for me felt exquisite. She kneaded the lotion into my skin, her hands hot needles of flame igniting me.

Sweat popped out on my forehead as I shivered. I floated. Disjointed, suspended. Honey ignored the now throbbing erection poking up at my boxers and kept working some kind of magic with her fingers on my limbs and torso. I tried to stay awake, flirting with the hypnagogic realization that as much as I needed to be touched, Honey needed to touch someone, to physically caress and cuddle with a man who was no threat to her, someone she'd long grown comfortable with. She was broken in her own way, but that line of thinking would have to wait, as I simply drifted off into some other eternity, deep asleep.

CHAPTER EIGHTEEN

I woke with Honey's arm draped around me. She stirred but didn't wake as I wordlessly dressed and left her a note and a door key. I biked to Audubon Park and willed my body into a cold run as I prioritized today's activities. I needed to get Eli's hair sample in for DNA testing; I needed to run an op against my boss, Twee; and I really needed to follow up on the Jimmy Nguyen/Tommy Boudreaux connection. Meaning I needed to staff up. There were too many leads to pursue, too many bases to cover as I found myself investigating two murders, not one. I couldn't simply call in favors from off- or even on-duty cops; I needed some dedicated assets. And I had a good idea who could provide some on the cheap.

Kendall Bullard met me for breakfast at Lil' Dizzy's over in the Seventh Ward by the I-10 overpass. He brought along three of his cousins, Cajun country fishermen from Houma who were eager to make a little easy money. They'd arrived in two beat-up pickup trucks that each needed about $10,000 worth of body work.

While eating eggs Sardou, I brainstormed with Kendall as his cousins ate biscuits and gravy like they hadn't seen food in weeks.

"Jimmy Nguyen's ride is a silver Range Rover with mirrored windows. A cop buddy tells me there are three locations where he's most likely to be found: his home, Gulf Coast Fish Company, or Club Bamboo."

"That be the RVB hangout on Chef."

"Exactly. It's a bar, but don't go in there if you're not Vietnamese and one of his boys."

I slid a piece of paper to Kendall that had the corresponding addresses. He glanced at the locations and nodded.

"So you just want us to watch, keep track of when he come and when he go?"

"For now, yes. If your cousins can be inconspicuous, it shouldn't be a problem."

"How 'bout we make like a clean-up crew? Set up near these here addresses and just start straightening some shit up. Nobody think twice they see us doing that."

"Great idea. There's certainly plenty of shit to straighten up in this town. We may run a tail on Jimmy later, but for now, just record his comings and goings." I gobbled down a big bite of eggs and creamed spinach heavy with Hollandaise sauce. "And if a very tall old guy with silver hair shows up driving a white Yukon, call me right away."

Kendall and his cousins nodded as they tucked in to the Creole breakfast.

Ron Charbonnet, the NOPD's Asian gang expert, had given me the three addresses for Jimmy Nguyen. But no one I knew, even

Twee, could help me out with a line on where to find T-Boy. A friend at Bell South ran his name for a landline phone number but came up empty. Even though Honey was off duty and about to take her mom to brunch, she was able to run a DMV check, which listed T-Boy's home address out in Destrehan. It turned out to be a private mailbox address in a mini-mall photo shop. None of the clerks could recall ever seeing the owner of Box 25, one Mr. Tommy Boudreaux, come in to get mail.

I figured I'd have to park someone out at Bayou Aviation—a good long way from New Orleans and a real pain in the ass—then decided instead to take a shot in the dark. Luckily, Lt. Eric Mondrian agreed to meet me for a lunchtime beer at the Three-Legged Dog, a slightly ratty corner bar in the Quarter, patronized mainly by locals. Mondrian, short and stocky with longish black hair, had been the NOPD's chief CIA liaison officer before transferring to CIB last year. On the side he dabbled in promoting MMA events, mostly on the North Shore, which is how we became friendly. I loved how so many NOPD officers had side businesses, even a bar, as I had had, with no complaints whatsoever from the department. Of course, the department paid squat, so they really couldn't complain too strenuously about their officers moonlighting to pay the bills.

I quickly gave Lt. Mondrian the bullet points of the Sam Siu case as we watched the chef grill burgers on the sidewalk outside the front door. The kitchen was still out of commission from storm damage, and the chef had fed a lot of hungry folks by grilling burgers on the sidewalk in the dark days after the Storm.

"Sure, I know Tommy," said Mondrian, sipping an Abita Amber. "Son of a bitch eats babies for breakfast."

"That can't be good for his cholesterol," I quipped.

"He's a rat bastard par excellence, far as I'm concerned. Effective as hell, though. Glad he's on our side. Although in the intelligence game, the notion of 'sides' gets kind of blurred sometimes."

"Where can I find him?"

"Beats me. Pretty sure he lived somewhere Uptown. I've got a cell number for him, but I don't know if it's still good." Mondrian scribbled a cell phone number on a napkin and slid it to me. "CIA station used to be at the One Canal Place complex. They used some obscure federal agency—Marine Fisheries Council—as their front."

"Is Tommy retired from the Agency?"

"Far as I know. About eighteen months ago. He's no longer station chief, I can tell you that."

"You know who is?"

"Yeah, but don't even ask me."

"What about the new address of the station?"

"St. James," Mondrian said, scowling, admonishing me for asking questions I had no business asking.

"Sorry, Eric. You know how it is. I'm trying to run this guy down, like, yesterday. If the cell number is still good, I'll think of something to draw him out." I finished my Sam Adams. "So when's the next event you're promoting? I know a guy who—"

"Hey, I just remembered," he said, hitting his fist on the table. "You belong to the New Orleans Athletic Club?"

"Been there a few times, but I never joined. They're still closed, aren't they?"

"Reopened a couple days ago. They got a boxing ring in there, you know."

"The lawyers and bankers like to slug it out, do they?"

"Didn't you know Roberto Duran trained in there for one of

his bouts? Anyway, Tommy's an avid boxer. The guy, his age, can still go three or four good rounds. And he's fucking taller than a giraffe. He used to go to the athletic club seven days a week. Was a regular in the bar there. He loved all that gentlemen's leather chairs and dark wood clubby bullshit."

"Sounds like I need to check out their membership plans."

The New Orleans Athletic Club was established in 1872 and sits on the edge of the Quarter on North Rampart Street. The impressive multistory building housing the club was built in 1929, and the same barber has been cutting hair on the same barber chair there for the last thirty-one years. Like in the rest of the city, tradition at NOAC means a lot.

Heather, a very buff twenty-three-year-old blonde, gave me the nickel tour as she extolled the virtues of club membership and explained payment options.

"How long have you worked here?" I asked, as we looked down from a small gallery with an ornate wrought-iron balustrade onto the two-story grand ballroom, now used as a group exercise area. About a dozen chubby matrons were going through some kind of step class on the polished hardwood floor.

"Four years."

"So you must know my old coworker, Tommy Boudreaux. He used to come in a lot and always told me I should join."

"Sure, I know Mr. Boudreaux. He referred you?"

"In a manner of speaking. I lost track of him since the Storm. Has he been in?"

"He was here last night."

"Really? So he's back in the city. I'll have to give him a call."

"He usually comes in around six o'clock, after work, I guess."

"Hey, if you see him, please don't mention me. I want to call him up and surprise him. Hell, maybe I'll catch him in the bar here."

"That would work. He stops in for a cocktail after every workout."

I purchased a trial membership, then immediately called Kendall. He said he could have a female friend parked across from NOAC within thirty minutes, keeping lookout for a white Yukon and a very tall game show host.

I was widening my net. Kendall and his people were in place covering Jimmy and my fresh lead on T-Boy. But I had some time before I seriously zeroed in on the gang boss and the ex–New Orleans CIA station chief, so I cruised over to the Warehouse Arts District. Twee had proven to be a little too shifty for my taste, so I'd decided to try and hedge my bets.

I had used computer software to track Twee Siu's comings and goings thanks to the GPS device Honey attached to her car. Twee lived in a trendy brick warehouse cum condo development. After confirming she was currently at Celadon, her beauty salon in Metairie, I entered her condo lobby. At least I tried to. Finally a doorman buzzed me in.

The fiftyish African-American gentleman behind the desk wore a polyester royal blue blazer and black clip-on tie. His gold plastic nameplate read LEVON. He looked vaguely familiar, but the name didn't ring a bell.

"Morning, Mr. Levon. Wonder if you can help me."

"I'll surely try, Officer St. James."

My gut tightened and I scrutinized him more carefully, sifting through the memory banks to put a story to the face.

"Darrian Johnson's the real name. This here name tag was on the jacket when I got hired on."

I nodded. "Breaking and entering. Somewhere off Napoleon and Baronne. What, five, six years ago I collared you?"

"Yes, sir."

"Oh yeah, and manslaughter. You were drunk, got into a fight, and killed some guy before you broke in, right?"

"Been out for two. Straight as an arrow, chief."

I nodded again, gauging my approach. "I need to get into one of the units here."

"This official business?"

"It's business. Dead president kind of business." I put two crisp hundred-dollar bills on the counter between us. "Twee Siu's condo."

"That cute little Asian ho?"

"That's the one."

"She some kind a freak, man."

"What do you mean?"

"I don't see what's going on inside, but I see what's going in and coming out. You know, hot little Asian bitches with some businessman-type guy. And the boys all look fat, dumb, and happy when they come out of that damn condo. They be passing a good time, for sure."

"Think she's running a brothel?"

"Not saying a brothel, but seems like they might be turning tricks or something, once in a while."

"So Twee brings these guys in?"

"No, that part ain't Twee. Different girls, man, not the same ones. But Twee, that girl go out every night and stay out late, I hear."

"Okay." I put a third hundred on the desk. "Another C-note if you shut down the video cams till I'm out of here." He smiled, scooped up the bills, reached into a metal lockbox, and handed me a passkey. Three hundred is a lot of green for a guy making eight bucks an hour.

"Anything for the police." Darrian pronounced it "Poh-lease."

"Hey, Darrian, why not erase the last hour for me on those tapes, too?" I didn't want any evidence of me parking on the street and entering the building.

"Will do."

"She got an alarm?"

"Yes, sir." Darrian used a key to open a locked wall console. He handed me a key chain with writing on paper inside a clear plastic slot. "But now you got the disarm code."

The foxes guarding the henhouse, indeed.

Twee's condo featured exposed brick, big windows, bleached hardwood floors, and the cool elegant lines of Scandinavian furniture. Immaculate to the point of being anal, the rooms shone spotless, like a display model. But condiments occupied the refrigerator, along with a half bottle of Mumm's Cordon Rouge champagne and ten frozen packages of Lean Cuisine in the freezer.

In the bedrooms, the beds looked like a hotel maid at the Ritz had just done them up. Clothes hung neatly in the master bedroom closet. A couple of short blond wigs relaxed upon mannequin heads on a vanity. Lots of women in the New Orleans alternative party scene wore wigs when they went out partying and I started to wonder if Twee had a freak streak.

I didn't find Sam's laptop during the walkthrough. It took twenty-five minutes after I began a second, more thorough search to find it in a linen closet under 1000-thread-count Egyptian cotton sheets. In another fifteen minutes I had swapped out the hard drive. The replacement contained all the programs and files I copied that night at Pravda, so if Twee booted it up, it would seem authentic. I returned the laptop to its soft cradle, then went to work installing listening devices into the hard wiring throughout the condo. That's when I discovered all of the cameras and bugs already in place. Even the bathrooms were wired.

I thought about what Darrian had said regarding the male visitors. I picked the lock on an armoire and found it crammed with sex toys and sex aids of every type, and the requisite French maid/leather dominatrix/Japanese schoolgirl costumes.

Now I really wanted to get to know Twee much better.

CHAPTER NINETEEN

Sometimes Fate is a beautiful thing. While still a rookie cop and fairly new to the city, I'd been on a VID—very important date—with the most beautiful African-American nurse at Charity Hospital, or any hospital for that matter. I'd taken her for a special four-course dinner at the Court of Two Sisters, spared no expense, and looked the picture of conquest certitude until the waiter informed me my card had been declined. My only card. *Merde.*

Showing my badge and explaining I was NOPD only seemed to dig me in deeper with the scowling waiter. He seemed reluctant to let me leave for a trip to my place for another card.

That's when a black gentleman at the next table stepped in and picked up my check without blinking. He insisted. He worked as a tech at the JP crime lab and so we were brothers-in-arms, in a manner of speaking. And even though he sat with his lovely wife and two of the cutest, most well-behaved little girls on the planet, I sensed that he was rooting for me to score with the nurse.

Kerry Broussard and I subsequently became fast friends and fishing buddies. He'd grown up in the Tremé, kept his nose clean, graduated from UNO, married, and moved his family to Metairie so his kids could go to better schools. He was a good Christian family man and maybe the most savvy crime tech in Louisiana. On important cases, I found myself using Kerry instead of the NOPD lab, which, unfortunately, sucked ass in certain areas.

I paid Kerry back for that dinner. He wouldn't take a dime from me for his lab favors over the years, but appreciated my donations to the church his family had attended for generations on St. Claude. I also taught both of his daughters aikido and became a regular for summer barbeques in their backyard. I always brought the potato salad and went to great pains to disguise the fact that it wasn't homemade but bought at Dorignac's.

Today I handed over Eli's hair strands in a plastic zip bag, as well as Sam's laptop hard drive. Kerry took them reverently, as he did with all evidence presented to him.

"So, Cliff, we got a hair sample here for DNA and you need me to retrieve all the deleted files on this hard drive. And you want to know the date and time they were deleted."

"Is it possible to retrieve those files, Kerry?"

"I know you like shrimp po'boys." "Poor boy" sandwiches originated in New Orleans and are ubiquitous here. Similar to submarine or hero sandwiches from elsewhere, they are split French baguettes slathered with meats, cheeses, or fresh seafood like oysters, shrimp, catfish, soft-shell crab, or crawfish that have been baked, steamed, fried, or barbequed. Even French fries find their way into poor boys. The Vietnamese *bành mi* sandwiches in the city are also made with fresh baguettes, but with unique Asian ingredients, including pepper-shredded chicken and shredded carrots and jicama pickled in a pungent sweet sauce. A muffuletta is perhaps the most quintessentially New Orleans sandwich, even though it was invented by a Sicilian immigrant and not a French, Spanish, or Creole chef. The city had lost a lot of its importance over the decades: Houston and Atlanta became the financial centers of the South; the sugar industry, tobacco, King Cotton were distant memories. But we still reigned as King of the Sandwich.

"Well, you've seen me eat, what? A hundred of them?" I said. "It's un-American not to like shrimp po'boys."

"The DNA from the hair sample I can't rush, it will take at least a week for me to get that. But by the time you're back with one po'boy for you and one for me, I'll have your computer files. Make mine dressed."

Kerry delivered as promised. He'd retrieved the deleted files from Sam's laptop and copied them onto a USB drive that now rested in my pocket as I fought evening rush-hour traffic.

I called Kendall and he reported that Jimmy was at his house in English Turn, the *très* expensive neighborhood on the West Bank. T-Boy had not yet shown up at NOAC.

So I slowly cruised back into the city and made a detour I had been avoiding.

The new sign on the old bar read BOXCARS and the logo was a railroad freight car festooned with a pair of dice showing double sixes. Sharon and Dice could change the name and the sign, but I knew it would be years, maybe decades, before locals stopped referring to the joint as the Jupiter Lounge.

I didn't want to go in, and hoped I'd never have to. The shabby exterior, de rigueur for most New Orleans neighborhood bars, hadn't changed. In fact, if you owned a bar that didn't look like it was about to collapse, you stuck out like a sore thumb. Bud, my missing-in-action contractor, had said Sharon and Dice chose a freight train motif interior design for the remodel. Nothing like aiming low.

I didn't look forward to screening the video file of Sharon stealing money in Sam's office—one of the files Kerry had retrieved—but it would be the first file I would check. If Dice were somehow complicit in Sam's death or the disappearance of the $400K, Sharon would be dragged into it. Not something I wanted to see happen. And if Eli told the truth about the rape, I could ruin Dice overnight, probably destroy his relationship with Sharon. We would just have to see how things played out.

I glanced in my rearview mirror and caught sight of a silver SUV slowly roll through the cross street behind me. Was it the same silver Escalade I saw pull into the JP crime lab parking lot a little earlier? There are lots of silver Escalades in the world. I should have written it off, but my place had just been broken into, so I pulled a three-point turn, and bailed after the SUV. I hung a right at Octavia, but the Escalade had vanished.

I started making calls as I drove toward the Garden District. I caught my personal banker on her cell and she told me to forget about trying to run down which bank loaned Sam the $500,000 and for what. She assured me that even if I could determine which bank issued the loan, no banker would share confidential details with a mere PI.

By the time I parked in front of CC's on Magazine I had Jim Shannon on the phone down in Costa Rica, where he'd just retired to after selling the Jupiter Lounge to Sharon and Dice.

You can't keep a good barkeep down, and Jim was already running an open-air bar on the beach in Papagayo. A real tiki bar, not a fake one like Sam had. It was early enough in the day that Jim wasn't yet pickled, just loose enough and happy that he had a higher quality of drunken clientele in Costa Rica than in NOLA, so he didn't mind me asking questions that were none of my business.

"Dice paid cash for the building, the fixtures. Sharon already had the liquor license, as you know. Simplest transaction I've ever done. We used the same attorney to handle all the paperwork."

"I never realized Dice had so much cash," I said evenly.

"Cash is a beautiful thing. I like cash. What bar owner doesn't? Including you, St. James. You telling me you never beat the tax man on bar receipts?"

"All I'm saying is that three hundred and fifty thousand is a lot of dough to pony up in cash."

"We did everything on the up and up."

"Yeah, I know that. The Hall of Records is a shambles or I wouldn't have bothered you."

"You want to know where the money came from? Beats me."

"Who was the legal entity, the purchaser?"

"Boxcars, LLC. Dice and Sharon are the LLC members, but you can check that on the state Web site, you know, that handles corporate licensing."

"Yeah, I'll do that."

"Don't ask me to speculate how a lifelong NOPD cop comes

up with the money, okay? I don't think you have to use your imagination about that. But I'll say this, I got the feeling the money was Dice's and not Sharon's, know what I mean?"

While standing in line at CC's for a triple caramel mochasippi to go, I counted no less than three silver SUVs drive past. So much for paranoia.

The note and key I left in the dojo for Honey were gone. Her black bra and panties lay neatly folded on the couch next to a pair of handcuffs, a Spyderco folding knife, and an extra mag for her Sig Sauer. An array of beauty products stood sentinel on the sink in the bathroom like soldiers on watch against an onslaught of ugliness.

Amazing what a girl can carry in her purse.

It was a little after seven and had been another slam-bang day that I figured wasn't going to end anytime soon. I retrieved my laptop and got right down to business. The thumb drive held three video files with the name SHARON ST. JAMES, all dated after our divorce. In the first video clip she looked haggard and a little desperate. She stole $157. An odd amount out of the $3,000-plus she counted. *Why not take an even $200?* Perhaps she had an overdue bill wearing down on her and she only took what she absolutely had to.

The same scenario held true in the other two videos. She took odd amounts of Sam's money, always less than $200. At the time she took the money I was sending her cash every month, even though the court didn't require me to. I guess I wasn't sending enough. My ego fed me the thought that Sharon only hooked up with Dice for financial stability: a dirty cop with dirty money and a pension was better than being on her own. I wanted to believe that was true and that she didn't, she couldn't possibly love the jerk.

I spent the better part of the next hour sifting through Sam's business records. Twee had lied to me; all of the Bayou Aviation records had been in Sam's laptop but had been deleted, probably by her. Bayou had fifteen employees and had been making a tidy profit as a helicopter repair and maintenance facility, as well as from shuttling men and material to and from offshore rigs. But there was nothing about a fish business with Jimmy Nguyen.

A large folder named SUNRISE, however, suggested Sam had his fingers in what could only be a smuggling operation. Meticulous record-keeping was Sam's strong suit, and there were dates and times of arrivals and deliveries of UNITS. *Units of what?*

I speculated "units" referred to either kilos of cocaine or Thai units of number-four heroin. Smuggling bundles of marijuana in helicopters didn't seem commercially viable, especially since Bayou brought in no more than twenty-five units per month. The units were all shuttled in from the same place—HALO-2. Possibly an abandoned offshore rig. Fuel consumption and cost per gallon for each round-trip flight to HALO-2 was noted, so it would be easy enough to plot out a maximum flight radius depending on which helicopter flew the run.

The files suggested, contrary to Kiesha's assertion, that Sam worked part-time as a dope smuggler, most likely in bed with T-Boy, Jimmy Nguyen, or Deon Franklin. Tough company. He'd taken out a half-million-dollar business loan just before he died. Logically, Sam's bank loan might have been to purchase another aircraft for Bayou, particularly if he was buying from a private party. But there wasn't too much that was logical about this case. I began to believe the worst about Sam, that the cash must have been to do a dope deal, probably behind someone's back. Considering the players involved, not a smart move.

CHAPTER TWENTY

While I continued to examine Sam's files, Kendall's cousin called in to report that Jimmy Nguyen had left his home in English Turn, driven to Gulf Coast Fish Company, and had just gotten into a reefer truck with two of his boys and was headed west. Seemed kind of odd that a crime boss would be riding in a box truck cab at nine o'clock at night.

On a hunch I checked the GPS surveillance software on my laptop; it showed Twee's car heading into Lafourche Parish, site of Tommy Boudreaux's Bayou Aviation. A return trip to Bayou for a black-bag job was on tap for much later this evening, but the schedule just got moved up to right now.

I called Honey on the sterile cell phone; she had finished with her mom and was ready for some night ops, so we agreed to a rendezvous.

As I drove toward the Windsor Court Hotel I picked up a silver SUV tracking me. An Escalade. And this time I was certain. I skirted past a Mardi Gras walking krewe on Poydras costumed like a bunch of vampires, raced up North Peters, and pulled into the circular drive of the Windsor Court Hotel to valet park.

I tossed my keys to a valet as I hurried into the lobby, then quickly exited the opposite side of the building onto Tchoupitoulas. I sprinted across to Common where Honey sat waiting in her black Jeep Wrangler.

"Were you followed?"

"Silver SUV. I lost them, but let's jam."

"Get a look at the driver?"

I shook my head. "FBI, CIA, Deon or Jimmy's boys, Twee having me watched . . . take your pick."

The razor wire–topped chain-link gate to Bayou Aviation stood necklaced with a heavy chain, the chain linked by a solid padlock. But a close look on this chill, ebony night showed us the padlock held the chain that held the gate, but the padlock wasn't locked.

"Dummy-locked," said Honey, keeping her voice down.

"Somebody without a key is either on their way in or on their way out."

"Or somebody has gotten lazy."

"That's T-Boy's white Yukon," I said. The SUV sat empty but nonetheless intimidating near the office door in the parking lot, dimly lit by a couple of security lights. The office windows appeared as dark rectangles and no hint of light leaked out from under the massive hangar doors. The buildings and grounds looked deserted and a little spooky; a low fog frosted the deep black delta night, icing the swamps all around. A good night to be up to no good.

Honey and I melted away from the gate and merged with the silhouette of a live oak just across the road.

"I don't see Twee's car, but the GPS tracker says it's here."

"Think she found it?" asked Honey.

"When's the last time you checked your car for a tracking device?"

"I don't have business with the CIA. Which apparently she does, since it seems she's here late at night meeting Tommy Boudreaux."

"This is all just getting curiouser and curiouser."

"Maybe she parked inside the hangar."

"Wait for me here."

"No way, I'm coming," stated Honey.

She followed me back to the gate, scanning all around as I quietly removed the lock from the chain and fed the heavy links through the galvanized fence mesh. I cracked the gate enough for me to squeeze through. "Honey, I don't have a career to jeopardize. You do. If I do some B and E, you can't be part of that."

"You mean like the B and E we did at the Tiki Hut?"

"That was different and you know it."

We both heard the sound at the same time, terminating further discussion. The faint *whump-whump* of moist air sliced by large, heavy blades, approaching from the south. We scanned the sky trying to pick up the running lights.

Honey pushed her way in behind me and re-dummy-locked the gate. "Is that 'copter coming here?"

"We'll know soon. Galliano airport is about ten miles north."

"Where's the helipad here?"

"This whole place is one big helipad. Runway is on the other side of the buildings."

"I didn't see any runway lights."

"Maybe for the same reason that helo is flying dark."

The parking lot security lights suddenly cut off as the sound of the approaching aircraft rapidly grew louder, the chopping sound acquiring a deeper, more powerful resonance.

"Pilot must be using night vision. Maybe Twee is parked on the other side of the building," Honey speculated.

"Move, we're in the open here!"

Airports, airparks, and airstrips require large expanses of flat, open ground, and Bayou, though carved from a swamp, was no different. Thirty open yards stretched between me and T-Boy's SUV, the only vehicle in the lot. Hundreds of yards of nothing but asphalt lay to my right. The same to my left, except about a hundred yards away a semitruck and trailer sat parked with what looked like a helicopter, covered with canvas, strapped to the flatbed trailer.

It sounded like the copter was now circling over the runway. If I tried to run around the large hangars in either direction I'd be completely exposed and any vehicles driving on the tarmac would see me instantly. But if I wanted to see what was going to come out of that helicopter, I needed to get a line of sight, and fast. Keeping cover but having a view meant going through the office building. Or over it.

I bolted on a dead run for the office front door, assuming Honey would follow. I heard the whining of the chopper's engines as the pilot increased power to maintain a constant glide angle as he approached. The heavy steel front office door, unlike the gate, was locked tight. The locks were serious ones that could not be picked quickly.

The helicopter engines screamed. The pilot was now landing

on the opposite side of the office/operations building I stood in front of. The one-story, low-slung cinderblock affair connected on either side to the two huge 10,000-square-foot, two-story-tall hangars. The hangars that bookended the office building loomed like monsters, but the office structure was low-slung and doable.

I shined a one-second burst of light from my Surefire and saw a way up. The iron bars securing the windows made a nice perch from which to grab on to some exterior electrical conduit. I found purchase and crab-walked my way up the wall, then struggled to pull myself onto the roof. Besides withholding a detective shield, the chief had thwarted my attempt to become an instructor at the NOPD Academy. So I taught defensive tactics to other departments on a pro bono basis, making a lot of friends in the process. I also taught something unique, something I felt departments sorely lacked training in: fence and wall climbing. I'd made myself something of the local master in that regard, so if I failed to make it onto the roof now, when it counted, I'd be pretty angry with myself.

Luckily, I got a leg over the roof edge and heaved my body up and over, rolling, then scrambling into a quiet, crouched run to the other side. Flattening out, I carefully peered over the ledge as I eased my micro-mini digital video recorder out of a cargo pocket and pressed REC.

A white Gulf Coast Fish Company box truck sat parked on the tarmac, its rear cargo doors open. A late-model sedan idled next to it. The helicopter had landed about forty yards from the vehicles and the pilot now spooled down the engine and shut off his turbines.

Two men from the box truck ran forward and opened the helicopter passenger door. Five passengers, each gripping a small piece of luggage, exited the copter. I distinctly heard snippets of an Asian language.

One man led the passengers to the truck and they climbed into the cargo compartment, then the heavy doors slammed shut behind them and the latching hardware engaged.

The other man, a stocky Asian, grabbed a satchel from the helicopter and jogged with it to the truck cab.

The truck lurched forward, its exhaust stack belching diesel smoke that smudged the pale, chalky fog with grayish wisps. I aimed the recorder at the scene, keeping as low a profile as possible. When I saw the pilot start to lock up his cockpit, I zoomed in and immediately recognized the man. He slung a heavy duffel bag, calmly walked over to the sedan, tossed the duffel in the backseat, then got in. Did the duffel contain his personal effects, or something else? The car squealed off angrily, turning tight after the truck.

I retreated back across the roof and ducked as the security lights flashed back on. The box truck stopped at the gate. As the truck driver jumped from the cab to heave open the chain-link gate, I zoomed in and recorded the figure in the truck cab: Jimmy Nguyen.

The truck driver got back in and revved the engine, rumbling the truck onto the asphalt and into the opaque night, the cargo safely ensconced inside.

The sedan screeched to a stop next to the parked SUV. The pilot got out of the car with jerky body language showing his irritation. He retrieved the duffel bag as he vehemently argued with the female driver in Vietnamese. *"Bạn cần phải ngăn chặn này."*

"Bạn đang là một trong những người cần phải dùng!" spat Twee, seething mad.

"Không dùng đó để anh ta."

"Tôi sẽ làm nhũng gì tôi muốn," Twee said dismissively, then rolled up her window.

T-Boy, not surprisingly, spoke perfect Vietnamese, and I considered who I would use for the language translation of the video I was shooting, when Twee laid rubber backing out, executed a reverse doughnut-and-a-half, and shot out through the gate with the proficiency of a PSD team driver avoiding an IED.

Whatever was said, they weren't very happy with each other. T-Boy tossed the duffel into his Yukon, then backed out, stopping in the road to close and forcefully lock the gate. He then slowly drove off into the chilly winter night.

In all the commotion I had completely forgotten about Honey. Where the hell was she? I dropped to the pavement, rolled perfectly, and came up at a run. At the gate I took gloves from my pocket and pulled them on, ready to hurtle over the razor wire, when Honey's voice caught me from behind.

"See any details?"

I wasn't happy to see her on this side of the fence. "Plenty. Human smuggling. Plus a satchel getting special attention from Jimmy Nguyen. T-Boy piloted the chopper and seemed very attached to a big duffel bag. Twee's driving the sedan. They were arguing."

"Jimmy Nguyen, Tommy Boudreaux, and Twee Siu. Now there's a triangle. We following?"

"Probably not in a timely fashion, since you're not waiting on the other side of this fence in your Jeep with the engine idling."

"I was doing some solid police work."

"And what would that be?"

"One. While you were climbing the wall? I planted a GPS tracker on Tommy's ride."

"Excellent."

"Two. That tarped helicopter? Sitting on that flatbed over there? I think it's stolen."

T-Boy had driven off slowly, heading north on Louisiana Highway 1 behind the other vehicles. We couldn't risk passing him to follow the box truck. And using only one vehicle to follow a seasoned operator like T-Boy for dozens of miles on a rural road would not have turned out well. So Honey and I decided to stay a bit longer and check out any other aircraft parked on the tarmac at Bayou Aviation.

We circled the buildings to where T-Boy had landed the copter. "Think T-Boy is heading for the drop point of the human cargo?" asked Honey.

"Somehow I doubt it. Jimmy Nguyen is probably handling that part of the operation. We're better off following the tracer on Twee's car or T-Boy's SUV when we're done here, and see where they've gone."

"Importing illegal aliens, huh?"

"It's lucrative," I said. "Southern Chinese pay upwards of fifty thousand dollars to have a snakehead get them into the States. The files on Sam's laptop indicated he was smuggling units of something. People, maybe?"

"Why not? Five bodies equals a quarter mil. Plus whatever was in that satchel you mentioned. Or the duffel."

We got the manufacturer's serial numbers off the data plates from three more helicopters and Honey called them in to a desk sergeant and asked him to check the U.S. Stolen Aircraft Recovery Systems database. I decided I could come back tomorrow night to break in and search the offices, so we drove back toward New Orleans in silence.

As we approached Larose, Honey's cell phone broke the quiet. "This is Sgt. Baybee." She paused to listen, then, "Thanks, McNair." She ended the call.

"The first 'copter I checked was stolen in Ames, Iowa, two days ago."

"The one covered with the tarp?"

She nodded. "Got curious about the registration numbers being rubbed out. So I got the serial number from the data plate in the cockpit."

"Any of the others boosted?"

"The one you said T-Boy flew tonight? Matches the description of a chopper stolen in California four months ago."

"But the serial number doesn't match?"

"Correct. Aircraft don't have VIN numbers like cars do. It would be easy to swap out the original data plate with a fake."

"So the helicopter on the flatbed just got down here from where it was stolen in Iowa. They haven't had a chance to swap out the data plate yet."

"Or repaint it with new registration numbers."

"Why would T-Boy steal helicopters?" I asked rhetorically.

"Because they're too expensive to buy?"

As we reentered New Orleans, the tracking device on Tommy Boudreaux's Yukon pinpointed him at a gas station in the CBD. Twee's signal entered the Lower Garden District and stopped right in front of my dojo.

"What the hell is she doing at my place?"

"We better go find out."

Honey put the pedal down and the Jeep shot forward.

"Seems like Twee is up to her eyeballs in no good. So why hire me to nose around?" I wondered.

"She could be an unwilling participant."

"Funny to hear you come up with a defense for Twee. Anyway, the sexcapades she's running out of her condo doesn't sound like she's an unwilling participant."

"She's using you, I guarantee it. Said it all along."

"You're probably right, but I still don't get it," I said. "It looks like she's a coconspirator in any number of federal offenses. She could do serious time in an unpleasant penitentiary. Why risk exposing herself to that by bringing me in?"

"Maybe you're not supposed to live long enough to do anything about what you uncover?"

"Thanks for that thought."

Honey double-parked on the corner in front of the dumpy, roach-infested neighborhood confectionery that had just reopened. With all the talk about the need for residents and businesses to "come back," there are certain people and outfits I'd like to see stay away. Such as my rat-hole local convenience store and its snarky Syrian owner.

"Why are you stopping here? Park up at the dojo."

"Get out," Honey said, looking away, refusing to make eye contact.

"Go on and pull up to my place. We'll both go in."

"Negative. She's waiting for you." Honey's tone had shifted; at least her unfounded jealousy was a constant.

"Are you coming back later?"

"Go on, move it. It should be interesting."

I left my laptop in her Jeep. A tenth of a second after I closed the door, Honey spun a U-turn and was gone.

I stopped in the market for props: a bag of Zapps Cajun-flavored potato chips and a forty-ounce bottle of Colt 45 malt liquor. When in Rome.

I approached my front door casually munching on the chips and holding the paper bag of rocket fuel, pretending not to notice Twee sitting in her car. As I fumbled for my key . . .

"Cliff."

I looked over and feigned surprise. "Twee! What's up? Everything okay?"

As I crossed toward her she got out of the Honda, then reached in and heaved up a desktop PC. "I brought Dad's computer from Bayou and . . . and I'm a little scared."

CHAPTER TWENTY-ONE

Twee sipped her second Grey Goose and Seven as I finished briefing her on recent events concerning Eli, Dice, and surreptitious FBI activities. I told her the exact time the shooting took place and told her the probable murder weapon.

She digested the info without comment and seemed to nurse numerous scenarios, none of which, I knew, she would share with me.

"My gut tells me I'm getting close," I said. Closer than she realized. "Does any of that have a bearing on why you're scared right now?"

She abruptly stood up and took off her black leather jacket. "I don't know. Maybe." She wore a tight black cashmere sweater that exposed a bare midriff. Her belly button was pierced with a diamond stud. The skintight black leather pants rose very low over her creamy hips. She wore a studded black leather cowboy belt with a sterling-silver ranger set. Black Kenneth Cole boots gave a few more inches to her five-foot-three figure, which was very nicely proportioned. Her hair and makeup and nails were picture perfect, of course, and as she paced in front of me I had to suppress a smile regarding the spin that I assumed I was about to be buried in. That she looked sexier than I'd ever seen her, I pushed from my mind.

"I got into a big argument with T-Boy over giving you Dad's computer. A big argument. Let's just say he threatened me."

"Okay."

"I'm wondering if he's up to something out in Lafourche. Something illegal with Bayou."

"You mean like not reporting income, cooking the books, that kind of thing?" It was fun to play dumb. At the very least I figured T-Boy to be using stolen helicopters to run a human smuggling ring and probably to import illegal narcotics. And from what I'd just seen, the woman standing in front of me was complicit.

"He said he's had enough with you snooping around and that I was to fire you, or else."

"Or else what?"

She sat back down. This time much closer to me on the couch. "Or else something bad might happen." She looked at me as her eyes moistened. "I don't know what to do."

She pivoted slightly, squaring her shoulders toward me, and put her right hand on my knee. I don't claim to know much about women, but one thing I have learned is that when you're sitting alone with them drinking late at night and they put their hand on your knee, they have opened the door and all you need to do is walk through.

Was Twee offering herself in an effort to shift my investigation toward T-Boy? If she was complicit, why would she do that? Was she using me to eliminate a business partner?

My response was measured; I needed to see where she was

going with this. I gently put my hand on her back, the kind of pat you might give to someone to let them know that everything will be okay. The soft cashmere was almost slick and I could feel heat emanating from between her shoulder blades.

She leaned in and pressed herself to me, her silky black hair against my face. An expensive citrus-tinged perfume invaded my nostrils as, interestingly, her right hand slid halfway up my inner thigh.

Then she attacked, her left hand forcing my face to hers as her lips and tongue ravenously forced themselves on mine. She pivoted and swung her leg over, straddling me. I remained passive, but certainly didn't resist as I fought getting lost in the lust of the moment. My instincts screamed that this was not a good idea, and as I considered how to break the moment before it was too late, the moment broke for me, via the sound of shattering glass.

She leaned back and spoke first.

"What was that?"

I moved her off me and grabbed my Glock. What I hoped was that a drunkard had stumbled into the walkway between my building and the neighbor's and had dropped their wine bottle. It wouldn't be the first time street people had set up shop in the narrow corridor. I walked quietly toward the front of my gym, listening for telltale sounds. What I heard was not promising, as more glass shattered, followed by a distinct *whoosh* that caused a knot in the pit of my stomach. It was the kind of whoosh that sounded like fire leaping to life.

All of my first-floor windows were bricked up except for a small bathroom window solidly barred with heavy wrought iron. I hoped I was wrong, but the worst-case scenario that came to mind was that the *whoosh* meant flames from Molotov cocktails thrown through that window. The door to the bathroom was closed and I touched it, sickened to feel a growing heat on the other side.

Twee stood and adjusted her sweater. Before I could say anything a large object came crashing through the blue tarp covering the hole in my roof, ripping the tarp free and crashing to the wooden dojo floor, disintegrating into a gray cloud of concrete dust. A cinderblock.

"Call nine-one-one and report an arson fire in progress," I yelled to Twee, but before she could respond, three Molotov cocktails rained down from above and burst into Rorschach-like splotches of flame.

Twee screamed and recoiled, but was heads-up enough to grab her purse. I practically kicked in the door to my utility room, popped the dummy wall, grabbed my boogie bag backpack and strapped it on. I spun around just as Twee ran up carrying Sam's desktop PC. Flames had already found the old couch where we'd just been sitting.

"Come on." I led her to the front door as she fished her cell phone from her purse with one hand while still clutching the PC. I tried to engage the dead bolt, but it was solidly frozen. The locking doorknob of the heavy steel security door was similarly fused. I considered trying to shoot out the lock, but the frame, as well as the door and hardware, were all extra-heavy-duty steel construction.

"They've jammed the locks or something."

"Is there another way out?" she asked as she pressed 9-1-1 on her cell.

"Just the back door. The windows are all bricked up except for the bathroom, which is already on fire."

We ran toward the back as three more green wine bottles filled with gasoline and stuffed with flaming rags hurtled downward and exploded onto the hardwood flooring. Gasoline spattered onto the canvas cage floor and the octagonal fighting ring that had survived the looters became engulfed.

As Twee screamed at the 9-1-1 dispatcher, I tuned her out, trying to focus as I pulled her along the west wall. We skirted the angry, spreading flames, then zigzagged through pools of fire toward the back door.

A small explosion signaled the bathroom door blowing out and more flames leaping into the mix. Smoke quickly filled the dojo. The heat rose exponentially and we broke into a heavy sweat. A pool of flame taking root into the wood floor blocked us from reaching the back door.

Twee terminated the 9-1-1 call. "Do you have a fire extinguisher?"

"Stolen by the looters, haven't had money to replace them."

A padded wrestling mat hung on the wall behind us.

"Twee, leave the computer." I lifted the mat, easing its nylon loops off the hooks that held it to the wall.

"But it might be important."

"If we both roast in here it won't matter much."

She quickly glanced around, taking in our tenuous situation, then put the computer on the floor. "Fire department is on the way, they know we're inside."

"We'll be well-done by the time they get here. We'll have one chance at this, so follow me and don't stop," I barked.

I moved forward using the heavy mat as a shield, giving us a crescent of protection, Twee on my heels, holding on to my sides. We scrambled faster, my unprotected hands seared by sheets of fire, but the mat deflected the heat and flame and we reached the back door. Patches of the rubbery/vinyl coating turned runny and melted, dripping onto the floor. I tossed the heavy mat aside as it smoked.

The back door locks were frozen. I kicked at the door, also made of heavy-duty steel to keep the bad guys out. Now it kept the good guys in. I knew I couldn't break through the door frame without a pry bar, and I was fresh out of those, or anything like them.

"Move to the side!" I pulled my Glock and emptied the magazine at the lock; a couple of ricochets zinged around the room. I slammed into the door, but it wouldn't budge.

"Are we trapped?"

It certainly looked like it. There was no crossing back the way we came. Then my screw-up hit me all at once and almost made me sick. I wasted my ammo on the door lock when I should have shot my way through the plywood covering the hole in my wall. And all my extra mags and ammunition were back in the utility room, which was now, as my firefighter pals would say, "fully involved." Then we both flinched as we heard gunshots.

"That would be my stash of ammunition cooking off."

"Cliff, you have to do something."

"I'm open to suggestions."

I glanced around for a tool, something to try and wedge the thick plywood sheet from the wall, when I saw it through the smoke.

A red plastic case containing a cordless power drill. *Bud, you magnificent bastard.*

I lunged forward, popped the case lid, pressed the trigger, and heard the sweet sound of a whirring chuck. I quickly tightened a Phillips head bit in place with a chuck key and went to work backing out the screws that anchored the three-quarter-inch ply-wood sheet to my wall.

Twee cowered with her back to the flames, dialed a number on her cell, and began yelling in Vietnamese.

The rising heat radiated unmercifully, and then the smoke thick-ened like a hot vegetable stock that's just had a bag of cornstarch tossed into it. I coughed, eyes watering, feeling for the next screw that I needed to back out of the wood.

There wasn't going to be enough time to remove all the screws. I could see little and dropped the power tool to the floor. "Twee! Get over here!"

She coughed as she felt her way along the wall and found me, holding on. "Please hurry," she pleaded with a whimper, as the unbearable heat pressed in tighter.

I wedged my Benchmade automatic folder between the plywood and the wall and levered the knife to give an opening for my fingers. "If I can open this, the outside oxygen is going to feed the fire and we won't have much time to get through."

I pulled with every ounce of strength I had, hoping the thick plywood wouldn't break and leave too narrow an opening for passage.

The wood gave a little. I screamed as did every muscle in my up-per body as I willed the wood to give us more. Then I leaned my body back, toward the fire, with my right leg against the wall, le-veraging more force. Sweat poured out of me like an open faucet, stinging my eyes and diminishing my grip on the wood. My head and neck felt like they were scorching and my shoulder started to cramp.

The wood didn't give. But it had to. *Goddamn son of a bitch! I won't die like this. The shitbags who did this will not succeed, I will not give them the satisfaction!* I repositioned myself and lurched my body mass using every ounce of strength I had . . .

The wood didn't give, but the remaining screws did.

The entire plywood sheet flew off the wall and I lost balance, twisting as I fell back to the floor. A rush of cool air fueled a roar of flame. Without thinking, I sprang to my feet, grabbed Twee, and dragged her into the moist chill of the evening. We stumbled into the back alley, eyes burning, coughing, shoelaces on fire.

In a haze of adrenaline shock I heard sirens approach in the distance, the sound of tires screeching away in another direction. I pulled the Glock for intimidation purposes. The magazine was empty and my eyes stung so badly I couldn't really see even if I had bullets to shoot.

A wave of heat and bright light caught us and I pulled Twee farther along the alley, behind a steel Dumpster. We collapsed like some drug-addled alcoholic couple, retching, choking, red eyes burning, holding each other. Twee Siu cried like a baby, so I held her.

For ten minutes we sat there, breathing good air, collecting our wits, calming down, listening to the sounds of firefighters arriving and attempting to fight the fire in a city suffering from extremely low water pressure, another by-product of the Storm and part of the New Normal that one simply had to accept because it wasn't going to get fixed anytime soon.

Finally I looked at Twee and wiped her smoke-smudged face that showed watercourses from a rivulet of tears. Eyes like reddish saucers, she was high on an adrenaline rush and I could see her brain going at a thousand miles an hour.

I started to laugh. Everything was just too funny. Especially Twee. In an attempt to manipulate me, she'd almost been roasted alive.

"This is funny?"

"I'd rather laugh than cry. Besides, none of my insurance covered the damage from the Storm. But I have lots of fire insurance. Thank God for shifty, stalling, slow-moving contractors who don't fix holes in walls. Burn, baby, burn!"

Twee laughed, too. Macabre gallows humor was great, as long as you survived the gallows.

She gently touched my chin and turned me to her. "Hey . . . you saved my life."

Then she kissed me. And this time, I kissed back. We broke off when footsteps and voices approached and a flashlight found us. Hands reached out and pulled us to our feet.

"Jesus, man, were you in that building?"

"I'm afraid so."

"Get EMS back here in the alley! Two victims!" the firefighter barked into his radio.

Twee and I both wobbled mightily and the firefighters sat us back down. They asked questions, trying to determine how badly we might be hurt, but my head was suddenly spinning and I couldn't answer coherently.

I tried to stand, but EMS had arrived and an oxygen mask was strapped over my mouth. I couldn't think, I just closed my eyes and let myself drift with Twee Siu drifting next to me.

We refused to go to the hospital and were treated at the scene for smoke inhalation and minor scalding. After a lengthy interrogation by police and fire investigators on site, we were free to go. I called Honey's sterile cell phone but she didn't answer. There was no voice mail set up so I'd have to call her back.

I had no place to go. And if the hit had been meant for Twee, then her options were limited as well. My Bronco was at the Windsor Court, my bike a puddle of molten metal inside the shell of the dojo, so Twee drove me to a house in Gretna, on the West Bank, where she said we'd be safe. She claimed the modest three-bedroom place couldn't be connected to her, but declined to elaborate. I felt so exhausted I could have slept on the street, so I didn't push it.

We both smelled like a bonfire. The house had a washer/dryer and I tossed my clothes in for a super-heavy-duty cycle. I found a shower in one of the bathrooms and carefully rinsed, the cool water soothing my red skin. Then the plastic curtain pulled back and Twee unexpectedly joined me. Naked.

I wasn't sure what to say, so I simply watched as she took a washcloth and washed my privates. When she finished she wordlessly handed me the cloth, and I returned the favor.

Then we found each other with the cleansing droplets streaming down and made love standing in the shower, awash with a renewed surge of energy that came from somewhere outside of us.

Still engaged, her arms around my neck, legs locked around my buttocks, I walked her into the bedroom. We'd just escaped an inferno, but Twee had her own raging fire to be placated. We met in a lover's union of extremes. Raw, tender, biting, scratching, gentle, sweat-soaked, hard sex. We both found ourselves screaming when we finally collapsed in spent elation.

As we lay in the afterglow in each other's arms, just before drifting to sleep, I asked her, "Twee, is there anything you'd like to tell me?"

She leaned over and kissed my nipple, then looked me in the eyes and said, "Yes, but I can't."

CHAPTER TWENTY-TWO

I woke up alone in the strange bed with no sign of Twee. My blue-faced TechnoMarine chronograph and an empty stomach both told me it was lunchtime. I moved my clothes from the washer into the dryer then checked the bedroom closets and drawers for something to put on, but everything was empty. So I nosed around naked and decided the house must be a rental property, furnished, that belonged to a friend or family member. I found pots and pans but no food; linens and towels but no clothes. I knotted a towel around my waist.

I wanted to call Honey on the sterile phone, but couldn't get a signal for that phone or my regular cell, which seemed odd. And there were no landlines in the house.

The noon news would just be coming on, so I turned on the flat-screen TV in the living room to check for reports about my place burning down. The lead story was an all-too-familiar one, yet a complete shock to me. The FBI had just arrested nine members of the old Marlin Duplessis mayoral administration on charges ranging from racketeering to grand theft to conspiracy. Nine cronies of Duplessis taken down, but the TV news reader stressed that the former mayor had not been arrested or accused of any wrongdoing.

"You rat bastard," I said aloud to myself. I'd been wrong. Duplessis wasn't being tailed by the FBI, he was being protected. His "centurions," he had called them. The mayor had been cooperating, dropping dimes on his best buddies from the old days to save his own sleazy hide.

I mentally hit the Delete key and erased his name from my suspect list. Duplessis wasn't a murderer, just a weasel.

A brief segment covered the fire on Magazine Street where a martial arts studio burned to the ground. Arson was suspected, but no one had been seriously injured. No one was seriously injured *yet*, but someone would be once I learned the identities of the would-be assassins.

I don't have nudist tendencies and felt uncomfortable with just a towel around me in someone else's house. I spotted what had to be a hall closet and decided to check in there for something to wear, maybe a jacket or something. It was the only place I hadn't yet looked.

The hall closet door was locked, and that seemed unusual. Who locks their hall closet door? I used a credit card to shim the tang and had it open in four seconds. The closet stood empty, but another door, a heavy steel door in a reinforced frame with a boxy five-button cipher lock, was set into the closet's rear wall. This made no sense. And the steel door was a serious door that couldn't be jimmied, similar to the doors in my dojo. This door was absolutely intent on keeping people out, so naturally it beckoned to me.

I grabbed my small B&E kit from the boogie bag and went to

work on the lock. This type of cipher lock had a key override advertised as being bump key and pick proof, but I knew better. Still, it was an impressive lock that posed a question that could only be answered by finessing the pins of the key lock, since I didn't know the cipher. So I worked the pins. The doorknob and the lock hardware were heavy gauge and stiff with increased tension, making my task extra difficult. I got past the first two pins with the bump key, but the mechanism was simply too tight. I reverted to picks.

A martial arts instructor got me interested in locks as a kid and I earned my locksmith certification at age eighteen. I knew locks, but it took an hour and seventeen minutes before I popped that lock open, walked through that door, and found what I couldn't quite believe.

The small, windowless room held a rack of the most sophisticated digital communications gear I had ever laid eyes on. State-of-the-art burst transmission technology that comms-freak buddies of mine had described to me. It made the FBI digital equipment in the Tiki Hut look archaic. I powered up other receivers, more familiar ones, and found they were preset to monitor law enforcement frequencies. What looked like an encrypted phone and fax setup sat on a console in the corner.

Opposite the communications gear, a substantial standing safe had redundant entry controls: keypad, card key lock, and biometrics—both fingerprint and iris scan. No way I could crack that safe. I could drill it or blow it, but I didn't have a drill or explosives.

This room held big secrets and I suddenly felt a chill along my arms. Instinctively I spun and checked around the door frame. I found some kind of motion-sensing pinhole cam that must have triggered as soon as I opened the door. No doubt a silent alarm had already been issued and my half-naked image recorded and sent into the ether.

Meaning I had to finish quickly and get out.

Drawers under a faux wood console had locks, but I got past those easily. The first two drawers held nothing but common office supplies. The bottom drawer suggested sloppiness or laziness on the part of the person who used this room. First there was the dossier of a young attractive Asian woman named Vang Tho, who looked very familiar. As I studied her face, I realized she was the receptionist at Twee's beauty salon Celadon. Her hair was styled differently, but it was the same female. Below the dossier lay envelopes containing foreign currencies and three passports—from Cambodia, Vietnam, and China—all jumbled unsecured in the bottom of the drawer. The photos in the passports were all of the same person, but not of Vang Tho, the Celadon receptionist.

The three passports, all issued in different names, all contained a photo of Twee Siu.

Oh, and Vang Tho's dossier was marked EYES ONLY and contained the seal of the Central Intelligence Agency.

I beat feet from the safe house in damp clothes and took a cab to the Windsor Court to retrieve the Bronco. Careful that I wasn't followed, I parked just below the levee across from Elizabeth's Café in the Bywater, where I checked my voice mail on the sterile cell. Honey had been worried sick and left me a series of messages. I powered up my regular cell phone. To hell with the sterile cell; Twee was CIA and had all of my numbers. If I was being monitored, so be it.

Honey didn't answer; I knew she was on Parade Duty, pulling a sixteen-hour shift, and probably had her hands full. Since I'd left my computer in Honey's Jeep, I used my phone to go online and check the GPS surveillance software. Except there were no signals to check. Twee and T-Boy had found the tracking devices.

I contacted Kendall and learned that Jimmy was out at the Gulf Coast Fish Company offices, and had been for most of the day. Kendall was there now with one of his cousins.

Then I tried Honey again, and this time she answered.

"Honey, it's me."

"Damn you, St. James! You just now call me?" she demanded, royally peeved.

"I couldn't get a cell signal at the CIA safe house."

As I thought it would, that remark neutralized her anger. I quickly brought her up to speed on recent events, leaving out the fact that I had hoisted the Jolly Roger over Twee's safe house bed.

"Whoever tried to whack us is no lone killer. I figure it was at least four guys."

"That doesn't eliminate any prime suspects. T-Boy, Deon, Jimmy, Dice. Any of them could put together a crew in seconds."

"I have to wonder if they were after me, Twee, or both of us."

"She's a dirty CIA officer. Holy shit."

"No kidding. I'm not getting paid enough for this."

"Get the hell out of town. Now." Honey sounded insistent.

"Negative. I got a fix on Jimmy. That's all I got right now, so I'm going to pay him a visit."

"Cliff, don't."

"I'll call you later."

"Officer Kevin Lee," she quickly interjected. "He's on duty right now out in the east. Vietnamese-American. He's expecting your call. Don't be stupid. Take him with you if you have to see Jimmy Nguyen."

"How long ago did he leave?" I asked Kendall.

"Maybe ten minutes."

I stood next to Kendall and his cousin and their trashed pickup truck, parked in a debris-littered parking lot across from Gulf Coast Fish Company. The lot was now partially cleared and I had to admire Kendall's ingenuity in conceiving convincing cover for the surveillance.

"He was in the Range Rover?"

"With three a his boys."

I picked up a piece of steel rebar and twirled it like a baton. I wanted to kick some serious ass, but whose?

"Good job, keep it up."

I drove east on Chef for a minute as my unfocused rage built. I spun a wild U-turn, pulled right up to the door of Gulf Coast Fish Company, then stormed inside with the steel rebar in my hand.

The office of Gulf Coast Fish Company on Chef Menteur Highway was nothing special, even though all the furniture and office equipment was new, as was the carpeting, drywall, wiring; everything was new, in fact, except for the foundation, the studs, and the bricks. When you're a fat cat crime boss like Jimmy Nguyen, dripping in dirty money, twenty feet of water in your business can be rectified fairly quickly. But even Jimmy's money couldn't erase the faint moldy smell that lingered as a reminder of the folly of living and working in bottomland swamp and pretending there wouldn't be an occasional price to pay for that.

The other aroma was of the piquant fish sauce variety, as the young receptionist ate a late take-out lunch of *hu tieu ko* at her desk. She and the other three employees present all looked up at me wide-eyed as I entered twirling the rebar.

"I'd like to see Jimmy Nguyen."

"Mr. Nguyen isn't in."

"I know that. I'm the gentleman who sent him to the hospital with a broken face. Tell him I said that if he had anything to do with burning down my place, I will burn down his house in English Turn, I will burn down Club Bamboo, and I will burn down this building. I will kill him and every last one of his homeboys."

I handed her my PI card. "Tell him I want to talk to him, now. You got that?"

The receptionist looked frightened. None of the employees moved an inch. They knew the kind of people their boss associated with, and they knew better than to get involved.

"I'll tell him," she managed to stammer.

I stormed out knowing that I'd be talking to Jimmy within the hour. You just don't walk into a crime boss's place of business and make threats without being promptly contacted. Or killed.

All wound up with no ass to kick, I called NOPD Officer Kevin Lee, a first-generation Vietnamese-American perfectly suited for his job. Born in Vietnam, raised in America, he was the kind of immigrant that benefited the United States: honest, hardworking, and willing to give something back to his new country. He had one foot in each culture and an innate, low-key sense of tact and understanding of how both of his worlds really worked.

Lee was in uniform and on duty, naturally assigned to Seventh District. We shared a small window table at Café Banh Mi, a shabby little sandwich shop off Chef on Alcee Fortier Boulevard in the Vietnamese enclave of eastern New Orleans, a couple miles from Lake Pontchartrain to the north and a couple miles from Lake Borgne to the south. Some older, out-of-work men, too frail to be out making cash money on a construction or cleanup crew, sat playing cards and chain-smoking as a battered, wall-mounted TV blared a bootleg copy of a Vietnamese variety show out of Ho Chi Minh City. Lee and I both sipped a *café' den dah,* iced, syrupy sweet, super-strong French-style Vietnamese coffee.

I looked out the window at the mostly empty businesses along the street, still grubby and debris-strewn. "You guys got hammered hard out here."

"Nineteen feet of water in my house. Only thing we were able to salvage was a set of china that was a wedding gift. Well, not really a set; a couple of cups and saucers and a plate or two. My wife was happy about that."

I nodded.

"The Vietnamese community is tight, they take care of each other, and don't wait around for a government handout to do it. Well, some of them do, but mostly these people have had hard lives in the old country. They're used to adversity. I think the reason we look like a ghost town out here is that most residents haven't come back yet."

"But Jimmy Nguyen has. His fish company looks like business as usual," I commented.

"Jimmy knows how to make money. I'll give him that."

"Think he was involved in Sam Siu's killing?"

"It's possible, I guess, but . . . you know about him and Twee, their past together?"

I nodded.

"I don't see him killing Twee's father over a business dispute. From what I know, Jimmy would do anything for Twee. So he's not going to kill her dad."

"But Sam took her away from him, right? Years ago."

Lee just shrugged. "She could have gone back to him. He knows that."

"Jimmy wouldn't kill Sam over a dope deal gone bad? Some kind of betrayal, maybe?"

"I don't believe Sam had anything to do with drugs. It's no secret who the players are around here. Sam was a decent, well-respected guy in the community. People were impressed with what he did during the Vietnam War—Vietnamese call it the American War—and how well he succeeded in city politics here. I mean, he did things for this community, kind of a behind-the-scenes money source for good causes that he never got directly involved in. People knew that, and that means a lot out here. And Sam Siu's name was never linked with drugs. I don't think Jimmy did him, whether drugs were involved or not."

"So if you don't think Jimmy would kill Sam, you definitely don't think he would kill Twee, do you?"

"Are you crazy? In a million years, never."

"Jimmy should be contacting me any minute to set up a meet. Can you come with me? I don't need you to protect me from him, but I might need you to protect him from me."

"I already told Sgt. Baybee I'd help you out."

I called Kendall and asked him to check with his cousins regarding a Jimmy sighting, then get back to me. Lee and I finished our coffees and stepped out into the gloomy light of overcast onto the gravelly parking lot. A chill breeze off the lake blew right through my jacket and carried a stench of stagnant water from somewhere nearby. The breeze subsided but the reek hung heavily in the air, refusing to dissipate. As I reached for a cigarillo to mask the unpleasant stink, Kendall called back.

"You in luck. My cousin say Jimmy just pull up to Club Bamboo."

"Good timing. I'll have to give your boys a bonus or—" A gunshot popped nearby, then more gunshots. Lots of them. Officer Lee and I exchanged a quick look. "Jimmy's at Club Bamboo," I told him.

"Sounds like where those shots are coming from."

We bolted to our vehicles. Two minutes later, I screeched into the large asphalt parking lot of Club Bamboo on the tail of Lee's squad car. Four bodies sprawled around Jimmy's Range Rover. Four fresh dead bodies. I was wrong; I wouldn't be talking to Jimmy anytime soon. His head still remained attached to his shoulders, but just barely. It would have taken a large-caliber slug to do this damage, and a quick glance to the pavement confirmed my conclusion: a spent shell casing from a .50-caliber semiautomatic handgun shone in the dull light.

I recognized the other three corpses; the men had all been with Jimmy the night they jumped me at the Bridge Lounge.

As Officer Lee called it in, I looked around for Kendall's cousin. His old pickup truck sat parked next door, but I saw no sign of the fisherman.

I crossed over to his truck, then saw the body facedown in the filth. Shot in the back. His cell phone just inches from his outstretched hand. The hit team must have realized they had a witness to the massacre. I bent down and confirmed that Kendall's cousin was dead. He had two kids back in Houma and had really liked the biscuits and gravy at Lil' Dizzy's. Like Kendall, he was a hardworking guy, not afraid of work, trying to make a few bucks to take care of his family.

I wanted revenge, and said a prayer for help so I would know where to find it.

I also didn't want to be around in case Dice McCarty showed up, but Lee asked me to stay while he checked out the bar, a known RVB hangout. He found three Asian bar girls cowering inside Club Bamboo, but of course, nobody saw nothing, nobody knew nothing.

Lee cut me loose. With Jimmy dead I had one less suspect on my list, but more questions than ever.

I gave Kendall the bad news in person. I couldn't have felt worse about it. With Jimmy terminated, so was the surveillance, but we kept a person posted across from NOAC. Kendall didn't say much. He and his remaining cousins had arrangements to make.

Twee didn't answer her cell phones, and the Celadon receptionist said she wasn't in. I called her cell back and left a message telling her about Jimmy. Of course, for all I knew, she had ordered his hit.

There was one more call I had to make, and I got lucky, NOPD detectives hadn't been there yet. In spite of it almost being Mardi Gras, my contact readily agreed to meet.

The influx of revelers into New Orleans for the first Mardi Gras after the Storm was a fraction of what it had been in past years. Today was three days before Fat Tuesday, meaning the most important, most prestigious krewes would now be parading. The parades over the next few days were the krewes everyone wanted to see, krewes with the most coveted "throws" of beads, doubloons, and other cheap Chinese-made souvenirs. The streets, restaurants, and bars should have been clogged with visitors from all over the world.

Well, this Mardi Gras season, there weren't that many cafés and bars that had reopened, and getting a hotel room took a minor miracle. The Ritz-Carlton hadn't reopened, the Fairmont stood empty though protected by security guards who took for themselves whatever the looters had left behind. The Hilton near the Superdome was still a shattered nightmare of broken windows and mold and rotten reek.

In spite of thinner crowds, the parades and key street closures still created nightmarish traffic conditions, even on my street, Magazine Street, which became the main Uptown route with the closure of St. Charles Avenue. I navigated every backstreet, alley, and shortcut to snake my way into the Lower Garden District before tonight's parade rolled on St. Charles, where the neutral grounds were already clogged with buzzed spectators: sober dads and moms hoisted young ones on specially crafted stepladders that would give them bird's-eye views of the passing floats; unlicensed food stalls hawked barbeque or gumbo or andouille sausage; coeds and frat boys checked each other's tattoos as they barbequed and hoisted beers from coolers; gangbangers strutted with their bitches.

No one looked like they had a care in the world; I felt exactly the opposite as I illegally parked opposite the ruins of my dojo.

"From what I heard, you almost fried in there. Is that true?"

I looked away from the video monitor and smiled at Barry

Morrison, the owner of an antique shop across from where my dojo had stood. "Two more minutes and I would have been extra crispy."

"You think it's funny?" Barry practically gasped.

"No, but I'm happy to be alive to joke about it now."

Barry's antique shop and the ones next to it had been repeatedly burglarized. The frustrated shop owners pooled their money and set up a network of inconspicuous but fairly high-end video cameras covering all angles of their properties and the street. The street views included my dojo.

I sat staring at some pretty good color footage of two men doing something to my front door, then slipping into the breezeway along the side of my building. I knew exactly who they were, but I zoomed in, flirting with pixelization, and got an even better view of their faces. I figured there must have been two more guys up on my roof, but the cameras didn't show that view.

"Mind if I copy this?" I asked, flashing a USB drive.

"Go ahead. I'm surprised the police haven't been by yet."

"It's Mardi Gras. They're busy." I inserted the drive and made the copy in a matter of seconds. "When the police do come by, would you mind not telling them I've seen the footage or made this copy?"

Barry wasn't born yesterday. He gave me a penetrating look. "Be careful playing with fire. It almost burned you once."

"Barry, you have no idea."

Honey and I met on her 10-40 in the parking lot of Superior Grill, right in the thick of the jacked-up parade crowd. I hated being there, but there was no other way to meet. Kendall and his two remaining cousins had insisted on coming along, and considering the circumstances, I couldn't really say no. It was a bit awkward at first as I filled them in on what I'd learned from the video surveillance cams.

"We gots to hit back," said Kendall. His cousins nodded.

"I can't be sure the same crew that torched my place killed Jimmy and your cousin."

"They be the same. You know that."

"What I know is that we have to be careful."

"Well, I might have the kicker," said Honey. "I pulled a big-time favor up in the State Police Crime Lab. They did a super-rush job. Deon's DNA from the cigarette butts you snatched? It matches the DNA taken from under Kiesha's fingernail by the crime scene techs."

"That's good news, but with our judiciary, that's still not enough to convict his ass," I said. "Half the judges are on the take, the DA is a racist imbecile. Deon's money will buy the best defense attorney and at least one member of the jury."

"It's more than enough to make an arrest."

"I know," I admitted.

"Coach, you looking to make an arrest here?" Kendall couldn't quite believe it. "If so, we say good-bye now."

I looked at Honey. She seemed to be thinking a lot more deeply than usual. "I'm off shift at midnight," she offered.

As I ran multiple scenarios in my mind vis-à-vis what I should or shouldn't do, could or couldn't do, it all came back to one thing: the faces of my would-be assassins I had seen on the tape.

"Okay, we drop the hammer at zero three hundred."

Everyone nodded.

I had a lot of chits with a number of NOPD officers and I

immediately started insistently calling them in. The entire department currently worked sixteen-hour Parade Duty shifts, but tonight was the night of my counterattack, sixteen-hour shifts or not. So I called in those favors owed, because you need all the help you can get when you take on the Devil.

CHAPTER TWENTY-THREE

Louisiana shone as one of the few American states holding out against the insane tide of political correctness. Ironically, it was partly due to the innate corrupt nature of the place that they were able to deflect the insanity for so long. For example, when the state finally passed antismoking legislation, Baton Rouge politicians craftily wrote in plenty of breathing room to subvert the intent of the law—at least in locations most sacrosanct to smokers: places where they drank alcohol.

Ahhh, the gray areas of Louisiana politics. Any stand-alone drinking establishment with gaming machines earned an exemption from the no-smoking rule. Most bars already possessed a couple of video poker machines, but those bars that didn't quickly got some, ensuring that their smoking patrons remained free to light up while enjoying their favorite adult beverage. Of course, the sales of new gaming machines may have also benefited, as some speculated, certain criminal elements, i.e., the Mafia.

I admired the classic Louisiana win-win-win scenario: the do-gooder antismoking fascists got their moment of triumph with the passage of a new law trampling other people's rights; smokers got to keep smoking in most bars; nonsmokers could go to hotel bars or the bars attached to restaurants and enjoy smoke-free air. The argument that bar workers shouldn't be forced to work in a smoky environment was a load of crap. Ninety-five percent of the bar workers I knew smoked; the other five percent should get into another line of work if it bothered them, or go to work in the smoke-free joints. If you're antimilk or lactose intolerant, don't work in a dairy.

For the party-hardy, free-thinking citizens of the state, the new law changed nothing, really. And in a region bound up in tradition, nothing changing is a good thing.

Police work, unfortunately, had changed. Locally and nationally. Most big-city departments have been defanged, deballed, pussified. Supersensitive to the slightest complaint from convicted felons, the honchos don't want police to be the police anymore, they want "community relations specialists."

A few years ago, when drug dealers had overrun the French Quarter and crime ran rampant, the city panicked, terrified the problem would keep tourists away. City "leaders" couldn't publicly admit NOPD officers were forced to coddle the pushers, or that the district attorney didn't really want to prosecute pushers, or that the judges were largely corrupt. So they allowed the Jefferson Parish Sheriff's Office to send in some deputies to help clean up the Quarter. The City Council did it as a publicity stunt, to allay criticism from the tourism industry, to make them look proactive, to signify they cared about the safety of the public's ass, and not just their own.

I worked the Quarter in those days. As an officer concerned for my future, I hadn't been playing rough with the dealers, and arresting them didn't solve anything, since they'd be back pushing the next day. So imagine my amazement when JP deputies showed up on Bourbon Street one night, outside their jurisdiction. They served in JP's infamous Street Crimes Unit, and they hadn't got the word they were only supposed to be there as window dressing.

I watched in amazement as the JP deputies proceeded to drag a crack dealer into an alley and beat the ever-loving snot out of him with the warning that if he ever came into the Quarter to sell drugs again, he would get a one-way ride to a very distant swamp. I think the dealer believed them; I certainly did, and the dealer never came back. In short order, the Quarter did a 180-degree turnaround and became safe again. Street crime evaporated. Drug dealing remained, but it wasn't overt; appearances, after all, mean everything.

So islands of old-school law enforcement remained in NOLA, fighting a rear-guard action against the tide of corruption and ridiculous political correctness. And certain elements of NOPD still took care of their own.

Like the elements that stood with me tonight—plus Kendall and his two cousins—as we surrounded Deon Franklin's after-hours club Chi-Chi's and broke down the doors, storming in through the rib joint.

We all wore civilian clothes and balaclava masks that concealed our identities. No one claimed to be the police. The patrons were rousted and dope and weapons seized. The customers, many of whom were blowing their FEMA money on chemical adulterants, got heaved out the door, where other officers encouraged them at gunpoint to get the hell out of the area. Not much encouragement was needed.

I hadn't entered. I remained standing with my balaclava mask on near Deon's black Mercedes with the python wheel spokes, right next to the heavy door that I knew led to his office and functioned as his private entrance. I monitored events inside via an earbud connected to a two-way radio on my belt.

Just when I started to second-guess my strategy, the door opened.

A big bull wearing an eye patch froze when he saw me. This was the guy I poked in the eye when I was wrestling around on the carpet with a bunch of Deon's boys. He held a heavy satchel and as he dropped it, I grabbed him, hit him hard on the side of his head, and flung him outside, headfirst into the Mercedes's grille.

I sprang into Deon's office and ran into Trey, leaning on a cane, probably due to the knee injury I'd given him. Trey stood out on the surveillance video torching my dojo. As he reached for his chrome-plated .45, pulling it out from under his silk blazer, I grabbed his gun hand and twisted.

Two shots rang out and Trey slumped in my arms, dead, but I hadn't fired. Then another shot tore into Trey's back and I realized the Big Bull who had beaten me pretty good, now standing across the room, had just pumped three rounds into his homeboy, trying to hit me. I fired the .45 three times in rapid succession, sending the projectiles into the chest of the Big Bull. He had been carrying a satchel, no doubt filled with drug money or other contraband. This guy also had a featured performance in the surveillance video taken from the antique shop across from my place. He was dead before he hit the floor and started leaking blood and other fluids onto Deon's $35,000 Oriental carpet.

Deon had been a tad slow to retreat behind his desk. He

fumbled for the big .50 semiauto in his shoulder holster as I drew a bead on him.

"Put the gun down or I'll shoot!" I yelled.

He didn't take my advice.

"Deon, don't!" When he raised the weapon, I shot him in the shoulder.

He dropped the heavy pistol as he fell back into the antique Chinese wardrobe cabinet behind his desk. He slid to the floor.

I jumped on Deon like a cat. I kicked his gun away and turned him over to face me. As I reached for the radio to call in "all clear," Eye Patch Bull stumbled in from outside. I wheeled, but he fired first. I put the last two rounds from Trey's .45 into the thug's center mass, dropping him.

Deon groaned. Eye Patch Bull's round had just missed me, but caught the Drug King of New Orleans in the chest. It never failed that gangsters—white, black, Asian, or Hispanic—simply weren't as good a shot as the police.

My First Responder training kicked in. The .45 round I'd put into his shoulder needed serious attention, but Eye Patch Bull's shot—also a .45—had created a sucking chest wound; Deon's right lung had collapsed. Air bubbles gurgled as pressure increased painfully on his heart. I was fresh out of chest tubes or one-way flutter valves, so I pulled off my balaclava and firmly pressed it down on the chest entry wound.

He flinched at the sight of me. "Shit, you supposed to be dead."

"New Orleans is full of ghosts, Deon. And your boy just drilled you in the chest."

"Your fault," he managed to stammer. Like some, he played the blame game to the hilt, and to the last. He was just a poor victim, after all, of a society that had forced him into a life of crime.

"No, you tried to charbroil me in my house, and now you're paying for it. Your fault.

"This is Papa One," I said into the two-way. "The office is clear, the office is clear."

"Ten-four," a female voice came back, a voice that sounded remarkably like Sgt. Honey Baybee. "The building is clear, the building is clear."

"Phase Charlie, Phase Charlie," I said into the two-way, then pocketed it. Phase Charlie called for most of the team to depart. Only Honey, Kendall and his cousins, and three other officers would remain in a loose external perimeter. I wasn't going to repeat my mistake of being in Chi-Chi's without backup.

"Deon, it's just you and me. And you need EMS, man, or you aren't going to make it. Tell me what I want to know and I dial the call." I held up my cell phone in my left hand. The truth was, Deon wasn't going to make it whether I dialed EMS now or not. "Why'd you go after me? It wasn't because I showed up here that night. So why?"

Deon looked away, a cold sweat breaking out on his forehead. "Don't know what you talking about."

"Video surveillance footage shows your boys torching my gym. What's up with that?"

He stayed silent.

"Okay, look. Hold this tight against your wound, I got to roll you on your side, keep you from bringing air in through your chest." He pressed down on the balaclava, I rolled him onto his side and he screamed. It hurt him like hell, but I was increasing what little chance he had for survival.

Much as I didn't want to, I dialed 9-1-1. And got a busy signal. I put the phone on speaker so he could hear the beep tone.

"Hear that? Nine-one-one is busy. It's the New Normal, Deon, nothing works anymore. You're fucking dying here, and they're too busy to take the call."

"Call them back."

"You talk to me, asshole, and I'll hit redial."

"T-Boy had me do it, he wanted you dead," he gasped.

"You work for T-Boy?"

"Had me kill Jimmy, too."

"So he's your boss?"

"He's got the best shit at the best price."

"He's your supplier, then?"

"More than that. Kind of senior partner. Said it was time to take out Jimmy and said you was getting too close."

"He wanted the Asian girl dead, too? Twee Siu. Sam's daughter, the girl at my dojo?"

"No, we was just after you. Hit redial!"

I did. Once again a busy signal.

"Was Twee involved in the dope business?"

"Don't know nothing about that."

Deon was fading quickly, so I kept the questions short and to the point. "Where does T-Boy keep his merch?"

"Damn fool keep it at his house."

"You know where his stash is and you haven't ripped him off?"

"His house is like a fortress, man! And I don't mess with T-Boy."

"Why'd you whack Kiesha? I see the scratches on your face. Don't lie to me."

He tried to look away again. I turned his head to face me.

"Deon, I'm not shitting you. Answer a few more questions or you'll just be a lump on the rug. PD has a DNA evidence match on you, man. They know you killed her. Why?"

"Tired of her shit and not paying."

"You killed her for not paying?"

"Said I was tired of her shit!" He coughed as bubbles of blood popped out of his mouth. "She got what she had coming."

"So you killed Sam, too?"

"No."

"T-Boy killed him, then?"

"Hell no!" Deon coughed again as his chest gurgled. His voice quieted as his eyes started to glaze over. "T-Boy was pissed Sam got capped, acted like he thought someone was moving in and he be next. But T-Boy is full of shit. I don't believe his mouth, I only believe the quality of his junk." Deon grimaced. "Redial!"

I hit the button and this time it rang. And rang and rang with no answer. I looked down and Deon had gone still as stone. I felt his carotid artery. Nothing. Even if they'd answered when I first called it wouldn't have mattered; his ticket had been punched.

"What's your emergency?" said the female voice, finally answering.

"The emergency . . . has passed."

I terminated the call and stood up. There were way too many dead people in the room. As I crossed toward the open door to Deon's private parking area I stubbed my toe on the satchel the Big Bull had dropped.

I checked and it was full of dope: pills, powder, pot. I emptied the contents onto the floor, doused it with good brandy from a bottle on Deon's desk, and set it on fire. The fire caught the rug, and I figured the whole place would be a charred memory in thirty minutes.

The satchel Eye Patch Bull had carried was full of cash. That I took with me as I called in Phase Delta on the two-way. I felt good.

Kiesha's killer, and the men who had tried to murder Twee and myself, were no longer polluting the Earth with their presence. And Deon's confessions were digitized on a memory stick. With more suspects crossed off my list, I turned my attention to Twee. I knew she had been playing me, the only question was to what extent: a jingle or a symphony.

CHAPTER TWENTY-FOUR

Twee had dropped off my radar screen. In addition to the GPS tracking device attached to her car, the listening devices I'd planted in her condo had stopped functioning as well. Her condo building's doormen all indicated she hadn't been there lately. She must have known I found her secret room at the safe house, and I wondered if she'd blown town or even the country.

She was AWOL at work, as far as I could tell from doing a brief recon, but just for giggles I walked into Celadon on Lundi Gras, the Monday before Mardi Gras, holding a valise.

The salon was packed with debs, their mothers, aunts, grandmas, and cousins, females of all ages and race getting cut, trimmed, teased, buffed, polished, waxed, and blown, last-minute fix-ups and makeovers for tonight's parties and balls. The receptionist had momentarily left her station to primp in a big mirror. She turned as I approached her from behind.

"You take a nice picture." I showed Vang Tho, or whatever her real name was, her CIA dossier. Her look of outright shock shifted quickly into utter fear, then panic. "Where's Twee?" I asked.

"I don't know. She hasn't been in." I could tell she now wondered if I was with the Agency.

"Show me her office."

"I don't have a key."

I put her dossier back in the valise, crossed over to Twee's office door, and kicked it in. The room was empty and had been sanitized since I'd last seen it. My boss had cleared out.

I sent Honey a text with a brief update. She'd be working her buns off on Parade Duty and was probably dragging her ass, since last night's raid at Chi-Chi's had pretty much assured she'd gotten no sleep.

Kendall and his cousins had returned to Houma with the corpse. They'd gotten their payback and now set about to grieve and bury the dead.

A couple of Kendall's girlfriends alternated shifts to provide coverage at the New Orleans Athletic Club, on the lookout for T-Boy, but essentially, I was on my own.

I'd picked up almost a quarter million of Deon's cash, meaning I wasn't concerned about getting paid by Twee. I considered backing away from the whole investigation while still in one piece and departing New Orleans for points unknown. Staying might have terminal consequences.

But I seriously wanted justice for Sam's murderer. And T-Boy needed to be stopped. I didn't care how many people he had assassinated in his years of service to our country, but I did care that he was running a drugs and murder racket with impunity in my town and that people I knew were getting killed. Not to mention that T-Boy had essentially put out a contract on me; it would be pointless to run, I simply had to take him out.

I needed to disassociate myself from the Bronco, so I parked it near the Iberville Projects, figuring the more enterprising residents would boost it within hours. I caught a taxi to Kenner and paid cash for a used truck at a lot on Williams. Perhaps the term "truck" didn't do justice to the size of the Ford F-350 dually, an extended-cab four-by-four with a five-inch lift and wraparound grille guard that came in handy if you ever hit a cow. Or a wino. I'd grown tired of being squeezed off the streets by all the greedy contractors in their monster trucks, so I decided to fight fire with fire. Considering all the bicycling I did around town on most days to mitigate my carbon footprint, I didn't feel guilty at having a truck as big as Rhode Island. Besides, the truck was black and gold, the colors of the New Orleans Saints.

Over by Lafreniere Park I paid way too much of Deon's cash to rent a cheaply furnished house across from a reform school in a so-so neighborhood that hadn't flooded. The landlord tagged me for about four times what the boxy, fifties-era one-story house would have rented for pre-Storm. But it had that special NF cachet—Never Flooded. Nonflooded dumps went for a premium in the New Normal where everything was upside down.

And perhaps it was cruel of me to refer to the institute of higher learning across the street as a reform school. Surely there was some less offensive term I should be using, some politically correct phrase, but I'd probably permanently blocked it out after hearing it the first time. No doubt the students would be upset if they thought someone was trying to reform them, and we mustn't upset the delinquents, I mean kids. My copper buddies and I called such schools CVCs, Crime Vocational Centers.

I bought new clothes at the dingy Wal-Mart on Vets, avoiding the street closures for the Mardi Gras parades in Metairie.

Housing, duds, and transportation successfully acquired, I called and set up a meet with Robert Galvez.

Lundi Gras. The day before Fat Tuesday. The city had shifted into a higher party gear last Thursday, when the parades started to roll every day, all day, even with all of the Storm misery still so fresh. Maybe because of it. A safe bet today was that every other car on the road was being driven by someone half in the bag. Tomorrow that figure would rise to three out of four.

Most locals' calendars would be filled with events large and small: cocktails with friends, king cake parties, lunches and brunches and dinners with family, office/work soirees, parade participation or attendance, concerts, dances, balls, and general carousing. A packed schedule would be even more demanding for a social pillar like Galvez. Regardless, he didn't hesitate to agree to meet, but I had to wait till 8 P.M., in Whiskey Blue at the W Hotel on Poydras. Even though I snaked in along the river all the way from the Bywater, traffic was abominable, parking impossible, until I waved a Benjamin Franklin at the young W Hotel valet. My new truck was slightly smaller than an M-1 Abrams tank, but money made everything possible.

At least I thought I was meeting Galvez in Whiskey Blue. He was either late or blowing me off, and I reluctantly faced the prospect of having to buy another twelve-dollar Jack and Seven, even if it was Deon's money. Cops would never hang in a place like

Whiskey Blue. I could get four bourbons at Peedy's for the price of one here. Of course Peedy's didn't have bartenders and cocktail waitresses who look like Russian and Brazilian supermodels. Whiskey Blue did, a clear sign that New Orleans was making some progress after all. I was making progress, too; I was paying attention to pretty girls again.

Just as I got my second bourbon from blue-eyed Mina and left her a hefty tip for looking so good, a big beefy guy who had to be a bodyguard collected me and my drink and took us to a suite on the twelfth floor. After another fifteen minutes, Galvez hurried in wearing a ten-thousand-dollar tux and what looked like a diamond-studded black velvet half mask. The bodyguard waited out in the hall.

"Cliff, I'm so glad to see you are amongst the living."

I stood and he took my hand. His graciousness never seemed forced, but clearly this was an imposition.

"I'm sorry about the timing here, sir."

"Call me Robert or the meeting is over," he said as he sat, gesturing for me to do the same.

"Robert, I need everything you can give me on Tommy Boudreaux. Where he lives, hangs out; gossip, rumors, facts, background."

Galvez took a deep breath. "Okay." He closed his eyes briefly as he collected his thoughts. "He has a big house up by Tulane somewhere. Asian wife, younger than him. Japanese, I seem to recall. One child . . . maybe around ten years old by now. As a couple they're very low-key. Tommy is usually out alone. I heard his wife is a traditional, stay-at-home mom."

"So you know him?"

"I've met Tommy socially, but he's a casual acquaintance at

best. To be honest, I don't like or trust the man, so I've steered clear. The intelligence game is a dirty business and doesn't appeal to me."

"I need addresses, names. Does he have an office somewhere? I mean, I need all this information yesterday, if not sooner."

"Tomorrow is Fat Tuesday. It's parade time, my friend. You know that no one is working right now, except the bartenders. It might take a couple of days to generate what you're looking for."

"I don't have a couple of days." I was distracted and on edge and he could tell.

"Are you all right? I heard what happened to your place in the Garden District."

I pulled a cigarillo and almost lit it, but stopped, remembering where I was. I felt embarrassed that I'd shown him how stressed I was. "Sorry to pull you away from your party, Robert." I stood.

"Please sit down and light one of those for both of us."

I lit the smokes and we sat in silence for a few seconds.

"I love Mardi Gras," said Galvez, glancing out the window for a view of the crowds on Poydras. "The parades, the balls, the pageantry, the tradition. For the tourists it might just be a drunken party, but to those of us from here, here for generations, it means something much more than that. It's our tradition, our culture. Iberville and Bienville celebrated Mardi Gras on the banks of the Mississippi back in 1699. We've been continuously holding Carnival balls here for over 260 years. I'm a good Catholic and I absolutely love the season and what it stands for.

"As you know, most of the krewes also function as charitable organizations. We work hard to help our community and put our money where our mouths are. Throughout the year, we meet, have lunches, dinners, perform good works. It's a celebration of our lives, of our commitment to living as fully as possible. The drunks on Bourbon Street dropping their drawers or showing their breasts are mostly from out of town. That is not a local tradition."

I wondered where he was going with the history lesson, but no way would I interrupt Robert Galvez.

"I'm damned proud to say that New Orleans has one of the most unique Carnival celebrations in all the world. It's an integral part of the fabric that makes New Orleans the special place that it is. And espionage, treachery, and CIA shenanigans are a part of that fabric as well. We've been kind of a free-fire CIA stomping ground for decades. The big fruit companies that headquartered here last century were literally arms of U.S. intelligence operating in South and Central America. And then all those Agency and mob players involved in the JFK assassination business operated right out of the French Quarter, just a few blocks away. It's easy to bend the rules and get away with murder—literally—in banana republics, and let's face it: we are more Caribbean than we are American down here."

"That's for sure," I agreed. New Orleans must have been a perfect venue for a guy like T-Boy to operate from all those years.

"I don't have a clue as to what Tommy Boudreaux's real business is. I hear he owns many companies. Are they CIA fronts? Not sure that I could even find that out for you. But I can tell you right now that he's been involved, no, instrumental, in bringing Asian refugees into the U.S. illegally, right here in southeast Louisiana, for at least the last twenty years."

"Yeah, I saw his operation in action out in Lafourche."

"Really? Do you know that they're Montagnards?"

"I didn't know that, but it makes sense," I said, recalling that

Tommy Boudreaux had hinted that Sam Siu himself was a Montagnard, said Sam had sung a Montagnard folk song on a dangerous rescue mission. And Twee told me Sam had exiled her to the Vietnamese Central Highlands to live in a Montagnard village with his relatives. "The cleanup crew Sam's daughter used to gut the Tiki Hut were Montagnards, too."

Galvez nodded. "I wouldn't call it an open secret, but there are a few people who know about this. And most of them, like myself, are sympathetic to what Tommy's been doing. The Montagnards have been victims of a cultural genocide inflicted upon them by the Communist Vietnamese government since the end of the war, and continuing to this day. But the U.S. government, as it has so often done, turned its back on our friends, on those people who helped us so much. So into that ethical vacuum stepped Vietnam veterans, especially former Special Forces members and ex-spooks who operated in Southeast Asia and worked closely with those very loyal Montagnards, or ''Yards' as we called them. You see, I'm an old Army Ranger myself, believe it or not. There is a loose association of support around the country to help get the 'Yards in, and then help them assimilate. I'm not active in that, I only contribute money. But jobs are provided, housing, different kinds of help to get them on their feet. I'm against illegal immigration, but I think it's outstanding that all these former soldiers have been doing this to help some old allies. To right a wrong. Aside from being CIA, Tommy Boudreaux is a former Marine and has been kind of a one-man transportation battalion in getting the 'Yards out of Vietnam or Cambodia and into the States via Louisiana."

"So Sam was helping bring his own people in. Fellow Montagnards who were legitimate political refugees."

"Yes. Sam worked with Tommy bringing them in and moving

them around the country. Some of those they brought in were probably Sam's blood relatives."

"No offense, Robert, but you sound like you're a brother-in-arms to T-Boy: fellow Vietnam War veteran, financial supporter of a clandestine Montagnard relocation effort. So why your dislike of him?"

"I don't make the mistake of confusing the artist with the art, or the man with the work a man performs. Tommy is obviously good at what he does, as his long CIA career attests, but I'd never have him over for dinner, if you know what I mean. In my opinion, 'assassin' is not an impressive job skill to have on a résumé. And since the Storm, rumor has it that Tommy has gotten a bit . . . hinky."

"Hinky?"

"Unhinged. A drug problem. Serious enough to cause trouble at home. But I don't like trafficking in gossip. You'll have to find out for yourself. I'm not one to bad-mouth people behind their backs. Even someone I don't particularly care for, like Tommy Boudreaux." Galvez snubbed out the cigarillo.

"Tommy tried to have me killed. And almost succeeded. That's not gossip, that's fact. I don't care if he's CIA, or ex-CIA, or a local legend. He's going down, unless he gets me first."

Galvez digested this. "I admire your guts. The Mystick Krewe of the High Priests of Augustus is having its ball tomorrow, Mardi Gras night. I'll get you tickets in case I can't come up with any addresses for you."

"Tommy will be at the ball?"

"I should think so. It's one of the best-kept secrets in town, but this year, Tommy Boudreaux . . . is Augustus."

CHAPTER TWENTY-FIVE

The feeling thickened soon after dawn on Mardi Gras morning. The Quarter, not exactly known for early risers, had come alive with snippets of costumed humanity flashing a fervent, smiling sense of anticipation, a barely concealed glee in knowing that one of the biggest, freakiest parties on the planet was about to kick off. The mood in the air felt akin to knowing that your team was about to win the World Series or the Super Bowl or the World Cup as you stood on the street waiting to embrace the joyful madness of it all.

A hot blonde in a thick sweater, wooden clogs, and a billowy peasant skirt, her hat a huge wheel of cheese with a nasty-looking butcher knife sticking in it, stage blood dripping from her nose and eyes, bicycled past me on a beat-up Schwinn Beach Cruiser as I stood on Bourbon holding a café au lait while brushing powdered sugar off my jacket from the three Café du Monde beignets I'd just wolfed down. The blonde never stopped smiling as she pedaled past me to wherever and whatever.

Some on the street simply scurried to work, but most folks

quietly, happily ambled toward an assignation with a good time. A couple of drumbeats from toward the river; three notes from a slide trombone over near Dauphine. The fun ran afoot.

This new perspective on Fat Tuesday and Parade Time almost made me smile. If it weren't for the fact that my life hung in the balance and I needed to stay focused and razor sharp until the Sam Siu train done pulled to a stop in the station, well, maybe I could have even enjoyed myself today, in spite of Carnival memories past.

But any celebration for me would have to wait. Instead, I reconnoitered a key building, checked egress routes, and polished a plan in my head that I hoped I could implement.

Six months after the Storm, the NOPD remained completely incapable of providing the bare minimum of police services to my beleaguered city. Hence, hundreds of Louisiana National Guard MPs still patrolled the streets in their Humvees, scores of Louisiana State Troopers remained semipermanently deployed, and dozens of out-of-state coppers on extended assignment from New York and Cincinnati, among other cities, shored up the badly broken police department. Even so, it wasn't nearly enough.

For the even greater needs of Mardi Gras, the Feds lent a hand as well.

So it was that FBI Special Agent Harding screeched her sedan into the rubble-strewn parking lot of the burned-out Taco Bell on South Carrollton, where I'd been waiting, shooting the shit with members of the local FBI SRT team. This unit was being held in reserve in case the shit hit the fan somewhere in the city on this, the biggest party day of the year. FBI vehicles and a gun truck peppered the parking lot.

Like her colleagues, Harding arrived outfitted for tactical operations, but unlike her colleagues, she wanted to bite my head off.

"Just who the hell do you—?"

"Shut up and listen or your career is over."

This got her attention.

I told her what I needed her to do, and when. I informed her of the role that Honey and other NOPD uniforms were to play as my plan unfolded.

I explained to Agent Harding how I was willing to get amnesia regarding her deliberate misrepresentation of the facts to SAIC Gunderson concerning the Tiki Hut surveillance as it related to Sam's killing. I made a show of flashing the memory stick I'd removed from the FBI computer that had been in the Tiki Hut and explained how I could use it to great advantage with the media. Then I showed her some hard video evidence of major criminal activity that fell under FBI/DEA purview. I served up on a platter to Harding and the Bureau an opportunity to score some major points.

She bit.

And I overheard her on a cell phone smooth-talking Gunderson into going along with the whole thing. There was no love lost between the FBI and the CIA—in NOLA Tommy Boudreaux personified the "Agency"—and Harding was every bit as ambitious as I had thought.

The three most important New Orleans Mardi Gras krewes, Rex, Zulu, and Augustus, have their fanciful balls the evening of Fat Tuesday. Rex and Zulu hold elaborate street parades before the balls and their throws of beads, doubloons, cups, and coconuts to the boisterous and drunken crowds from their expensively decorated floats are highly prized. The Mystic Krewe of the High Priests of Augustus is a smaller, more exclusive and sedate nonparading krewe that holds an elaborate masked ball on Mardi Gras night. In short, Augustus members were A-listers who made no pretense of wanting to commingle with the great unwashed.

Every year, Augustus members vote via secret ballot to elect a new leader, a new Augustus. The mantle supposedly falls to the most deserving male member, a man who has demonstrated good local citizenship and philanthropy and service to the community. How a cheapskate, drug-dealing, murderous racketeer like T-Boy could get the call was either a testament to his masterful duplicity or an indictment of New Orleans's cultural paradigm.

Regardless, if all went well tonight, I'd be playing the spoiler at a place I absolutely loved: the Hotel Monteleone, the grand dame of the French Quarter. I'm a huge fan of the great old hotels of the world, and the Monteleone is one of the most magnificent examples of Beaux Arts architecture in the city, with arched and pediment windows, exquisite symmetry, sculptural details intrinsic to the facade, and a rusticated and raised first floor. Designated not only a Historic Hotel of America, but also a Literary Landmark, due to the many illustrious writers who have graced its suites over the centuries, the Monteleone was the obvious location for an old-line krewe such as Augustus to have its ball. I looked forward to a post-arrest cocktail in the Carousel Bar off the lobby.

I entered the hotel's Tennessee Williams banquet hall around 11:30 P.M. carrying a double-edged prop sword. One edge represented reason, the other sword edge represented justice. I wore the mask of a blindfolded female with long hair and a golden robe over my street clothes. To complete the outfit I should have been carrying a set of scales, but that simply wasn't practical.

All krewes have a theme every year, and most krewes this season chose topics criticizing or satirizing FEMA, the U.S. Army Corps of Engineers, MREs, blue tarps, and other painful icons of the Storm's aftermath. Being a conservative outfit whose membership was carefully controlled, Augustus shied away from controversy and would never choose to make sarcastic political points. As I looked around the hall I spotted this year's nonoffensive catchphrase: "Renaissance: Rising From the Ashes."

The Monteleone's grand hall glowed resplendent with purple, green, and gold bunting and banners. The majestic Augustus krewe emblem hung suspended above the small stage where a costumed chamber orchestra played their last set. The Augustus krewe emblem never changes, but every parade season a logo is created to accompany that year's theme. This year the image was a resplendent phoenix, its colorful wings spread out benevolently and protectively over a new Crescent City rising from the rubble on Old Man River, the Mississippi.

The phoenix image prevailed everywhere in the ballroom, but I couldn't help thinking that exactly the opposite was about to transpire for Tommy Boudreaux: he was going to fall to the ashes, not rise.

I circled the huge room bustling with conviviality, all members bejeweled and attired in exquisite Roman costumes and elaborate glittering masks. Most attendees sat at round tables draped in gold silk, others worked the room, emerald-encrusted goblets in hand, while a few couples danced with practiced, formal precision on the polished parquet floor.

Waiters and waitresses in purple satin kept the libations flowing, scurrying from table to table in an intricately controlled frenzy.

I didn't really get the appeal of this kind of party, but then, a guy like me they wouldn't want in their circle anyway, so I'm sure the feeling would have been mutual if they'd known an interloper was among them.

The interloper had not only entered, I was on the prowl.

It neared midnight, the witching hour that closed Mardi Gras and ushered in Lent and the sacrifices and devotion that supposedly came with it. But the party, even at this late hour of the Carnival season, roared in full swing, drowning out the lighthearted high notes of Vivaldi's Flute Concerto in G Minor.

I sensed that the krewe members simply didn't want the season to end, even after what must have been an exhausting several weeks when Mardi Gras season officially begins, as it always does, on January 6—Twelfth Night, also called Epiphany's Eve, marking the coming of the Epiphany and concluding the twelve days of Christmas. The Augustus krewe members, and especially this year's chosen court, had celebrated countless cocktail parties, brunches, high teas, coffee klatches with the ubiquitous king cakes, rehearsals, banquets, and dinners both formal and casual. I'd heard that for business networking and social climbing, there was no better venue than Augustus.

At midnight, following the traditions of this krewe, Augustus will take center stage and announce that this season's Mardi Gras is over. He'll take the arm of this year's Queen, always a pretty, young, up-and-coming Uptown debutante, as the crowd bows en masse and the curtain drops symbolically in silence.

And the devout will end it just like that. They will put down their drinks and go home. In the morning they'll attend mass where a priest will mark the sign of the cross upon their foreheads using ashes created by burning the Palm Crosses from the previous year's Palm Sunday. For the faithful, this is an act of repentance. As the priest makes the sign of the cross in ash he recites, "Remember that you are dust, and to dust you shall return." I found it to be a worthy sentiment but hoped I'd be able to close out this Passion Play without returning to dust anytime soon. I was reminded of the lyrics from a country-western song: "I want to go to Heaven, but I don't want to go tonight."

Ash Wednesday marked the first day of Lent, and the forty days leading to Easter traditionally meant refraining from foods and festivities, and instead performing acts of penance, prayer, and almsgiving. A nice concept.

The less devout revelers in the Monteleone banquet room tonight would simply adjourn to their private suites at midnight and keep their drink on till deep into Ash Wednesday. Based on what I'd seen over the years, I harbored plenty of doubts that sacrificing or truly giving something up was possible for many NOLA residents. The lifestyle here was simply so *très "Laissez les Bons Temps Rouler."* Let the good times roll.

I couldn't imagine T-Boy was part of the truly devout, but you never know. What I did know was that he wouldn't be leaving the hotel a free man.

As I turned to snatch a goblet from a passing tray of drinks, I caught sight of my prey.

Augustus rose from a table and returned to a more serious arena, a raised platform near center stage where his own large imperial table awaited. A dozen of the high and mighty, including this year's Queen, sat around the regal circle looking pleasantly sated and engaged in lively banter.

As I edged closer I could make out more detail. Augustus sat down and immediately held court at his grand, golden-trimmed table, the centerpiece of which was a floral arrangement sprouting up from a porcelain replica of the Colosseum. The finely detailed papier-mâché face mask that concealed his true identity bore a strangely stern, almost malevolent countenance. *How appropriate.* Verbose with drink and chattering with a clipped energy buzz that seemed far removed from the more measured and controlled man I had met, he appeared to be jacked up on coke or maybe crystal meth. I watched closely as his elegantly masked consort—not the Queen—carefully poured him a flute of Louis Roederer Cristal Rose Champagne. He downed the thousand-dollar-a-bottle draft as easily as a glass of cool water on a hot day.

Midnight beckoned. The music concluded and Augustus seemed startled that it was already that time. He reluctantly rose from the table, as did his Queen, as I inched forward. Young court pages in white tights and cummerbunds trimmed in gold appeared on the platform to lead Her Majesty to center stage.

I had now moved to within a few feet of the royal table. As Augustus stepped down from the platform to join his Queen he looked at me and held out his hand.

"Who is that?" he inquired. "Not Mercury, are you?"

"No, I'm Justitia, Roman goddess of Justice," I said, impulsively taking his hand and locking him in a viselike handshake as I removed my mask with my free hand, exposing my identity.

"And tonight, T-Boy, justice will prevail."

I could see his eyes and mouth through the mask openings. His lips tightened, his eyes flashed. His body jerked instinctively away, but I held him fast. I could almost feel his reaction, as if I had stabbed him in the heart with my sword. "Deon Franklin sends his regrets at being unable to be with us tonight. Of course, he's not really able to be anywhere these days, except his special room in Hell. It's fortunate we were able to have a long chat just before he expired."

I released my grip as more court pages moved in and led the stunned Augustus to the stage, which had been cleared of the chamber orchestra musicians. In just a few seconds, the crowd had gone from dull roar to respectful silence.

Still reeling, Augustus limply took the hand of his young blond Queen and managed to intone the traditional announcement, closing the ball and the season. Then the curtain came down on T-Boy and the lights came up in the hall, ushering in the harsh reality that the party was over for another year.

I tore off the robe where I stood, then quickly made my way backstage where the Queen had already been ushered away. A phalanx of FBI agents led by Harding, and a couple of NOPD uniforms led by Honey, surrounded T-Boy. I'd insisted to Harding that NOPD—represented by Honey—share the collar. And Harding insisted Tommy Boudreaux be taken quietly at the conclusion of the ball and not in an embarrassing way to the social elite of the Augustus krewe.

Harding and Honey stepped up to T-Boy, who still wore the mask and cloak of Augustus.

"We just executed a search warrant at your St. Charles Avenue home, Mr. Boudreaux, and found a kilo of heroin, thirty-two pounds of marijuana, and other illegal narcotics in your garage. We also found a cache of illegal weapons and $727,000 in cash." Harding looked like the cat who swallowed the canary. How satisfying to bust the rich and powerful.

As T-Boy craned his neck to take in his predicament, Honey

moved in closer. "Thomas Boudreaux, you are under arrest for importation of a controlled substance, felony possession of a controlled substance with intent to sell, felony grand theft of rotary aircraft, interstate transportation of stolen property, possession of illegal firearms, and suspicion of conspiracy to commit murder," she said, then grabbed his right hand.

He tried to break free, but Honey put him in an armbar compliance hold as other officers closed in and easily cuffed him. "We'll add resisting arrest to those charges."

As an officer read him his rights, T-Boy drowned him out, shouting, "Are you kidding me? Do you know who I am and what I have done? Do you know who my friends are? I'll be out in an hour and you'll all lose your jobs!" T-Boy scanned the cluster surrounding him, the unwavering visage of his mask made threatening by the fire from his burning eyes, which now locked on me. "Some of you will lose more than that."

The officers and agents led T-Boy toward a rear stairwell exit. Honey cut free and crossed right to me, beaming.

"You did it! I can't believe . . . you son of a . . . I'm so proud of you." She looked like she was about to kiss me.

"I'm not sure what I've done, but at least T-Boy is out of the game."

"Why did you have the FBI bring me in for the bust?"

"You found the stolen helicopters. You helped me every step of the way. You had everything to do with it and deserve a lot of credit."

"I don't think so. We'll talk later over a Grey Goose and—"

Just then I saw T-Boy grab the pistol from the duty holster of the officer to his left as the group paused at the stairwell entrance.

"Gun!" I yelled.

Everyone seemed to freeze for a moment except T-Boy. He locked his left forearm around the hapless officer's throat as he held the 9mm Beretta to the officer's temple. "Hands up, everyone, or I kill him!"

T-Boy spun so no one stood behind him. Taken completely off guard, Harding and her FBI team actually raised their arms into the air.

Honey and I stood about twenty feet away and we both pulled our weapons and trained them on T-Boy, who did something that made no sense to me; he backed himself into the corner.

"I said drop those weapons!"

"I'd rather just shoot you in the head," I said, "and save the taxpayers a lot of time and trouble."

"Fire a shot and this officer dies."

"Maybe."

"Jesus, man, drop the gun," said the NOPD uniform, almost whimpering, as he wet himself.

"You carried a handcuff key to a Mardi Gras ball? T-Boy, I am impressed."

"I'm an old Boy Scout. Drop the guns, St. James. You and the lady next to you."

"That's not going to happen."

"St. James, Sgt. Baybee," said Harding. She and her agents still had their hands up. "Drop your weapons, he can't escape."

"The hell he can't. There's about a quarter million drunken people within six blocks of here right now. All he needs to do is get downstairs and we'll lose him." While talking to Harding I saw T-Boy whisper something to his hostage, then remove his arm from around the man's neck. "Besides, I think he'd shoot me if I . . ."

The hostage blocked my view, but T-Boy moved his hidden arm and I heard clicks and then the hall and stage area plunged into darkness. He'd hit the circuit breakers. Three muzzle blasts lit the area like brief strobe flashes as he fired, and I swear I heard a bullet whiz past my ear. I heard Honey groan, I heard bodies go down, including mine, footsteps scrambling, yelling, a door open and close.

"Honey! Who has a light?" In pitch-black I groped my way to Honey's form on the floor. I felt for her duty belt and found her flashlight pouch. I pushed the button and the beam lit the room just as one of the FBI agents got their flashlight on. Harding was barking instructions into her radio to seal the building's entrances. Other agents scrambled toward the fallen hostage.

I shined the light on Honey. She was unconscious. "Harding, call for EMS! Sgt. Baybee's been shot!"

CHAPTER TWENTY-SIX

Harding and an agent scrambled over to where Honey lay still as another FBI agent hit the circuit breakers and the lights came back up.

"Stay with her, I'm going after that son of a bitch," I barked.

"Thompson," she yelled to the agent at the circuit breakers, "go with him."

As Harding worked the radio to deploy her agents, Thompson and I ran into the stairwell, then stopped to listen. Dead silence.

"He couldn't have made it to the ground floor already. He either went up one or down one, probably to go for a different exit. He'd know we'd have somebody waiting at the bottom of this stairwell."

"I'll go up, you go down," said Thompson.

I flew down the stairs and exploded through the stairwell door onto the second floor. T-Boy's Augustus mask lay discarded next to an antique table. This floor was filling quickly with terrified masquers hurrying down the main staircase from the just-ended ball, chattering about gunshots.

Which way did he go? T-Boy was a New Orleans native and this was an old-school New Orleans hotel; he probably knew the place well. He'd certainly known the placement of the circuit breakers backstage.

I caught sight of a pink upholstered Queen Anne chair close to the main staircase with Augustus's gold silk cape draped over the back.

T-Boy, the former "Hey diddle diddle, straight up the middle" Marine and audacious CIA field operative. The bastard probably took the most propitious route and ran right out the front door. So I headed that way, too.

Partygoers packed the crowded lobby. Patrons stumbled in and out of the famed Carousel Bar near the front door and inebriated throngs lurched past in some kind of spacey elation. I made it outside through the heavy brass and glass doors onto the banquette, the sidewalk, and grabbed a doorman uniformed in a gray double-breasted overcoat with gold trim and lots of brass buttons.

"You see a guy named Tommy Boudreaux run out here a minute ago? Very tall, silver hair, maybe seventy years old." I pressed twenty bucks into the doorman's hand.

"Yeah, I know Mr. Boudreaux, he just left."

"Which way?"

"He ran up Royal, that way."

Royal and Bourbon functioned strictly as pedestrian streets during Mardi Gras. Royal, always the less crowded of the two, was now packed tighter than Tokyo Station at rush hour. T-Boy had headed deeper into the Quarter, but the going wouldn't be quick. The streets and sidewalks were so jammed with party hounds that just covering a block could take fifteen minutes.

This was absolutely the worst time to be on the street, because the hammered masses were being cleared from Bourbon. Every Fat Tuesday at midnight a ritual played out that I always looked forward to. NOPD on horseback entered Bourbon Street from Canal, backed by an army of street sweepers and garbage trucks. A mounted captain announces to the crowd, "Ladies and gentlemen, Mardi Gras is over. Go home." Those words rang heavenly to a tired, crowd-weary copper's ears.

That announcement had just happened a few minutes ago, and now scores of thousands of people surged onto other streets as the Quarter methodically cleared out.

I struggled past a high tide of drunken coeds, groups of looped Hispanic laborers, an old couple in wheelchairs, wigged-out middle-aged women in clothes they were too old for, blotto underage Goth punks, wannabe gangbangers, screaming frat boys. I leapt over a rolling bed being steered by four gay guys—a fifth gay guy in drag laying on the bed, come-hither style. Costumes of every type from every era pressed at me. I sliced between a cluster of half-naked strippers and a pack of construction workers haggling a deal with them. Everybody in the world seemed to be there, drunk, mostly happy, and not wanting to go home.

And yet, I counted on T-Boy standing out from this raucous mass. It's not easy to upstage a Mardi Gras street party, but T-Boy stood six foot six with a shock of white hair. I shimmied halfway up a cast-iron lamppost and caught sight of him just as he fought the mob to turn right onto Bienville.

I bounced off revelers and knocked a few down as I got to the corner. I moved as quickly as possible to carve through the mayhem and track T-Boy as he veered left onto Chartres.

The swarm ran thinner on Chartres, but it was still crowded

fat with tipplers. I ran in spurts before having to slow to break through more heaving, potted humanity. I gained on T-Boy, who loped along at a jog about a half-block ahead.

Suddenly a marching band, probably invaders from Frenchmen Street, waded onto Chartres between myself and T-Boy. The male and female musicians looked like walking cadavers, escapees from some Tim Burton nightmare, playing a brassy, boozy version of Bob Dylan's stoner anthem "Rainy Day Women #12 & 35" as pedestrians marched beside them cheerfully slurring the chorus, "Everybody must get stoned!"

I bulldozed through the center of the motley ensemble, knocking a trumpet player on his desiccated ass.

When I broke out from the musical horde, I'd lost sight of T-Boy.

I hustled forward with all the speed I could muster and my side started to cramp up as I got to Jackson Square. I scanned 180 degrees and was about to unleash a string of expletives when I picked up the flash of white mane as T-Boy crossed in front of St. Louis Cathedral. Before I could move forward he spun suddenly and saw me. I stood maybe thirty yards away when he opened fire. I dove and rolled as I hit the pavement.

Pedestrians shouted alarms and scattered clear. I came up with my Glock in time to see T-Boy kick in the door to Muriel's Restaurant and storm inside.

Muriel's occupied a historic building whose origins dated back to the very founding of New Orleans, at a strategic location overlooking the square. The restaurant was closed but staff would still be there cleaning up, and screams from inside confirmed this to me. I'm not much for waiting around for the hostage negotiators to show up, so I moved inside with my Glock pointing the way.

Busboys and waitresses ran past me for the door, eyes impossibly wide. I then realized some of their fright was directed at me; the left sleeve of my white shirt was soaked red with my blood. Once I saw I'd been hit, I felt the burning, then immediately put it out of my mind.

T-Boy had cut a path through the main dining room, knocking over tables and chairs, and I followed as if tracking an animal. One wounded animal tracking one panicked animal.

Another gunshot and screams. I hurried into the indoor patio area that loomed two stories tall with a mezzanine above. A terrified female bartender crouching behind the bar looked up at me.

"He just escaped from the FBI. Which way?"

"The stairs," she whispered, pointing to the dark entryway to my right.

"Clear out," I told her, covering her flight.

I knew the way to the stairs all too well. The building supposedly had a ghost, and a table was always set with flowers and wine for one Mr. Pierre Antoine Lepardi Jourdan, at the base of the stairway. I carefully entered the gloomy stairwell. T-Boy had apparently bumped Mr. Jourdan's table, knocking over the wine. *Bad mojo for T-Boy.* On impulse, I quickly righted the glass and poured a refill from the bottle on the table. I silently asked Mr. Jourdan's assistance for what I was about to face.

I mounted the dimly lit stairs and heard the familiar intonation of a Gregorian chant that was always piped into the spooky stairwell. As if for a dramatic effect, but one that I could have done without, the wood creaked below me as I slowly climbed.

I moved onto the top landing, eased out of the stairwell onto the mezzanine, and looked down over a wooden railing into the patio area from where I'd just come. The workers had all cleared out, the place empty. I backed up against the wall until the wainscoting pressed against my buttocks. To my left were the entrances to the ornate, antique-furnished banquet rooms, to my right lay another small bar and some salon rooms. I glanced down and saw that my left sleeve was now drenched with blood. I'd have to check the wound soon, apply a tourniquet, but not yet. *Which way to go, right or left?*

I heard a dull thud to my right, so I slowly moved in that direction.

Sirens approached in the distance but I pressed forward.

Time slowed down. I heard my own breath, heard my heart beating as I cautiously entered the outer salon room, appointed with red velvet antique chairs, old steamer trunks, a thick red Oriental carpet, heavy wooden furniture, plush old red velvet couches, and cheetah skin–covered pillows. Red satin padding covered portions of the exposed brick wall, giving the room an 1800s brothel feel, which was what the building had once been. But no ladies of the evening presided as I willed myself deeper into the shadowy drinking space.

The entrance to the inner salon room was blocked by heavy red velvet drapes. These curtains needed to be opened for T-Boy's final act to play out here, in a former New Orleans whorehouse drinking room. It somehow seemed fitting that an old-guard spook like Tommy Boudreaux would play his final hand in such an old-guard venue that had no doubt witnessed many a conspiracy hatched between these ancient walls.

I stopped to listen. All I could hear was my blood dripping on the Oriental rug. I willed my breathing to relax. I strained to hear the slightest sound, but eerie quiet reigned. I fought wooziness trying to creep into my consciousness. My finger tensed on the trigger. I knew these rooms; there was no way out. If he stood on the other side of the curtains, I had him. Or he had me. He might be crouched in a shooting position with his gun trained on the drapes, ready to bust a cap right up my ass. I could wait, or force the issue right now, take a chance with my own destiny. It made sense to wait, but to hell with that. Maybe he had turned left out of the stairwell and was hiding in one of the banquet rooms, or even dropping back down onto Jackson Square; I could be wasting time here. I knew of one quick way to find out, and decided that if he waited on the other side of the perfect folds of these lovely aged drapes then either he would kill me or I would kill him, elderly war hero or not.

A lot of people died because of Tommy Boudreaux, and he'd just shot Honey, not to mention myself. I'd worn the mask of Justitia, goddess of justice, for good reason. Justice in New Orleans was often reserved for "Just Us," just those with money and power and connections, regardless of race. The high and mighty manifested their own perverted version of justice. The citizens here have become inured to the fact that vicious culprits get off scot-free on an almost daily basis. The good folks of the city don't like it much, but that's simply the way it was; it wasn't going to change in a city that resists change in every fashion.

But I'm not from around here.

So I heaved a heavy pillow through the drawn curtains as a diversion, simultaneously snaking under the hem line of the thick red drapes, into the inner salon room, my finger tightening on the trigger.

I instantly sighted on a supine body sprawled on a settee, but didn't fire. I didn't have to.

T-Boy's face seemed frozen with a questioning look, with both hands clutching at his chest as a two-bit ghostly pallor consumed his million-dollar tan. The NOPD Beretta rested on the floor. I moved in close, my Glock pointed at his head, and felt his carotid artery.

Tommy Boudreaux lay still as stone, quite deceased.

Harding and her team arrived eight minutes later. The EMS crew that declared T-Boy dead, probably from a heart attack, bandaged my arm. The bullet had gone through, missing bone and major blood pathways. Harding told me Honey had been taken to Touro Hospital. Her body armor saved her life, but she probably had broken ribs and was being checked for internal injuries.

Harding agreed to cut me loose. After all, I'd delivered her boy on a platter and the Bureau could take the glory along with NOPD. But before I went to see Honey, I decided to follow a hunch.

CHAPTER TWENTY-SEVEN

I knew most of the Hotel Monteleone's plainclothes security people. One of them got me T-Boy's suite number and a passkey. It was the suite where Truman Capote had often stayed. Of course, Capote had claimed he was born in the hotel, a patent falsehood. Staff had gotten his mother to a hospital to deliver, but quite possibly he'd been conceived at the hotel. Maybe that had earned him a discount.

I turned the key and quietly entered the opulent suite to find T-Boy's masked consort, the woman who had sat at his table all night, reclining on a chintz-covered sofa in the main sitting room, still in costume, drinking champagne. This must be the Japanese wife Galvez told me about.

"Did you confirm my husband is dead?"

She refilled her coupe with Cristal, then filled one for me. I almost dropped the fine crystal stemware when I noticed that her petite, primly manicured hands incongruously bore old scars.

Then Twee Siu took off her mask.

Bruises and scratches marred her beautiful, sad face. She had two black eyes.

"Aww, shit," was all I could manage.

"Did you personally confirm Tommy's death?" she repeated.

"Yeah, he's dead."

I quickly checked the large multiroom suite to make sure we were alone. The rooms ran heavy on chintz, colorful fresh flower arrangements, and lush Queen Anne styling. Not really my taste, but some people get off on the over-the-top richness of it all.

Twee seemed cemented somewhat heavily to the sofa. I remained standing, jacked up on adrenalin, then paced the area across from her.

"Twee, have you been officially notified of what just happened?"

"Tell me what Deon said before you killed him."

She wanted to play like she was in control, so I let her. I gulped down the champagne to take some of my edge off. "I didn't kill Deon, but he talked. He said you weren't the target in the arson fire."

"Tommy panicked and went after you. I gave him hell that I almost got killed. That's why my face looks like this; he was high when I confronted him."

"Deon said your husband was his supplier and partner. Claimed T-Boy ordered your ex-boyfriend Jimmy killed. But Deon said he didn't cap Sam and said T-Boy didn't do it, either."

"Deon wouldn't know whether Tommy killed my father or not."

"What do you think?"

"If only you had known Tommy years ago. I mean, I grew up

just loving this tall handsome man who was so smart and full of confidence, so brave, and larger than life. He treated me like a princess. When I was twelve I wanted to marry Tommy and I knew I would. I just knew it. He was the knight in shining armor."

"Sorry you got what you wanted?"

"We have a wonderful son, Bradley. He's living in Houston with my mom. New Orleans is not a good place for kids right now. And Tommy . . . he's a bona fide legend at Langley. Things that are still classified that he did to serve this country, that no one will ever know . . ."

"He recruited you?"

"I recruited myself. What I told you was mostly true. I got in trouble with the law, Dad and Tommy took me to Vietnam. But just for three months. Then it was to spy school at Camp Peary and a year and a half at the Monterey Defense Languages Institute to learn Lao, Khmer, and Chinese. We married after I got pregnant with Bradley. I was nineteen."

"It's kind of impressive that no one seemed to know that Twee Siu was Tommy Boudreaux's wife."

"A few people knew. But Tommy and I were experts at tradecraft. Double, triple lives. Lots of travel."

"I guess that explains all the wigs at your condo. You never really lived there, did you?"

"I worked hard to make it look like I did. But I spent most nights with my husband and son."

"The doorman at your condo said you went out late almost every night," I remembered aloud.

"I had a second car I kept in the condo parking garage. I'd put on a wig and drive that car Uptown, see my family, and sleep in my real bed."

I nodded. Having two vehicles explained why my GPS bug never tracked her to the home she shared with T-Boy. "So, did you replace Tommy as the New Orleans station chief?"

"You know I can't acknowledge those kinds of questions. Tommy retired from government service about a year and a half ago, but no one thinks people in our line of work ever retire. That helped keep me off the radar screens."

"The safe house in Gretna?"

She just shrugged. "I've run some ops out of it. Keep sensitive documents there. Tommy didn't know about it. Wish you hadn't broken into the communications room. I need the passports and file back right away."

"I'll return them tomorrow. The girl, Vang Tho? Great-looking chick. She works for you at Celadon. I figure you must be running a net of female agents. Sexy young honey-trap specialists would make sense. I figure your beauty school and salon are some kind of training ground, and your condo is what . . . a place for dress rehearsals? I found your hidden cameras, the sex toys. Do your girls only operate locally, or do you insert them back into Vietnam, Cambodia, China? It's sexual blackmail, right? And maybe prying secrets from Asian government officials though pillow talk?"

"T-Boy said it was a mistake to hire you, said you'd uncover too much. I'm the one who made him agree to talk to you. We fought a lot over you. I've known for some time that he had gotten into using drugs; that's when he started beating me. But I was in denial. I thought he was just buying from Jimmy or something, and I was trying to get him to quit using. It obviously occurred to me Tommy might be smuggling dope, but I just couldn't accept that he would do that. We had plenty of money, more than plenty.

Anyway, I took a chance and hired you. I owed it to Dad to find his killer. And to my son. I told Tommy I'd divorce him if he didn't cooperate."

She didn't answer my allegations, but didn't deny them, either. "Why the stolen helicopters?"

"I didn't know about that, but Tommy is a tricky, deceitful, veteran spy. Old habits die hard. And he's cheap. So I guess he did what Oliver North was accused of doing during Iran-Contra and stole some aircraft to augment his operation. Anyway, about a year ago he tried to get Dad into the drug-smuggling business. No way Dad would touch that. But I guess Tommy felt invincible and started dealing anyway. He never told me what he was doing and I'm very angry he exposed Dad and me and Bradley to all kinds of potential blowback. Keeping large quantities of hard drugs in our house!" She shook her head in disbelief. "Maybe Tommy just needed something exciting to do after retirement, I don't know. I've asked myself a thousand times why he had to do something so stupid and wrong."

"What's the story with Sam's half-million-dollar loan?"

"Down payment on a used Bell Jet Ranger in Mexico."

"Why couldn't you have told me that before?"

"Maybe the CIA was going to lease that helicopter from him after he bought it. But then, I never said that and we're not having this conversation."

"So Jimmy's involvement was for domestic transport of the illegals?"

"Yes. Some of the Montagnards stayed local. . . ."

"Like the group that gutted the Tiki Hut?"

"Exactly. But most of them went to the Fort Bragg, North Carolina, area."

"Home of U.S. Special Forces."

"I got Jimmy to do it on a pro bono basis. But I guess it was no surprise that he and Tommy went into the dope biz before too long, to take advantage of the smuggling routes."

"Does your headquarters know?"

"I don't know who knows what. I just know that the man I loved stopped being the man I loved. Before, I would never have cheated on Tommy, I would never have had sex with you. Then everything changed so radically. And I stayed in an increasingly abusive relationship for the sake of my child. But when Dad was murdered I started to suspect Tommy might have killed him because Dad refused to go along with the dope business."

"And you couldn't really share those suspicions with the Feds or the local police."

"Tommy had too much influence. Can you imagine what he would have done to me if I had gone to the authorities and pointed my finger at him? I had to pretend I didn't suspect him at all, and that meant bringing in a determined outsider, someone he had no influence with, someone tough who had a shot at bringing him down."

"So I was your guy until I uncovered your secret room?"

"Using you was always a calculated gamble."

"Twee . . . I can't definitively say who killed Sam. Not yet."

"But it had to be Tommy."

"We'll see." I lit a cigarillo and exhaled, staring at a vase of flowers. "I guess I'm having a hard time wrapping my head around the notion that you hired me to find your father's killer, all along suspecting that your assassin husband was guilty."

"Tommy devolved into a wife-beating, drug-dealing dope addict, in bed with vicious murderers. I stopped loving him long ago and wanted him excised from my life. I wanted you to prove his guilt or innocence in the death of my father, my son's grandfather. If I had told you that up front it would have colored your investigation. Can you wrap your head around that?"

I refilled my coupe with more Cristal and took a healthy quaff. I shrugged. Who knew what to believe? Other than the fact that Twee had used me like a dishrag.

She looked me straight in the eye. "I need you to be discreet with some of the things you've learned, Cliff. Do we have an understanding?"

"I think the understanding is that I stay healthy in return for getting a little selective amnesia. That's fine. I have no desire to stink up any Agency black ops or blow anyone's cover."

She sized me up carefully. Twee was a righty, but I noticed she held the champagne glass in her left hand. Her right hand, her gun hand, had disappeared into the folds of her elaborate gown. She'd had the drop on me for the last several minutes. I closed my eyes and took another sip. I stood out in the open in the oversized suite, too far from her to make a move. This one was in God's hands and all I could do was surrender to it. I'd learned in chess that sometimes the best play was to do nothing significant, but to simply move a meaningless pawn. So I simply took another drink of the greatest champagne on the planet. There are worse ways to go than to get shot drinking Cristal.

"I'm sorry Tommy shot you and your friend. But I'm glad you didn't have to kill him. Kind of ironic he would die of a heart attack like that."

She pulled her right hand into view and I could see the bulge of a weapon under a fold of her gown. I exhaled silently; she wasn't going to cap me. "Did the FBI call you?" I asked.

She smiled a sad smile and didn't answer my question. "Tommy's time was up."

Twee's words haunted me. She had wanted Tommy "excised" from her life. I couldn't help thinking about the champagne she had been so carefully pouring him at their table in the ballroom, and how the intelligence services were known to use exotic drugs to induce heart attacks in unsuspecting victims.

I now understood that I hadn't been hired to find Sam's killer at all; I'd been brought in as an expendable snoop to get the goods on some of Tommy's dirty dealings, to flush him out into the open, as part of a larger plan Twee had initiated to get rid of her husband. Langley would be less inclined to investigate the death of a disgraced agent than they would a legendary hero. A death that also conveniently avoided an undoubtedly messy divorce and custody dispute. And left the entirety of a significant estate in the hands of the widow.

As I drove across town I checked my voice recorder to play back the conversation with Twee, but it was unintelligible, masked with white noise. The same held true for my video. Twee must have been using a jammer in her hotel suite to make sure her revelations, true or not, never saw the light of day.

Twee Siu was something else. I wrote it off to pure dumb luck that I'd survived our association together, but the ultimate truth of Twee's machinations didn't really matter to me at this point. And when dealing with spooks, ultimate truths were always a moving target. What mattered to me was that the game was still on, the night very young, and Sam's killer still at large.

CHAPTER TWENTY-EIGHT

The docs protested, but I sprang Honey from Touro Hospital. She had one cracked rib, a bruise as big as a watermelon, and the feeling that she just lost a fight with a locomotive. They also rebandaged my arm, so we were now the walking wounded, or rather, the driving wounded, as we made our way Uptown in my new, politically incorrect ride.

I drove extra slow, but the bumps from the pot-holed streets hurt Honey like hell.

"Gunderson, the FBI honcho, is going to have a long talk with the mayor about you tomorrow. He wants to make sure Chief Pointer gets the message that the FBI holds you in the highest regard. And the press coverage tomorrow will be very favorable."

"You arranged all that?" she asked.

"I have my moments. But I'm not sure that where we're heading right now is going to bring out the best in me."

I pulled over and parked. I looked into her eyes, then gently caressed her. I felt her resistance, so I gently kissed her face, her forehead, her eyes. "Please, just let me hold you," I whispered, close to her ear.

She relaxed her muscles. We didn't kiss, but held each other in a lover's caress for a long time. Finally I pulled back and looked her square in the eye. "Thank you for coming with me. For emotional support. It's going to be ugly."

The bars in New Orleans close whenever they want. One bar on Decatur Street is open twenty-four/seven as evidenced by the absence of a front door. And while some bars in town close at midnight on Fat Tuesday to honor the religious spirit of the season, bar owners have the option to keep the party pumping into Ash Wednesday. That was certainly the case at a place now called Boxcars, aka the old Jupiter Lounge on Freret Street.

Boxcars rocked with a loud, packed gang of sloppy, happy drunks, none of whom, I was sure, could pass a sobriety test. Most looked to be of legal age and most either sported the purple/green/gold colors of New Orleans's Mardi Gras or were draped in beads or wore some type of costume or all of the above. All were at least partially clothed.

As Honey and I angled through the wobbly throng I was surprised to see Dice, looking fairly sober, working behind the bar. Sharon, my ex-wife, stood back there, too, although she appeared to be several sheets to the wind. A couple of extra bartenders and bar backs brought in for the expected crowd worked frantically.

Dice towered over a group of gamblers as he shook six dice in a leather cup. Then he spotted us. He stiffened and put the cup down without rolling. Sharon also saw us. She kind of tottered behind the bar, so I motioned for her to come forward. I hadn't seen or spoken to Sharon for more than a year, but I was shocked to see she looked a decade older than the last time I'd seen her. Too much booze, and maybe drugs, I figured.

The place had three good-sized rooms, all done over in a kind of freight train motif. There were old black-and-white railroad crossing signs, flashing red signal lights, and even a liberated orange-and-white-striped crossing gate. Dice had saved money on his design costs by simply stealing railroad items that then became "memorabilia."

Several of the walls were done up to look like freight cars from Union Pacific, Southern Pacific, and the Illinois Central Lines, complete with spray-painted gang graffiti. The entrance from one room to another was done through the sliding wooden doors of a "boxcar." I spotted a framed black-and-white photo of the famed City of New Orleans locomotive.

Customers sat at simple, sturdy wooden tables and chairs. A workingman's bar, there were no allusions to club cars or dining cars or sleepers, nor of famed passenger trains like the Orient Express or the Trans-Siberian. A hobo would have felt at home here.

Honey and I made for the game room, followed by Dice and Sharon.

Six drunks were throwing darts in a patently unsafe manner in the game room. I walked up to them and said, "Hey, you all need to go now. This room is closed."

Dice lunged toward me. "Don't talk to my customers like that! Who do you think you are to—"

When he laid his hand on me I spun him around, kidney punched him, then hit him so hard in the small of his back everyone in the room heard the wind get knocked out of him and the big man dropped to the floor like a freshly cut pine.

The six drunks scrambled out as Sharon stumbled toward me screaming, "You son of a bitch! Get out! Get out of my place!"

Honey stepped in front of Sharon and in spite of being injured and very sore, she applied the minimum amount of pressure to bend back Sharon's wrist and control her like a marionette. "Shhh," said Honey softly, mellowed by the pain medication. "You need to listen to what's coming."

"Let me go, bitch!" Sharon struggled, so Honey applied more pressure, easily stopping Sharon in her tracks. Sharon glared at her with a hate that melted into fear. She looked toward me, afraid of whatever was coming.

I pulled Dice to his feet and threw him onto a couch against an exposed brick wall. He was recovering faster than most men could from that punch. I hoped I wouldn't have to fight him since my left arm wasn't feeling that great as blood soaked through the bandage.

"Where did you get the three hundred fifty thousand in cash to buy this place?"

"None a your business."

He rocketed off the couch toward me. Using simple aikido, I stepped aside and guided him using his own momentum so he slammed into the side of a foosball table, knocking the heavy piece onto its side. He floundered like a grouper on a boat deck. I didn't come here to administer a beating, I just wanted answers. So I pulled an ASP collapsible baton from my pants and used the tip to apply pressure to a sensitive point on his wrist. He shrieked in pain.

Sharon cursed and made to break free, but Honey stopped that notion fast.

"Answer my questions and I'll leave. Where did you get the money?"

"Screw you."

I applied more pressure, extra hard this time, and Dice caved like the blowhard bully I knew him to be. "Stop! I'm corrupt, all right? I'm corrupt."

"You also gamble away every penny you make or skim, like it's burning a hole in your pocket."

"Not since I got with Sharon."

That comment took me aback. *Does the guy really love her that much?* "Don't waste my time, Dice." I started to apply the pressure and he started talking.

"I saved it in sixteen months. By shaking down every drug dealer, stealing their stashes, selling them, taking payoffs right and left, strong-arm tactics, a little bill collecting for the mob, broke some arms and legs, couple of burglaries a month. I looted some jewelry stores in the big hotels right after the Storm and made a killing. And I would do it all again."

I looked to Honey, then to Sharon, the woman I had so loved. I doubted Dice had ever told her exactly where the cash had come from. Sharon wasn't dumb, she knew Dice was no straight arrow, she must have suspected. But still, she now heard from the horse's mouth that he was worse than a common criminal, because he hid behind a badge. I could see the wheels spinning inside Sharon's alcohol-soaked brain.

"I did what you didn't have the balls to do. I did what I had to do to take care of my woman."

I had Dice on the ground, in a hold, but his words cut me deep. *I did what I had to do to take care of my woman.*

Then I looked at Sharon again and realized I'd been wrong, she had known exactly where Dice's money had come from. She was complicit, in a sense. "So we'd still be together if I'd been committing felonies to bring in money?" I asked her.

"Everybody else does it," she offered, defensively, looking away. I thought she might be a little ashamed that she'd become such a sell-out. It hit me that her descent into alcoholism, the bartender's curse, had been meteoric. The woman I now looked at was a lush. She had never worked at our bar drunk when we were together, especially at an important time like Mardi Gras. Toward the end of the marriage she drank more heavily, but I wrote it off to the stress of the breakup. But now as I looked at her, the smile, the spark of life, her pixieish energy were all deadened by the sea of booze. The woman standing in front of me needed a detox treatment and counseling.

I suddenly felt like a complete fool. I had been holding a torch for a woman who no longer existed. I could have just walked out of the bar and kept walking. But Dice squirmed below me and Dice deserved what was coming.

"Dice, why didn't you mention stealing money from Sam Siu's pile of cash?"

Dice tried to get up but I sent searing pain into his nervous system and he went limp.

"You rotten bastard. We stole from Sam because we had bills to pay!" screamed Sharon. It was like there was another being inside of her, controlling her speech, her body language. The Sharon I had loved no longer resided in that human body.

"Well, that certainly justifies it," I said. " 'Your honor, I knocked over that bank because I didn't want to miss my car payment.' 'Well, in that case, son, charges dismissed.' "

"If you had been a better provider . . ." she slurred, eyes glazed over.

"We took a gamble, opened a bar, and it didn't work out. And if you hadn't run off with another man, this pathetic little prick right here, I would have paid those bills for you."

"Sure you would have, except we never had money during our entire marriage."

I had learned long ago there was no point in arguing with a drunk. "Sharon, you need a twelve-step program. You need help."

I turned to Dice.

"Hey, Detective, I know you stole the four hundred K from Sam's safe. You also deleted those video files on his laptop that showed you and Sharon stealing money he asked you to count."

"I didn't."

"Please, I have proof of that. And you killed Sam and stole the money, didn't you?"

"I deleted the files, but I didn't kill Sam or steal the money."

"Where's your fifty-cal auto?"

"I sold it."

"You lying bastard, do I have to hurt you again? Does Sharon know about the kid you have with Kiesha?"

Dice went limp; I could literally feel the fight go out of him.

"What?" Sharon hissed, as she also stopped struggling.

"You remember Kiesha, don't you?" I said to Sharon. "She was Sam's old lady, the pretty black girl at the Tiki Hut. Dice turned her into a snitch when she was only thirteen, and she gave birth at fourteen after he raped her. Their daughter is up in Atlanta being raised by the grandma."

Sharon's mouth was moving but nothing came out. Finally, she sputtered, "Dice?" She wanted to hear her man say it wasn't true.

"When's the last time you had sex with Kiesha?" I asked.

"St. James, please."

"About a month ago, right? According to her boyfriend Eli, right? She was your fuck buddy." I applied more pressure.

"Yeah, that's right," he managed to choke out hoarsely.

Dice began to whimper, and I released him. He sobbed in a way that actually made me feel sorry for him for a second. But the second passed quickly. Sharon's face had fallen and she suddenly looked very old.

"I'll bust into your gun room if you don't come clean. Bud told me where he built it. Now where's the AMT AutoMag?"

He sounded weak, beaten. "I gave it to Kiesha. Before the Storm. Told her to sell it, use the money for the kid."

"She's your daughter, Dice. She's not 'the kid.' Her name is Kaitlinn." I nodded to Honey and she released Sharon. I handed the photo of Kaitlinn to Sharon.

"You have one month to get your child support caught up and keep it caught up, or what you did is going to go a lot farther than this room. Know what I mean?" I glanced at Sharon. Honey was essentially holding her up as she swayed on her feet. "And if you really love Sharon, get her into detox. Now show me the gun room."

The .50-caliber pistol wasn't in the gun room or anywhere else in the building. Dice and Sharon had stayed silent as we searched the entire premises.

As Honey and I left the bar, we looked back at Dice and Sharon. They stood like two static pillars of misery in a kinetic crowd of blissful drunks. For the first time since falling in love with her, I felt absolutely nothing for Sharon, except pity.

I gently put my good arm around Honey's shoulder, and she gingerly put her arm around my waist. "A crooked cop with a gambling habit, an alcoholic bar owner . . . I think they'll make it in this town."

CHAPTER TWENTY-NINE

I parked my Ford F-350 illegally on the neutral ground on Esplanade not far from Port-of-Call, and even closer to Eli's rusted-out van, which needed a set of tires and a new windshield.

At 6:10 A.M. Ash Wednesday the massive post–Mardi Gras cleanup effort was still underway to remove tons of cans and bottles that were discarded or dropped, never-caught strands of beads and doubloons, and plastic cups, junk food wrappers, used condoms, party hats, and every other kind of garbage imaginable. Power washers hosed down urine- and vomit- and blood-encrusted sidewalks and streets as the whole city nursed a collective hangover.

The hot sweet breath of Sgt. Honey Baybee seared my ear as she dozed snuggled up to me in the truck cab, her head tilted toward and leaning against mine. The position felt a little painful, but I liked it. The fact that I felt pain kind of baffled me, but I didn't have long to consider that notion, since Eli had just emerged from a staggering group on Royal Street and approached his van.

I gently woke Honey with a kiss. "Honey, it's time."

Eli had trouble standing, he was so stoned. He managed to open the rear cargo doors when I got to him. Instead of cuffing him I simply led him to the front passenger seat and helped him climb in. He couldn't even speak.

I entered the cargo area, snapped on a pair of blue latex gloves, and tossed the van. In less than two minutes I found Dice's .50-caliber automatic with the initials DM engraved onto the slide.

How ironic that a gun given to Kiesha Taylor by the man who raped and impregnated her was subsequently stolen by her boyfriend/husband who used it to kill her one true love, Sam Siu.

Two cardboard boxes in Eli's van contained Sam's missing VHS surveillance videotapes. One of the tapes probably showed Eli using a purloined key to let himself into the Tiki Hut and surprise Sam while he was in the shower.

But why take a year's worth of tapes? The answer hit me as soon as I asked myself the question. Eli had worked part-time as a bar back at the Hut. He stole the tapes to eliminate every shred of hard evidence that he'd ever set foot in the place. It wasn't particularly logical, except to Eli.

A tattered old gym bag—the stiff kind that looks like a black half-moon with handles—sat stuffed with cash under a grubby moth-eaten army-surplus wool blanket. The gym bag had been Sam's and it didn't take a detective to figure that out; Sam's name was written on yellowed paper slipped under brittle but clear vinyl below the handles. I counted every bill; $400,000 exactly. Eli lived like a penniless pauper, yet he hadn't spent one cent of the money he stole from Sam. Go figure, as he was in no condition to explain that to me right now. Or to tell me why he had to kill Sam at all.

But then Eli didn't have to tell me, because as I stood there in the breaking dawn it became crystal clear. I'd been so distracted by Sam's links to drug dealers, intelligence agents, crooked politicians, surveillance operations, by the missing cash and by the fact that almost all NOLA murders are drug-related, that I had overlooked the oldest motive of them all: simple jealousy. Kiesha had started dating Eli to make Sam jealous, but the wrong man became jealous; Eli had fallen for her and *he* became jealous.

Eli couldn't stand for Kiesha to have a meaningful relationship with another man, and she clearly had loved Sam deeply. He must have killed Sam in order to have Kiesha as his own, even to have her in the bizarre, dysfunctional way they lived their lives. What a waste.

As a private citizen, going through Eli's truck after he opened the doors was not illegal. I didn't need a search warrant. And I could now inform police of the existence of criminal evidence, which they could legally seize. I waved Honey over and she arrested Eli for suspicion of murder in the death of Sam Siu.

EPILOGUE

I sat at my corner table in Pravda sipping a steaming latte and reading an article in the *Times-Picayune* Business section about how Marlin Duplessis, our dear former mayor, had just been named to the board of a well-known media conglomerate. Ornette Coleman was tearing up a jazz standard on the house sound system as I digested the news of Duplessis's good fortune.

As I skipped to another article, Honey entered and sat abruptly next to me, wearing Special Weapons and Tactics BDUs. Without saying hello, she flipped through my newspaper, extracted the Sports page, and went right for the box scores.

"DNA came back on that body."

"Murder rate is through the roof. Which body are you talking about?" I asked distractedly, not really interested, trying to understand the newspaper story explaining arcane Wall Street financial structures that had been peddled to the gullible and greedy, who now demanded that we taxpayers bail them out. And people thought we were crooked down *here*.

EPILOGUE

"The one the tree-trimming crew found in City Park. Up in that oak tree."

"Did you see where Duplessis just got named to the board of—?"

"It's Sam Siu."

I put down the paper. "What?"

"The body in the tree. Sam Siu."

"Really?" It had been a while since I'd thought about Sam. The case wrapped months ago. Eli confessed, and as I'd suspected, his motive was pure jealousy. He said he'd taken the money from Sam's safe as an afterthought, to make it look like a robbery that had gone bad. He hadn't even known the money was there. I didn't understand how taking the money would have shifted suspicion away from a junkie desperately in need of cash, but then, Eli didn't exactly have both chopsticks in the chow mein.

T-Boy, Jimmy, Deon, and Kiesha were dead. Dice was keeping up his child-support payments and still lived with Sharon, who I'd heard was trying to sober up. Their bar was doing so well he transferred out of Homicide to Auto Theft so he wouldn't have to pull so much overtime.

I coached Kendall three nights a week when he was in town; he'd made the jump to the UFC and just won his first bout in Las Vegas. And even though I'd lost my best street source since he no longer bounced on Bourbon, I felt like a proud parent, he was maturing so beautifully.

Twee's bank in Metairie handed me $30,000 in cash from the escrow account for solving Sam's murder. I'd returned her three passports and the CIA dossier on Vang Tho to an unfamiliar receptionist at Celadon, which, I recently heard, had changed owners.

Then there was the $400,000 of Sam's money from Eli's van. I had wanted to return the cash directly to Twee; $400K represented a lot of temptation to sticky fingers that might have an op-portunity to examine the "evidence." But Honey insisted on going by the book. She put her own lock on the gym bag before logging it into the evidence warehouse and took photos of the officer who signed for it. Subsequently, the money had been returned to Twee in its entirety. Sometimes the system works, and it's encouraging to get confirmation of how many good people still work in NOPD.

A week after Eli's arrest I finally got Twee on the phone. She was thrilled I'd gotten the killer, but I didn't sense any grief over the death of Tommy Boudreaux, her husband.

Twee insisted I take the four hundred thousand. She called it blood money Sam had been killed for. Initially, it really belonged to the bank, since it was a loan. With Sam declared legally dead and Bayou Aviation shut down, the bank had already seized assets to collect the debt. Twee said it would be simpler if I just took the money. As I predicted, she had inherited all of Tommy's estate, to-taling north of $30 million; nice work for a guy in civil service all his life. And a nice payday for Twee.

She obviously wanted me to have the money as a sweetener, an inducement to keep my mouth shut regarding certain things I'd learned. She had the cash delivered to me in an armored truck. She included a nice note thanking me for my services and discre-tion. The armored truck I could have done without. Nothing like letting the neighbors know I'd hit a trifecta.

I wasn't tempted to keep Sam's cash, because I'm not a guy who's for sale. I'd keep my mouth shut because I'd given her my word that I would, and that was that. So I anonymously donated a quarter of it, $100,000, to several charities that provided free health care in temporary facilities throughout the city; those out-of-town medical volunteers were the saints who came marching in to help us when most of our hospitals were destroyed and our doctors had evacuated and weren't exactly returning in droves. So many individuals and organizations had given so much to help us in our dire time of need, it was nice to give something in return.

I used another chunk of Sam's cash largesse to buy Honey a shotgun house in the Bywater next to Vaughn's Lounge. Honey had refused to accept the gift. I forced the issue, insisting that if I beat her at chess, she'd have to take it. I now have a place to crash every Thursday night after Kermit Ruffin's live music jam and gumbo party at Vaughn's.

I caught a Sunday service with a great gospel choir at Kerry Broussard's church on St. Claude and made an extra-large donation to help them with building repairs.

I distributed cash to certain NOPD officers as college tuition money for their kids. They had risked their lives and careers to help me when I needed them, and what goes around comes around.

I gave Kendall and his cousins and girlfriends a nice bonus for services rendered, and made sure that the widow of his cousin who'd been killed out at Club Bamboo got an extra-large cash chunk. It wouldn't bring her husband back, but I could only do what I could do.

Officer Kevin Lee helped me locate a local Montagnard association, whose members included Michael the florist and the others who had gutted the Tiki Hut. The 'Yards had had a rough time assimilating into American culture, challenges with education, language, work. I donated the last portion of Sam's money to their group. They cried like babies and said they would use the cash to buy building materials to build themselves a community center. It felt good that Sam's money was, in a way, continuing the work he had been doing to help his people.

EPILOGUE

Deon's money I kept. I used that and Twee's $30K to give me some cushion and to pay off my condo in the Quarter, which I'd moved back to after my disaster-relief-worker tenant packed up and went home to Kansas. Fire insurance money was on the way to rebuild my dojo.

Honey's star had risen exponentially in the department after Eli's and T-Boy's high-profile arrests. She wanted to stay in patrol, but a couple of captains dangled a carrot to convince her to become a detective. She got slotted right into homicide. The carrot? They put Honey on the SWAT team.

Honey slammed shut the brief window of openness and intimacy she had shown me. Not sexual intimacy—we'd never become lovers—but that crack in her hard shell that for a time seemed to indicate she was inviting me in, that we would become a couple; that crack had resealed and our relationship reverted to one of close friendship. I knew she loved me, and I'd come to realize I loved her too, but timing is everything and for now I simply accepted we were best friends. I long ago ceased believing I could ever understand a woman.

Thanks to referrals from Robert Galvez, I was flooded with sensitive but lucrative PI work for the very elite of the local community. And true to his word, I'd sat at the head of Galvez's table at Galatoire's, with Honey at my side looking every bit the Uptown lady, if only for a few hours.

But Honey's news solved the last piece of the Tiki Hut Sam puzzle. I had seen plenty of animal carcasses, including horses and cows, snagged in tree limbs after the Storm's towering floodwaters had receded. Sam's corpse apparently had floated out of the Tiki Hut in the churning flotsam and jetsam and perched in a remote part of the large park that was still closed to the public. I figured he'd now be put to rest in the Vietnamese community in New Orleans East, and I looked forward to attending the funeral. From his death I had learned what a good man Sam had been in life. I wish I could have been a better friend to him when he was alive, but I felt his spirit must be happy that he had been right; he sent his daughter to me for assistance and I had delivered, bringing his killer to justice.

The city was still broken, of course, but it was broken before the Storm. Its many faults are part of its charm, I am often told. What's charming about losing your transmission in a pothole the size of Iowa, I'm not quite sure, but then, I'm not from around here. I've only lived in the city for nine years, and in some circles, that "newness" on my part doesn't earn me the right to comment one way or the other.

Unlike the city's failings, my many faults have nothing to do with being charming, I'm afraid. One of those faults is a restlessness that has taken root inside me. It's not that I want to leave New Orleans due to wanderlust so much as it is a feeling, a knowing, that something is coming my way, something big that I will grab on to and run with wherever it might lead.

Funny, but in a way Sam's death had given me my life back. Solving the case enabled me to process the reality of my divorce and to let go of Sharon. I sat here a free man, cognizant of the responsibility that entailed.

I held up two fingers to Michelle, the Goth chick owner, and pointed to my latte, indicating that it needed sweetening with a touch of Irish whiskey. My usual table at Pravda had morphed into my Permanently Reserved Table, complete with an engraved brass sign. I'd made a deal with Michelle to run my PI business out of a corner of the bar. I'd installed a printer/fax/phone/answering machine and laptop into a locking, steel-reinforced wooden cabinet specially built to look like a Russian antique.

I leaned back and fired up a Partagas cigarillo just as percussive bursts and bellowing brass ripped the ambient noise; somewhere on the riverfront a second line had busted out and was heading this way.

Through the window I saw a woman who managed the coffeehouse on the corner saunter by. She had been pierced so many times there was more hardware in her body than in aisle 12 at Home Depot. She had more tattoos than the First Marine Division, and was the granddaughter of an infamous Mafia don who still owned a large portion of the Quarter. It all seemed so perfect. As Bob Dylan once said about New Orleans: "The city is one long poem."

I looked over to Honey. As usual, she hadn't even given me so much as a sideways glance when she entered. So I reached over and pinched her fine ass through her SWAT-issued tactical BDUs.

"You look so hot in that uniform, I can't tell you."

"That's sexual harassment," she said flatly, still scanning the scores.

"In America it is. But we're in New Orleans." I pronounced it, "Nu-whohr-lins."